GETTING OUT OF HAND

SAPPHIRE FALLS

ERIN NICHOLAS

THE SAPPHIRE FALLS SERIES

ABOUT GETTING OUT OF HAND

Genius scientist Mason Riley can cure world hunger, impress the media, and piss off the Vice President of the United States all before breakfast. But he's not sure he can get through his high school class reunion.

Until he meets the new girl in town.

Sleepy little Sapphire Falls has been the perfect place for Adrianne Scott to escape her fast-paced, high stress city lifestyle. Now she's happy helping revitalize her new hometown and has the simple goal of starting her own candy shop on Main Street.

Straightforward. Easy. No pressure.

Step one: use her marketing skills to raise the funds they need.

Step two: convince the gorgeous genius to help her.

Step three: keep her boss, the Mayor, and Sapphire Falls' It Girl from breaking his heart. Again.

Step four: don't fall for him herself.

But Mason sure doesn't look—or kiss—like a science geek. Chemistry like this with a guy like him is a recipe for disaster for a girl looking for an uncomplicated life.

Good thing no one falls in love in a weekend.

1

Mason Riley studied his best friend's tight butt and long legs and reflected, not for the first time, on how much easier his life would be if they were attracted to one another.

"Oh, you're going," Lauren said, as she turned from retrieving the garlic bread from the oven.

"I'm not going."

"You have to."

"No, I definitely do not."

"Come on. It's your hometown."

Initially, Mason had thought he was attracted to Lauren, but they had a hard time spending any time together that didn't quickly divert into work talk. They'd tried. But they were too compatible in their work life to ever get beyond it.

And then there was the small detail of Lauren being a lesbian.

Technically, she was bisexual, but of her last three lovers, two had been women and those two relationships had spanned almost a year.

"I've lived happily for the past eleven years without

spending time in Sapphire Falls. I can't imagine why that would change now simply because they need something from me," he said.

Lauren slid the bread into a basket and handed it to him.

"Mason Riley, your hometown needs you."

He frowned as he carried the bread and wine to the table. "Too bad."

"You inherited that land what, two years ago? You haven't even seen it."

"Not true. I spent hours and hours on that land growing up."

"You haven't seen it since you've owned it."

"It's a big old farmhouse, a barn and three hundred and sixty acres of fields. I imagine it looks much like it did when I last saw it."

"You should be doing something with it. Or letting someone else do something with it," Lauren said.

He glanced at the letter lying conveniently in the center of the table. "They want to build on top of it."

Lauren set two plates of chicken parmesan on the linen placemats and took her chair. "It's a legitimate offer. You have land that you're not using and they need land to build on. Why shouldn't they ask you?"

"It's a town of twelve hundred people. What could they possibly be building that's worth investing in?"

"Why don't you go find out?

He took a bite of chicken.

"It's your hometown," she tried again.

That really didn't matter. It might mean he was an ass, but it really didn't matter that it was where he had grown up.

It didn't make him feel special, or intrigued, or flattered to be on the list of five specially selected possible investors. He knew the other four men on the list. Too well. They'd been in high school with Mason. They'd all done well enough to be included on the list, but he knew for a fact that he was worth three times what the other four were—put together.

So they wanted him to invest. And they wanted his land.

He'd loved that farm and Milton Johnson, the man he'd worked for every day for nearly six years during junior high and high school, but he had few positive emotions for the town where the farm was located. He hesitated to call it his hometown. He didn't know that he'd ever really felt at home there. But it remained that he'd spent his formative years in the tiny Nebraska town. And now they needed him.

It was interesting. To say the least.

He'd been an outcast growing up. He'd skipped two grades, making him two years younger than the peers he went to class with. That made him weird. He'd been far more interested in the crops and animals he worked with on Milt's farm than the dates and parties the other kids spent their time on. That made him weird. He'd been awkward around girls, hadn't been able to discuss pop culture and didn't care about Friday's ballgame. That made him weird.

That was years ago, of course. But he hadn't been back to Sapphire Falls since he'd finished his doctorate degrees, made his money, discovered the genius of custom tailored suits or realized that there was a fine science to women and seduction —and science was something he was plain made for.

Mason poured wine into both glasses and then took a long drink of his. He watched Lauren stab a green bean and chew, clearly thinking of a new argument.

"Why do you care if I go?" he asked.

"I just want you to." She didn't make eye contact as she pushed her chicken around her plate.

"How is this about you, exactly?"

"It's about you. I think you need to go back there and blow them away."

"You think my two PhDs will impress them?"

"Maybe. But they've always known you were smart. What they don't know is that you now know how to dress, how to talk to women, how to order wine, how to—"

"Got it. And let's not forget to mention that without you, I would be sitting in the corner, alone, dressed in ten-year-old sweat pants, lamenting the utter lack of anything positive in my life."

Her gaze traveled over him, and Mason grinned, knowing what was coming.

"I really did do a hell of a job."

Lauren wasn't technically as smart as Mason, but she was smarter than ninety-six-point-four percent of the population, which meant she was hard to argue with. Making things even more difficult was the fact she could be impressively charming or incredibly manipulative, depending on what the situation required. Both of those things had helped them expand from a research lab funded by grants to an actual business that made a profit consulting with and developing projects for everyone from overseas governments to local farmers.

Innovative Agricultural Solutions, or IAS for short, was the perfect combination of all the things he and Lauren were good at and loved. This was where he was appreciated, needed, successful.

Why would he want to go back to Sapphire Falls even for a weekend? He had every intention of flat out ignoring the letter.

"They said in the letter that it's the alumni weekend. They've invited you to all the festivities, to see what the town is really like and hear about their plans for the land. Aren't you the least bit curious?"

Mason took a drink of wine and shook his head. "No."

"You have to be," Lauren insisted. "You haven't been back in over a decade. You have to wonder, at least a little, what's going on. Isn't there anyone you would want to see again?"

4

No.

It didn't matter that Hailey Conner still lived there.

Nor did it matter that the letter to the potential investors had come from her. The mayor of Sapphire Falls.

Oh, yeah, the land would mean a lot to her.

But it didn't matter.

He had a sophisticated lifestyle, the respect of the state and nationwide agriculture community and the attention of women that would make jaws drop in Sapphire Falls. He'd gained confidence and the ability to participate in social situations without embarrassing himself. He could out dress the models in GQ. He never had to look at price tags before buying anything and his taste in wine, entertainment, women and nearly every other facet of life was perfect.

He didn't need to impress Sapphire Falls, or Hailey Conner, to feel good about himself.

Lauren continued to chew, her eyes on the wine bottle. Finally, she swallowed, set her fork down and regarded him with a serious look. "Honey, you have to go because...I need the time off."

"You need the time off? You're coming with me?" He knew that wasn't the case. Lauren didn't spend the night in towns that didn't have a Starbucks and a Macy's. Sapphire Falls had coffee at the diner, Dottie's, and at the Stop, the gas station/convenience store/pizza place/ice cream shop on Main and First—though not good coffee. The closest shoe store was twenty-two miles away.

"I need the time off from you."

He selected a green bean as well and chewed as he watched her. "I have no idea what you mean by that."

She tipped her head to one side. "The hell if you don't."

Mason took a sip of wine and shook his head. "No. I really don't." He did. But he did not want to go to Sapphire Falls.

"I can't take time off if you don't take time off," she said. "And you know it."

"You don't need time off. We have a lot to do."

"Look, Mason," Lauren said. "Alex is a little intimidated by you."

"Alex needs to man up." Alexia was a tall, beautiful, willowy blond who was absolutely, no question, all woman.

"Ha, ha. What Alex needs is a weekend alone with me without you interrupting us."

Mason knew exactly what she was talking about but he wasn't about to admit it. "I don't interrupt. I call you about work. If you're in the middle of...things...when I call, that isn't my fault."

"The last eight out of ten times that we've been making love, you've called."

"Not on purpose. Though if you had a webcam, I would very likely email."

"Again, you're hilarious." Lauren drank the rest of her wine, set the glass down on the table and leaned in. "You owe me. I made you rich, hot and un-weird. Now I want you to leave town. Is that so much to ask?"

"It's also not my fault that you take my calls and return my texts," he pointed out, not wanting to admit or deny that he owed her. He did. Big. And he knew that no matter how wonderful Lauren was, she was going to cash in sometime. Maybe this was a good way to get it over with.

Lauren looked down. "You're right."

"I am?" He hadn't expected that.

"I shouldn't answer when you call. But I never know for sure. I mean, what if you need me? Or what if something huge happened at the lab? Yes, I'd want to know." She looked up with the most desperate expression he'd ever seen on her face. "I can't help it. I love Alex, but I also love what you and I do together, Mason. So I can't ignore the calls. Which is why you have to leave town. Far away. For several days. Because when you're here, you work. When you work, amazing things happen. When amazing things happen, I want to know. So you have to leave."

He knew they were co-dependent. Pathetically so. Everyone knew that. They practically shared a brain. A big, amazing, no-one-else-could-do-what-they-do brain. They'd met in college and had been inseparable ever since. They worked together. Neither really socialized, so they didn't need to do that together. But they ate at least a meal a day together—at work—saw each other at least a day a weekend—while working—and went out of town together—to work-related conferences and meetings.

And everything had been fine until Lauren had met Alex. Alexia had seen Lauren at the grocery store and had hit on her. Lauren had fallen hook, line and sinker, leaving Mason without a chef or someone who would put up with his eccentricities— of which there were many—or a partner who was at work constantly.

It was all quite inconvenient frankly.

"I don't want to go." He'd never pouted, even as a child, but he really didn't want to go.

"Why not? Mason, God, you should want to go. Show them all how wonderful you are, how great you turned out, how hot you are now."

"Yeah, you know I appreciate the compliment, but it's a little empty from you. You don't know hot unless it has long blond hair and wears red lingerie."

Lauren laughed. "I don't mind black either."

"Hair or lingerie?"

She grinned. "Either."

"Exactly."

"And I do, quite obviously, know hot. I created you."

ERIN NICHOLAS

Lauren had known Mason for exactly three days before she'd taken him to the barber and the mall.

The results had been...transforming.

"I don't appreciate the I-owe-you bit, babe."

"I know." She grinned. "And I don't really feel that way, you know. But I do expect a thank-you note from all of those women in Sapphire Falls."

He sighed and cut into his chicken. There was no reason to answer and no point in arguing. He'd do anything for Lauren, and if all she wanted was a few days with Alex—a very sweet woman who made his best friend incredibly happy—then he could get lost for a long weekend.

But not in Sapphire Falls.

———

Three things intrigued Adrianne Scott about Mason Riley. Two of those things had caught her attention as she'd written up his profile for inclusion on their list of potential donors for the building project. One, he was a genius. Literally. He had an IQ of 163. Second, he'd grown up and graduated from Sapphire Falls High but hadn't stepped foot in the town in eleven years.

Third, and very interesting—he hadn't dated Hailey Conner. Her boss. The mayor of Sapphire Falls. That almost made him more unique than the IQ thing.

"Why are we only inviting men you've had sex with?" Adrianne asked.

The first four men on the list were past boyfriends of Hailey's. One had been her first love, one had been a friend who'd turned into more, one had taken her to two proms, and another had stolen her from the guy who had taken her to two proms.

Adrianne had heard all the details.

But her favorite piece of information was Hailey saying, "I never dated Mason. He wanted to go out, but I wasn't interested."

It was ridiculous that Adrianne cared who Mason Riley had or had not dated in high school, but she did. The only reason she could really give for that was that she was fascinated by the guy.

"And I didn't say I'd had sex with them all," Hailey protested. She tossed the photo she'd been looking at on top of the five manila folders that lay on the table between them. "But I'll give you three reasons these guys are all on our list. They like me. They're from here. They all have money."

That was all true. Hailey seemed to have great taste in men. All five of the men on their list of possible donors were successful, intelligent and good-looking.

"You're sure Mason likes you?" Adrianne couldn't help but ask. "You turned him down, right?"

Hailey shrugged. "Yeah. But he's the most successful of any guy who's ever even asked me out, so I thought we might as well ask."

"Sure, why not just ask? It's only a hundred thousand dollars," Adrianne commented dryly.

"And a chance to come home for all the alumni activities and reconnect," Hailey added.

"Yeah, don't forget the free barbecue," Adrianne muttered.

She loved the idea of Sapphire Hills. The shopping area they wanted to develop would be full of unique shops, offering everything from wine to purses to furniture. They'd come up with the name over margaritas and wine about six months ago. It would be on top of a hill. Kind of. The Sapphire part they were still trying to figure out. Of course, Sapphire Falls, founded in 1892, also didn't have a blue waterfall—or a waterfall of any other color—within a hundred miles. But Sapphire Hills would boost the local economy, pull tourists in and give them a claim to fame.

Of course, they already had a kind-of claim to fame.

"Tyler Bennett is such an ass," Hailey said with a groan, tossing one of the photos of Mason onto the table.

Right on cue. The subject of Tyler Bennett being an ass came up on a daily basis.

Hailey had never had trouble getting a guy to return her calls before, so she was completely out of her element having to talk to Ty about the project through his people. She was in touch with his lawyer, primarily, and the guy was either immune to Hailey's charms...or he actually had Ty's best interests at heart. They wanted to be sure everything was happening by the book, and happening successfully, before they committed any of Ty's money or his name.

"Why does he have to be the most famous person from Sapphire Falls?" Hailey asked. "I swear, if I end up with wrinkles because of him, he's paying for the Botox."

The way she scowled whenever she talked about him, wrinkles were a real possibility in a normal person, but Adrianne wasn't convinced Hailey's skin could actually wrinkle. Like her hair seemed incapable of frizzing.

"I'm not sure he meant to end up famous," Adrianne said.

Tyler Bennett was an Olympic silver medalist, born and raised in Sapphire Falls. That would have been enough to make him the most famous Sapphire Falls native, but he'd also landed himself in the media with some post-Olympic antics in Vegas and New York and a tumultuous romance with a big Hollywood star.

It was all a little ridiculous, but it was enough to make Ty a sort-of celebrity, which meant that he could attract some attention and traffic to Sapphire Hills. If he was a part of it.

He wasn't willing to sign anything or make any commitments—or public announcements—until they had the building built and mostly paid for.

That was the part that was pissing Hailey off.

That he planned to put his name on it via a sports bar called Bennett's was what annoyed Adrianne.

How a sports bar fit with candy, coffee, furniture and jewelry was beyond her. But she was determined to make it work. If anyone could convince people that beer and burgers fit with handmade greeting cards and locally produced jams and jellies, it was her and Hailey. And if those beers and burgers pulled people in to buy the cards and jelly, then she was all for it.

But first, they needed money. A lot of money. Money that was not magically appearing as Hailey seemed to have expected it to.

So Adrianne was assisting in efforts to find funding. It was right up her alley. She had a marketing and finance degree and had spent five years in sales and marketing for her family's candy company. Her father had always said she could sell sand to a sheik.

Finding investors had been her idea. So had asking people from Sapphire Falls who had gone on to bigger, more lucrative things, but who had a soft spot for their hometown.

Hailey had been in charge of making the list.

"Don't forget that Mason's got the land too," Hailey said.

"The land?" Adrianne frowned at her. "The farmland you want to build on is Mason Riley's?"

Hailey nodded. "Kind of. He inherited it from the guy who lived on it for years. But he's obviously not using it."

"That doesn't mean he wants you to pave over it," Adrianne pointed out. She'd been out to the build site a number of times and it was beautiful. Peaceful, rolling fields, lots of trees and a gorgeous big old farmhouse complete with a wraparound porch and a swing. She remembered being tempted to sit on that old swing and watch the sun set over the fields.

She'd kind of hated the idea of building a shopping center and parking lot there. Sure their plans were for a collection of quaint shops with their own porch-type fronts with flower planters, wind chimes and wicker furniture. But there was something about that house and the porch that got to her.

But Hailey insisted it was the perfect place to build. What did Adrianne know?

"Did you choose the site because you thought Mason would donate it?" she asked.

"That makes sense doesn't it?" Hailey asked. "If we can get it for free from a guy who isn't here and doesn't intend to ever be here, isn't that better than having to negotiate with Ken Stevens for that lot down by the highway? And then putting up with Ken afterward?" Hailey rolled her eyes. "That's the only other place that's big enough. And Ken's a dick. And he's asking way too much. Everyone says so."

Everyone meant Hailey's dad and Drew Thurman, a high school classmate of Hailey's who'd appointed himself one of her advisors because he had an opinion on everything, and Betty Newman, a life-long Sapphire Falls resident with slightly more money than pieces of gossip—which meant she was quite wealthy. In fact, Betty had agreed to match whatever they could raise for the building project. But that also, apparently, gave her a vote in everything from where they were building to the color of the shingles.

"And you know he wants to have one of the shops for his loser son to open a taxidermy business."

Adrianne stared at Hailey. "What?"

"Ken Stevens," Hailey said impatiently. "He said he'll only sell the land if we promise to give one of the shops to his son, Eddie. Eddie's going to do taxidermy."

"Which is stuffing dead animals," Adrianne said to clarify.

"Yes. That's exactly what it is. Which should go nicely with the specialty coffees and gourmet candy that we want to sell there, don't you think?" Hailey asked. "The advisory board feels very strongly that Mason's land is a better choice for several reasons."

Ah, the advisory board had evidently given itself a title since she'd last seen them.

The four of them were a force to be reckoned with though. They loved to argue with one another—and anyone else who dared open their mouths—loudly and for long stretches of time while having coffee and donuts. It was exhausting, and Adrianne had long ago given up trying to give any insight or opinions. Now when they had meetings she found something else to do. Far from the office.

She'd left Chicago to escape that kind of ridiculous fighting, stress and wasted time. Sapphire Falls was supposed to be quiet and calm and simple. Dammit.

Of course, with all their meetings and donuts, she'd assumed the issue of where they were building the damned thing had been finalized a long time ago.

The whole thing drove her crazy, but Adrianne was committed to the Sapphire Hills project for reasons that went beyond being Hailey's assistant or believing it was a good move for the town. It would give Adrianne a place to start her own shop. Something she'd been thinking about more and more over the past year.

Working for Hailey had been exactly what she needed when she'd come to Sapphire Falls. She'd escaped Chicago and the pressures of her family's business just before it killed her. Literally. Her mild heart attack at age twenty-seven was a medical anomaly, but it had scared the shit out of her. She'd checked out of the hospital, given up smoking, quit her job and started yoga all on the same day.

A week later, she was in Sapphire Falls working as the assistant to the mayor—a cushy job in a sleepy little town with lots of fresh air and nice people.

She was healthy now, happy, converted to small-town life. It was time to buy a house and some land. And open a shop. She wanted to be secure without stress, and thanks to Sapphire Falls, she knew that was possible.

It could happen.

It was why she was here. And why Sapphire Hills had to happen.

"Tell me about Mason," Adrianne heard herself say.

What? Why did she want to know more about Mason? From Hailey or anyone?

She had the basic information they needed to include him on the list of invitations—he was from Sapphire Falls and had money to donate. That was all she needed. Period.

But she wanted more details.

It was ridiculous.

He was some guy whose name showed up on the list Hailey had written on the back of her grocery receipt.

Adrianne had wanted to know about all five men Hailey had decided to approach about investing. So she'd begun her research on the Internet but quickly discovered the most comprehensive information on the guys could be found at the diner downtown. All the local men aged seventy and older congregated at the diner every morning for coffee and gossip. They had all lived in Sapphire Falls forever and kept track of everyone and everything.

They were able to report where each of the men were now, what they were doing, how much they were worth and the probability they would invest.

Except for Mason Riley.

They knew where he was and that he made a lot of money. Beyond that, they were no help.

Mason's family had moved to Sapphire Falls from "some big city" when he started kindergarten. His parents doted on him but socialized very little with the rest of the town. When Mason graduated from high school, they'd moved away, back to "some big city."

Neither he, nor his parents, had been back to Sapphire Falls since.

What she had found out from the Internet—which no one in Sapphire Falls seemed to know—was that he had two master's degrees and two PhDs. He was a world-renowned agricultural engineer. His company had done a number of projects for various government and private groups. And they had made him a lot of money. They had also gotten him selected to head a task force for the White House. They had gotten him published in six different scientific journals.

But she didn't need to know anything about him beyond the fact that he was from here and had enough money to make a sizeable donation to their project.

It didn't matter that he was—

"A dork."

Adrianne blinked at Hailey. "I'm sorry?"

"Mason Riley was a dork. A nerd." Hailey shrugged and took a long drink of her iced tea.

"Because he was so smart?"

"I suppose. And because he was...different. He was nice. Sweet."

Hailey smiled softly at the picture of Mason. It was from high school and he did look a little nerdy. The pictures Adrianne had seen online were of a very handsome, sophisticated man with dark hair and dark eyes. If she looked closely, she could see the resemblance between the successful man and the geeky boy, but she had to look very closely.

Adrianne was grateful for the Internet. All the other men had responded to their invitations to attend the town's annual festival and alumni reunion along with some special events for investors only. With their RSVPs, they had been asked to provide a current bio and photo. They'd heard nothing from Mason.

But Hailey definitely had an affectionate look on her face for the Mason in the photo.

"He was weird?"

"Yeah. Typical nerd, for sure," Hailey said. "He was so... beyond all of the rest of us. More mature. Interested in politics and world events and science and machines. He knew nothing about football or baseball. So around here, he didn't fit in well with the guys. He also didn't care too much about girls, really. I mean, he never flirted, never looked at a girl's butt, never went out. Of course, people thought he was gay for a while."

Adrianne rolled her eyes and sipped again. Of course.

"But the weird thing was..." Hailey trailed off, looking at the picture, and sighed.

"The weird thing was..." Adrianne knew she had to hear this.

"He was a great kisser."

Adrianne knew it was stupid, but she felt her heart drop at those words.

"You kissed him?"

"Yeah. Once. On a whim."

"At a dance?" Damn Sapphire Falls and their dances. What was in the punch they were serving these kids anyway?

Hailey sighed again and Adrianne had to resist the urge to sigh in frustration.

"No. Not a dance," Hailey said.

That made Adrianne feel better.

"And?" Adrianne asked.

"He was great."

"You mentioned that."

"I mean, he didn't date, flirt, make out." Hailey lifted her gaze from the photo to Adrianne. "How'd he get so good?"

How indeed? The fact certainly didn't make him less interesting to Adrianne. Or, apparently, to Hailey.

———

T he minute Mason walked through the doors to the Come Again, the only bar in Sapphire Falls, he knew he'd made a mistake.

He could have bought a plane ticket from Chicago to anywhere and been, well, anywhere else by now. Instead, he stood inside the social mecca for a town he had hoped to never visit again. Not only was he back in Sapphire Falls, but he'd seemingly found the bulk of the town's population all at once.

He was hungry. The Come Again was the only place that made food at this time of night. Unfortunately, it was also the only place that had a dance floor, and that was apparently a big draw tonight.

It only took him thirty seconds to notice Hailey Conner.

She was being escorted around the surprisingly large dance floor by Kevin Marshall in a traditional two-step. She looked gorgeous. Her hair hung to the middle of her back and was held away from her face by a gold clip, the lights above the dance floor making the blond highlights glow. She was smiling, but her eyes were unfocused and directed over Kevin's shoulder as if she was only pretending to pay attention.

"Mason? Is that you?"

And so it began.

Mason turned to find Drew Thurman standing toward the back of the crowd gathered around the dancing. Drew had been their class president and Mason knew, from the alumni newsletter that surprisingly found him no matter where he moved, that Drew had taken over his father's plumbing business. As far as Mason knew, Drew had never been more than one hundred miles from Sapphire Falls.

"Hey, Drew."

"Holy shit! It is you." Drew came forward, took Mason's hand and pumped it up and down enthusiastically. "I wouldn't have even guessed it was you if I didn't know you were invited. They said they hadn't heard from you though so I didn't think you were coming."

"I didn't know I was coming until the last minute," Mason admitted, pulling his hand from the other man's firm grasp.

"Well, damn, man, it's good to see you."

Sure it was. The only conversation Drew and Mason had ever had was the daily ritual when they passed each other in the hallway on the way to their fourth period classes. Drew would ask, "What's up?" to which Mason would answer, "Same stuff."

They'd done that routine for two years.

Mason assumed Drew knew his name only because he had apparently been a topic of conversation over the past few days because of the investment opportunity.

"I thought I should come and see about this big plan," Mason said. He could admit, to himself only, that he was curious. Not curious enough to truly entertain the idea of giving money, and definitely not curious enough to make the trip without Lauren's pushing, but curious.

"Oh, it's big all right," Drew replied with a large grin. "Gonna be great for the whole town. They're promising to buy local. That means I get to do the plumbing and stuff."

Sure, that sounded cost effective. Exactly what a potential investor was looking for.

"Come on, I'll buy you a drink. Hailey and Adrianne are officially the people in charge, but they're busy." He gestured toward the dance floor. "So I'll be the one to first welcome you back to town."

The song ended as Mason followed Drew, weaving through the crowd on the way to the bar. The dance floor was surrounded on all sides with spectators and they all turned to the podium set up on the far side of the room.

"Okay, boys," Jack Morgan, the local banker and city council member for nearly thirty years, said. "Get ready to cough up some more cash."

Everyone cheered and Mason found himself interested in spite of himself.

"Come here, girls," Jack said.

Hailey and nine other women of varying ages, sizes and attire lined up in front of the podium, posing, smiling and blowing kisses, winking and waving at the audience. All except one. A curvy blond stood next to Hailey, barely smiling and not flirting or strutting at all. She was the only one Mason didn't know.

Mason found himself studying her as Drew handed him a beer. He didn't like beer outside of one microbrew he'd found in Chicago. He preferred martinis and scotch. He gave his attention to the woman in hopes of avoiding further conversation with Drew. Since he and the man had absolutely nothing in common, avoidance seemed the best way to prevent an awkward situation.

The woman was very pretty. When Hailey was around, Mason had always had trouble noticing anyone else. Or anything else. Like open locker doors or chairs in his path, for instance. He assumed by the way they acted around her that other men had the same problem. Perhaps they were more graceful than Mason about it, but men still acted stupidly around her.

But Mason found it quite easy to keep his eyes on the woman to Hailey's right. She turned and said something to Hailey. Hailey shook her head and the blond rolled her eyes and visibly sighed.

"Charlene is first, boys." A short redhead grinned and waved. "Who's in?"

"Ten bucks," somebody yelled from the right side.

"Twenty," someone else called.

"What's going on?" Mason asked Drew, unable to keep from addressing the other man after all.

Drew took a long draw of beer and then said, "It's an auction. Kind of like those bachelor auctions. But the guys are bidding on dances with those girls. Later, the women will bid on ten guys. The money goes to the building fund."

Mason was sure the men were not bidding because of the building fund, but he refrained from saying so.

"You one of the guys they'll be bidding on?" Mason asked, already knowing the answer.

"You bet." Drew grinned. "It's great for the ego."

Charlene ended up partnered for the next dance for thirty dollars.

Linda, a forty-ish blond in tight black jeans, promised the next two dances for thirty-five dollars and Betty, a cute little white-haired lady with enough jewelry to fund the entire building campaign times three, went to stand next to a tall bald gentleman who was grinning widely in spite of having spent fifty-three dollars on two dances.

Then Hailey stepped forward.

"And who's next on Miss Hailey's card?" Jack asked the crowd.

Several hands went up and Mason noticed that the guy she'd been dancing with was one of them. Mason leaned an elbow on the bar and took a sip of his beer while keeping track of the bid while it climbed.

Finally, her previous dance partner agreed to pay eighty-one dollars for three dances and all the other hands fell.

She looked less than thrilled but still gave the guy a huge smile as she went to stand next to him.

"'Kay all, Adrianne's next."

A hand shot up in front before Jack even asked for a bid.

Jack chuckled and started the action at thirty dollars. It quickly climbed to two dances and fifty dollars.

Adrianne. Mason had no idea who she was, but it was obvious she was damned popular. She was no Hailey Conner, and in Sapphire Falls she never would be, but at least the guys around here hadn't missed the silkiness of the blond waves that fell to her shoulder blades, or the sweetness of her smile, or the perfect curve of her ass—

Mason straightened. What the hell was that? His type was about four years younger than Adrianne, twenty pounds lighter and not from Sapphire Falls.

"What's her story?" he asked Drew.

"Adrianne Scott," Drew said with an appreciative sigh. "She's new."

"Yeah. I noticed."

"Been here a couple of years. She's friends with Hailey. Everyone wants her."

He'd noticed that too. And it bugged him.

"She's not dating anyone?"

Drew chuckled and shook his head. "Nope. Not for lack of trying. She never dates. The first guy to kiss her gets a hundred bucks."

Mason raised an eyebrow. He didn't necessarily approve of guys kissing a woman to win money, but then again, he was quite sure that no man would want to kiss Adrianne just for money.

"Everyone wants her."

The guys in Sapphire Falls might have more taste than he'd given them credit for.

He drained the beer he didn't want and disliked immensely and decided to place a food order to go. This was all of no interest to him.

"Okay, sixty-five dollars and three dances with Miss Adrianne Scott. Going once—"

Then she laughed at something the woman next to her said.

And Mason was in trouble.

Well, hell.

"Three hundred dollars," he called out.

2

Every single pair of eyes in the room turned to look at Mason at the same time.

He'd never been the center of attention without a microphone in front of him and a conference logo behind him before. Certainly never in Sapphire Falls.

He stepped forward. He'd opened his big mouth, couldn't really go back now. He should probably be more surprised that he'd bid like that, but he wasn't. He was a genius after all, and while his brain and mouth almost never disconnected, paying a few measly bucks for a chance to dance all night with Adrianne Scott and hear that laugh again was a genius move.

"Did you say three hundred?" Jack demanded, pointing a wooden gavel at him as if challenging him to take it back.

"Yes, sir," Mason replied, looking at Adrianne when he added, "For the rest of the dances tonight."

Adrianne's cheeks were pink and her eyes wide. She wore no makeup to enhance the features that were completely captivating him. Her hair was loose and she wore a simple white cotton tank under a denim shirt with blue jeans. Simple, unadorned, and yet he had never been more drawn to a woman.

Jack looked around the room. Obviously, it was unprecedented for a man to monopolize a woman for the entire evening.

"But it's only—" Jack started.

"Four hundred," Mason answered, still watching Adrianne.

"I don't—"

"Maybe we should let the lady decide," Mason interrupted, walking toward Adrianne.

"I can't," she said, shaking her head as he advanced. She was breathing a little fast and she darted her tongue out and wet her bottom lip.

He took another step toward her. "Then what are you worth?"

She swallowed and glanced around. "There's only three dances left," she said. "I can't let you pay three hundred dollars for that."

"I offered four," he reminded her, moving in closer still.

She smiled and he couldn't stop staring at her mouth.

"I meant that even three was too much."

He was directly in front of her now, and only those within about ten feet of them could hear the conversation. "I didn't tell you what I expected those dances to be like for four hundred dollars."

A drianne was having a hard time breathing. A man hadn't done that to her in a really long time. She liked it and hated it at the same time. She pressed a hand over her heart, which was, not surprisingly, pounding. She took another deep breath. It might be safer to say no. But she made the mistake of looking up into his eyes and knew instantly that she was not going to say no to this man. No matter what he asked of her.

He was something. He wore khakis to everyone else's jeans and a blue button-up shirt instead of a T-shirt. And he moved with purpose and confidence in front of this crowd even though he wasn't one of them. He was tall, his smile was sexy, his voice was sexy—

"How about you loan me that other hundred and I'll bid on you next hour?" Adrianne asked.

He cocked an eyebrow, having noticed her eyes on his mouth. "I'm worth two hundred less than you are?"

She shrugged. "There are ways of finding that out, I suppose," she said without thinking.

Dammit. She was flirting. She didn't do that. Not with guys in Sapphire Falls, for sure. She hadn't flirted in almost two years with anyone.

He gave her a lazy smile that clearly said he was willing to prove anything she asked and Adrianne felt her stomach flip.

She felt his gaze follow every move as she shrugged out of the denim shirt she'd worn unbuttoned over the spaghetti-strapped white tank and tied it around her waist.

"He wins," Adrianne told Jack over her shoulder. "Make it a slow one."

She took the man's hand and led him to the edge of the dance floor while they waited for the other women to be matched with dance partners.

"Is this dance auction a new invention? Because it's an effective fund-raising technique."

"Yeah, it's been part of the festival for the past couple of years. At least it's better than a kissing booth, which was also suggested," Adrianne said, smiling up at him.

He gave her a small smile in return, but his eyes were focused on her lips. Her heart tripped and she pressed her hand against her chest.

"How is dancing better than kissing?" he asked.

His voice sounded a little husky. Which was dumb, because she didn't know him well enough to really know what his voice usually sounded like.

"Um." She rubbed the pads of her first three fingers in a circle on her chest, willing her heart to slow. With a deep breath, she dropped her hand. "A dance lasts longer than a kiss, for one thing."

He leaned in closer, his eyes on hers now. "I think maybe you've been kissing the wrong guys."

Yeah, definite heart pounding. "Wow. Who are you?"

"Mason—"

Her eyes widened. "Riley," she finished for him.

Mason Riley. Of course. She'd looked at a dozen online photos. How had she not recognized him? Probably because he hadn't been smiling like that online.

If this was how they grew nerds in Sapphire Falls, it was a wonder all the girls didn't take the honors classes.

He looked surprised. "You've heard of me?"

"You're here about the investment proposal."

"How did you know that?"

"I'm...on the committee. I wrote your profile."

"My profile?" He frowned. "Making sure I measure up to the standards?"

"Making sure we're not wasting your time."

"Or yours," he said.

She shrugged. "If you were pulling in minimum wage at a fast food franchise, we might not consider you a good match for our needs," she said truthfully. Hailey might consider no one off-limits when it came to batting her eyes and asking for the world, but Adrianne wouldn't let her guilt or coerce anyone into donating money he didn't have. That was why she'd insisted on doing the profiles herself.

"What are your needs, Adrianne?" Mason asked.

She glanced up to find him studying her. She licked her lips. Her needs were pretty specific both right now and in regards to the Sapphire Hills project.

One required several thousand dollars. The other required Mason Riley, a few less articles of clothing and a sturdy horizontal surface.

She eyed the wall behind him. Maybe it didn't have to be horizontal.

"I need—"

"Okay, everyone!" Jack Morgan interrupted. "Grab your partners and get out there. Miss Adrianne requested something slow so we'll start with this..."

The music started and Adrianne was glad for the distraction. This guy was really doing a number on her pulse, and she didn't like it.

The distraction lasted another ten seconds, until she stepped into his arms.

She fought the urge to sigh as Mason pulled her up against his long, lean body and began swaying. Then she decided to just enjoy the rush it gave her. There was no sense being intimidated by it or over-thinking it. Her heart was racing a little, but her chest wasn't tight or painful and she could still take a deep breath. She tested it out right then, to be sure. Yep, still breathing.

"You've made quite a reentrance," she said as they started around the dance floor, following the pattern of the other couples.

"You think so?" he asked.

"You didn't tell anyone that you were coming. Then all of a sudden, you're here. Like magic. After all this time."

"I didn't decide to come until I was on my way out of Chicago."

He was looking right at her as they talked, but he seemed

much more interested in something in her face rather than in what he was saying.

"You couldn't decide?" she asked.

"Oh, I decided within five minutes of reading the letter," he said.

"To not come," she said, without a question mark.

If he meant to distract her from the topic with the way he pulled her even closer and spread his fingers on her low back, it worked.

"Um, what..." She struggled to remember what she was saying as Mason's thighs moved against hers. He was built for a woman to press up against. For sure. "What made you change your mind?" she finally managed to ask.

"I decided that I was curious."

"About?"

"Everything."

An old girlfriend?

She wasn't sure why that was what first popped into her head. But she did wonder. He wasn't married, that was all she knew. And he'd been a great kisser, according to Hailey—who would definitely know—so who knew who he'd had a crush on or dated or...

Oh, crap.

Again, her heart thumped, but not in a good way this time.

He'd wanted to date Hailey, but she'd never said yes.

"Everything?" she finally managed to ask.

There were a few changes in town. They'd raised money and put in a new public swimming pool. The downtown area had undergone a makeover about six years ago with new storefronts, new sidewalks and new signs. They'd also seen a small explosion of new houses built on the outskirts of town.

"Did you stay in touch with anyone?" she asked.

"No."

"So you were wondering about people and..."

"How everyone would react when I walked in here."

She felt one corner of her mouth turn up. "And paid four hundred dollars for three dances with a stranger?"

"I thought I paid three hundred."

"Was it worth it?" She really didn't know where this bravado was coming from. Besides being out of practice, she was also dressed in denim, her new favorite fabric. Since moving to Sapphire Falls, it was practically all she wore, and she was in love. She was never going back to high heels and power suits and cocktail dresses. But she had never in her life flirted with a man while dressed in denim.

"I'm thinking this dance auction is the best idea anyone's had in a really long time around here," Mason said.

"I'll take that as a compliment."

"Please do."

She smiled up at him and he smiled back, a lazy, sexy smile that made her warm all over.

Crap.

She couldn't flirt with this guy. She shouldn't be flirting with any guy, but especially not one she was going to be asking for money in a couple of days. He was here for the building project. Her job—or at least part of it—was making that building project happen. She needed to convince him that it was a good investment and did not want him to think that she was coming on to him to get money out of him.

"I think it's so great that you're here."

Mason's eyebrows rose. "Do you?"

"Of course."

"Why is that?"

The song changed, almost without them noticing. They continued moving without interruption to their steps or their conversation.

"Yes, definitely. You're going to add such legitimacy to the project."

"What do you mean by legitimacy?"

"If you decide to invest, the other guys will surely think harder about it."

He frowned. "How do you figure that?"

"Well, there's the fact that you graduated when you were sixteen. You were a genius then, and I doubt you've gotten any dumber. Not to mention all the things you've accomplished since you left. And you're a hometown boy like them. They have as much reason to support it as you do."

Mason leaned in a little closer. "I'm not sure I'm really a hometown boy."

She looked at his earlobe instead of in his eyes. "Of course you are. You grew up here. You graduated from here—"

Mason pulled her up tightly against his body, eliciting a soft ooph from her and stopping her words.

"You know exactly what I mean, don't you, Adrianne?" Mason asked quietly. "You did my profile."

She looked at him. She could lie. She could try to ignore what he was talking about, avoid the discomfort. But she felt herself nod.

"I wasn't anything special here. I was different but not special. Until the other day when I got the letter. Now they need me...and want me. How could I not come and check it out?"

"And how does it feel?"

"Right now, I'm feeling really good about being back."

Adrianne didn't think that they could get any closer together, but Mason somehow pulled her up against every available millimeter of his body. His gaze was hot on her and yet she felt goose bumps all over.

"Oh?" she managed weakly.

"Definitely."

Yeah, she was feeling pretty good too.

The second slow song ended and the tempo kicked up into a country swing.

They stood, plastered against each other, staring at each other until another couple bumped into them. Mason's only response was to lift one corner of his mouth, and she saw the knowing look in his eye. Then, without warning, he spun her out away from him, and pulled her back in, but the twirling of the country swing was too upbeat and quickly changing to allow anything more than their hands to connect.

She caught his eye and opened her mouth to say something, anything that might tell him how glad she was that he was here.

But then he was accosted. By a bunch of men.

Adrianne found herself shoved out of the way as five men pushed in and started gushing all over Mason.

"I thought you were dancing with Mason," Phoebe Sherwood, her best friend, said as Adrianne took the chair next to her at a table on the near side of the dance floor.

Adrianne frowned. "I was." And wished she still was.

She'd met the guy like a minute ago and she already missed him. Yeah, that was normal.

"You looked like you were having a good time." Phoebe gave her a wink that said she knew exactly how much Adrianne had been enjoying herself.

Unfortunately, Adrianne was never going to be a champion poker player. She had a hard time keeping her emotions to herself.

"He's...a good dancer." It was so stupid that she wanted to say more than that. He was a lot of things. She was sure of it. But that was stupid. She didn't know the guy at all. Her experience with him was fifteen minutes long. The fact that she felt a connection to him was...stupid.

"He's a good dancer," Phoebe repeated with something in

her voice that made Adrianne suspicious even though she couldn't define it.

"Yes. He's a good dancer," she said again. She watched Phoebe twirl one of her tight red curls around her finger nonchalantly.

Except that Phoebe was rarely nonchalant. She was nosy and bold and outspoken.

"Grant Hanson is a good dancer."

Adrianne proceeded cautiously though she couldn't pinpoint why. "Yes, Grant's a good dancer."

"You've danced with him a number of times."

"Two or three," Adrianne agreed.

"Lance Corbert is a really good dancer. You've danced with him too, right?"

There were always weddings and anniversary parties and street dances going on in Sapphire Falls. The people were dance crazy and it was simply easier to join in than fight it. Plus, she liked dancing.

"Yes, I've danced with Lance."

"How about Tim Gordon? He's a good dancer."

Adrianne sighed. "Do you have a point?" She knew Phoebe did. She just wondered how long it would take to get to it.

Phoebe leaned in, elbows on the table, and pinned Adrianne with a direct look. "You've never looked at Grant, Lance or Tim the way you were looking at Mason while you danced with him."

Adrianne knew exactly what Phoebe was talking about. And it was stupid.

She decided not to play dumb. Instead, she groaned and slumped down in her chair. "I know."

"Is it safe to say then, that Mason is a little more than a good dancer?"

He was. In fifteen minutes, the guy had managed to get to her like no one ever had.

It wasn't like Mason Riley was the first guy she'd looked at like that. It had happened twice before. Because she'd been in major lust. Twice.

"This is really, really bad," she said, dropping her voice to a loud whisper. "And impossible. I just met him."

"Chemistry is like that." Phoebe sat back and took a long drink of her rum and Coke.

"Chemistry?" Adrianne narrowed her eyes. "You know about chemistry?"

Phoebe was single. Had been single as long as Adrianne had known her. She dated. But she was most definitely single.

"Of course I know about chemistry." Her eyes focused on something, or someone, over Adrianne's shoulder and Adrianne turned.

Matt Phillips was leaning against the bar directly in Phoebe's line of sight.

She spun to face her friend. "Matt?"

Phoebe didn't look all that happy as she shrugged. "You can't help who you have chemistry with. It just happens."

"But haven't you always been friends?"

"Since fourth grade," Phoebe confirmed.

"And you've fallen for him?"

"Since I was a sophomore in high school."

"Does he know?" Adrianne asked.

"If he does, he's not doing anything about it."

"Are you?"

"Doing something about it?"

"Yeah."

Phoebe swallowed the rest of her drink. "Not yet."

"Why?"

"Timing is everything."

Adrianne sighed. "Yeah. So true. I almost said something stupid to Mason right before the guys cut in. Glad they saved me. And now he's talking to Hailey, so I'm safe."

Phoebe's eyes widened. "What did you almost... Hailey's talking to him...what...wh—?" She craned her neck, trying to find Mason.

Adrianne laughed at Phoebe's obvious frustration with not being able to follow both trains of thought at once.

"She found him?" Phoebe finally demanded. She sat straight in her chair and scanned the room. "How long ago?"

"Found him?" Adrianne repeated. "She was standing right there when he made that ridiculous three hundred dollar offer to dance with me."

"Yeah, but she couldn't get to him while you were dancing with him. Where are they now?" Phoebe lifted her butt out of her chair a few inches, trying to see over the people at the bar.

"Right after the guys interrupted our dance, she pulled him over to the bar. They've been sitting there ever since."

"Holy shit, Adrianne. We can't let her do that."

Adrianne frowned and swirled the water in her glass. "This is Hailey, remember? Everyone lets her do whatever she wants. Even me. Especially me." She was Hailey's assistant after all. "Basically, my entire job description can be boiled down to letting Hailey do whatever she wants. That and clean up the messes she creates."

"Why do you let her do that stuff?" Phoebe asked—for the millionth time since Adrianne had moved to Sapphire Falls. "Stand up to her."

Adrianne knew that it could seem that Hailey walked all over her. It drove Phoebe crazy.

But it wasn't a big deal. Usually.

In her past life, Adrianne would have never let someone order her around and dump all of the work on her. She'd had twenty-two people reporting to her at one time and she'd been on top of each one of them. She was certain at least eighteen of them had regarded her as a demanding bitch. The other four hadn't liked her but had wanted to be her. All twenty-two had respected her.

And she was over it.

Here in Sapphire Falls, things were small and simple. There weren't millions of dollars at stake. There wasn't a family reputation riding on anything. Her own self-respect wasn't wrapped up in sales figures and new accounts and getting all the credit so her superiors thought she was worthwhile.

Here, the most pressing matters were if they should replace the stop signs on Main or if it could wait for the next budget year, what color to paint the new fence around the soccer fields and, now, Sapphire Hills.

She loved that. She had a stress-free schedule, a beautiful view of Main Street out her window and an office chair that heated up and massaged her back with the press of a button.

And coffee and donuts on advisory-board-meeting days.

Life was good here.

Adrianne could put her foot down, demand Hailey say please more often, but why? Adrianne liked her job. It even had its rewarding moments. She took pride in a job well done, even if no one knew she was the one who'd done it.

And Hailey was mostly harmless.

At least, until it came to Mason Riley.

"Well, we're going to prevent this pending mess." Phoebe was texting someone as she spoke.

"What do you mean?"

She hit send on her phone and then focused on Adrianne. "Honey, we have to keep Hailey and Mason as far apart from each other as we can."

Adrianne shook her head. "What are you talking about? Hailey invited him here."

"Yeah, I wish you'd told me that."

"Why would I have told you that?"

"You're not from here. There are lots of things, history and stuff, that you don't know. You should really tell me everything."

Adrianne snorted. Phoebe would love that. She was the high school English teacher, and Adrianne was stunned by the things that she found out at that school. But she didn't quite know everything.

"I can't tell you everything."

"Well, anyway, we can't let her spend time with him now that he's really here."

"But he probably came because she was the one that invited him, or at least came with the expectation of seeing and talking to her."

"Doesn't matter," Phoebe said.

Matt slid into an empty chair at their table. "They're at the end of the bar."

As his comment seemed in response to some inquiry, Adrianne guessed he was the recipient of Phoebe's text of a few seconds ago. "Hailey and Mason?" she asked.

Matt nodded. "And they made plans to meet at the building site tomorrow morning at ten for a private look at the plans."

Phoebe scowled. "What's she drinking?"

Matt hesitated. "Mojitos," he said, almost apologetically.

Phoebe's hand met the top of the table with a sharp smack. "Okay, we have to intervene. Now."

"Mojitos mean something?" Adrianne asked.

"Flirting. She always drinks mojitos when she's flirting," Phoebe said.

Adrianne gave Matt a puzzled look but he nodded in affirmation. "It's true. She drinks red wine with girlfriends, light beer when she's hanging out at parties or barbecues and mojitos when she's flirting."

Adrianne couldn't believe that they knew that. Or that it was true. And how had she missed it? Probably because she'd never cared, or hadn't known she needed to care, about what Hailey drank.

She couldn't help it. She craned her neck to find Hailey and Mason. Hailey had stolen Mason away from the guys who had stolen him from Adrianne, but Adrianne told herself that they were high school acquaintances. It made sense that she would greet him. Her enthusiasm was directly proportional to the amount of money he could potentially donate to Sapphire Hills. It all made sense.

The flirting not so much.

"Why do we..." She caught sight of Mason's dark head above the others at the bar. Then someone shifted and she could see his face.

And the way he was looking at Hailey.

"Crap." She slumped back down in her seat and wished for more than water as she tipped her glass back. Hailey might be flirting with Mason, but he was looking at her with what Adrianne almost had to label as affection. Double crap. Her stomach felt heavy and sick.

"What?" Phoebe asked, looking over her shoulder. Her back was to the end of the bar where Hailey was perched on a high stool next to where Mason leaned on the bar. He was facing the room and Adrianne. Phoebe could only see the long mane of blond hair against Hailey's bright red, tight dress, but there was no mistaking that was her. Adrianne knew that hair toss. It was Hailey's signature.

"He likes her." Adrianne knew she sounded dejected and knew that was ridiculous. She barely knew the guy and he and Hailey had a past. She could hardly expect him to ditch Hailey to hang out with her. Plus, there were plenty of other people clustered around chatting and laughing. It was a reunion. He was a part of that. He was from here.

Adrianne wasn't.

"He does like her," Phoebe agreed, looking almost as unhappy as Adrianne felt. "That's the problem."

Adrianne agreed it was less than ideal. For her. But why did Phoebe care?

"Do you have a thing for him?" she asked.

Phoebe looked confused. Then she laughed. "For Mason?" She glanced at Matt. "No, not for Mason."

"Did you date him in high school or something?"

Phoebe was even more amused by that. "No. Mason didn't date anyone. And that's not why I want to keep them apart."

"Then why?"

"They have a history," Matt inserted. "Not a good one."

"They seem to be getting along fine now," Adrianne muttered, tipping an ice cube into her mouth and chewing hard.

"It won't last," Phoebe said. "Which is why we have to keep them apart."

"I'm confused," Adrianne said, watching Mason smile at something Hailey said.

"Hailey will flirt with him just long enough to get what she wants. Then she'll tell him that they should stay friends, Mason will get mad, pull his donation and we're screwed. It's better if he has nice feelings for her, but not too much contact."

"How do you know she'll only want to be friends with him?"

Looking at him, Adrianne could think of at least sixteen really good reasons Hailey might want to see him again, and his broad shoulders and heart-tripping smile were just two of them.

"Because she had more than one chance with Mason in high school and always kept him very much at arm's length. Everyone knew it. If there was any doubt, there was one pretty public denouncement that I remember."

"Ouch."

"Yeah, I'll tell you that story sometime," Phoebe said. "But right now we have to run interference here. Seriously. We can't let her get him all worked up and then break his heart. We need his money and we have a better chance of getting a real check in the bank if we keep them simply saying hi on the street and nothing more."

Adrianne hated, irrationally, that Mason's heart was at risk with Hailey.

But Phoebe wasn't known for being melodramatic. She was a straightforward, smart, funny woman who had lived in Sapphire Falls her whole life and who Adrianne liked a lot. Adrianne had absolutely no reason not to believe her.

The problem was that Mason had given Hailey more than one chance in high school and he was here now looking at her like she was incredibly interesting. "But how do we do that?" Keeping Mason away from Hailey seemed like a great idea at the moment. Really any moment Adrianne could foresee in the future too. "If he wants to spend time with her—and vice versa—there's not much we can do about it."

"Oh, we're gonna do something about it," Phoebe declared. "I have a plan."

Adrianne crunched on the last ice cube from her glass. "Whatever. Go for it."

"I need you."

Adrianne looked at Matt, but they were both looking at her. "Me? For what?"

"To step in."

"For?"

"Hailey."

"I have no idea what you're talking about."

"Someone has to fill him in on all of the plans, and how great Sapphire Hills is going to be and how much we need his help."

"That has to be me?"

"You know the plans even better than Hailey does. You'd do a better job selling it anyway."

That was completely true. It wasn't even arrogant to say it. It was a fact. Adrianne was great at sales. Especially when she was passionate about something. She was passionate about Sapphire Hills.

"But he agreed to meet her. How do you propose we change that?"

"Hailey's not going to be able to make it. We can't leave the poor guy out there all alone, and he does need to know the plans. So you'll meet him instead," Matt said.

Adrianne wasn't sure she should ask the next question, but she heard herself say, "Why can't Hailey make it?"

"Something's going to come up."

"Something?" Adrianne repeated.

"Some...mayoral emergency," Phoebe said.

Matt winked at her and Phoebe grinned.

"A mayoral emergency in Sapphire Falls?" Adrianne asked. "That she won't need her assistant for?"

"Don't worry about it. We're a team. You play your position and let us play ours," Matt said with a this-is-gonna-be-good grin. "Focus. Commitment. Execution. That's what we need from you."

Adrianne rolled her eyes at Sapphire Falls's head football coach. "You've been to too many coaching clinics."

Matt chuckled and took a drink of his beer.

"You want Sapphire Hills too, right?" Phoebe asked Adrianne. "What about your shop? You want that to happen, don't you?"

Adrianne sighed. She really did. "Of course."

"Then you need to help make it happen. If you're not part of the solution, you're part of the problem. Or something like that."

Adrianne knew she was going to regret this. "What do I need to do?"

"Show up at the build site at ten in the morning and be prepared to wow Mason."

"Okay," she said slowly. "Wow him?" she repeated.

Phoebe regarded her for a moment. "Wear your blue sundress," she finally decided.

Adrianne felt her eyebrows rise. A sundress? That was her church outfit. "Why?"

"You have great legs and breasts."

She turned to look at Matt. "Did you say I have great breasts?"

He shrugged. "You do. Sky is blue, ocean is deep, you have great breasts. And legs."

Adrianne wasn't sure what to say. She glanced at Phoebe wondering how she felt about the observation by the man she was in love with. She seemed lost in thought.

"Don't you think I should try to wow him with information about the project and the building plans?" Adrianne asked.

"Sure, sure." Phoebe waved that away. "That's a given. Don't show up in cut-off sweat pants and we'll be good."

Adrianne thought there was a compliment in there and then started to protest Phoebe's assumption she would show up like that anyway. Then she realized that yeah, it was possible. It was a construction site, not the dinner theater or even her office. Cut-off sweat pants would be appropriate. "I could wear—"

"But we have to get them apart tonight too before any more damage is done," Phoebe cut her off. "We have to do something now."

Adrianne couldn't help but glance in Mason's direction again. "How are you going to do that?"

Phoebe definitely had a twinkle in her eye when she looked at Adrianne. "I have an idea."

"Oh boy." That didn't sound good. "Tell me."

"Can't."

"Phoebe—"

"It's better if you don't know."

She was probably right. "Phoebe—"

"I have to say one thing—he was looking at you while you danced too."

That made Adrianne pause. He had been looking at her. Not as a dance partner or even a very interesting new acquaintance but like...he'd really like to do body shots off of her.

And he didn't seem the type to generally do body shots.

"What do you mean?" she asked, wondering if Phoebe had noticed the same things she had.

"You know how I said I noticed how you were looking at him?"

Adrianne nodded.

"He was looking at you like that too."

Adrianne swallowed. Okay, she'd noticed. No matter Mason's history with Hailey, there had been some definite heat between them on that dance floor that wasn't one-sided. "You sure?"

"I was surprised you both got off the dance floor with all your clothes on."

Adrianne felt her cheeks heat and put her hand over her heart. "I—"

"Get up." Phoebe got to her feet and reached to pull Adrianne out of her chair.

Adrianne stood. Phoebe looked at her. Adrianne spread her arms. "Okay. Now what?"

Phoebe picked up her shot glass and splashed the butterscotch schnapps down the front of Adrianne's shirt.

"Hey!" Adrianne stared at her friend. "What the hell?" She started to reach for a napkin, but Phoebe stepped on her foot. Hard.

"Ow!" Adrianne glared at Phoebe. "What's wrong with you?"

"Come on." Phoebe yanked on her arm, causing Adrianne to trip over the leg of her chair.

"Dammit, Phoeb—oomph." She lost her train of thought as she spun and bumped into Mike Corbin. His beer sloshed out of the mug, a large spot landing on her thigh. "Sorry."

Mike smiled and skirted around her as Phoebe pulled her forward.

"Let's go."

"What is going on?" Adrianne demanded of her friend when there were no people or chairs between them.

"What?" Phoebe called over her shoulder.

Adrianne found herself limping the next two steps due to her sore toe. "What is going on?"

"What?" Phoebe asked again from a step ahead of her.

Adrianne raised her voice. "What. Is. Going. On?" she practically shouted. As the song ended. Several people turned to look. Phoebe pushed her into the table to her right and Adrianne knocked the bowl of popcorn on the edge to the floor.

She mumbled an apology and turned to blast her friend. Only to find herself face to face with Mason. She froze for an instant as she met his gaze. Dang. There was something about this guy that could stop her in her tracks. And she didn't mind.

He was still standing with Hailey, but his attention was fully on Adrianne.

"Hailey." Phoebe grasped the other woman's arm with her free hand. "Adrianne needs a ride home."

Hailey was talking to Christine, one of the bartenders. But her knees were very close to Mason's crotch. Her bare knees— thanks to the short skirt and how she'd crossed her legs.

Phoebe wasn't one to be ignored. "Hey, Hailey!" she said louder. "Adrianne needs a ride home."

Adrianne barely registered the words as she continued to

stare dumbly at Mason. But she did hear her name. And the word home.

Hailey stopped mid-sentence and swiveled toward them as she realized Mason's eyes were no longer on her. She looked Adrianne up and down. "Why? Are you okay?" she asked Adrianne.

"Look at her," Phoebe said before Adrianne could answer. "She's got schnapps and beer down the front of her, she can't walk a straight line and she doesn't know what's going on."

"She doesn't drink," Hailey said with a frown.

"She's a mess," Phoebe said, conveniently not quite lying.

Adrianne opened her mouth to protest that she was a mess. Or drunk. She didn't know what Phoebe's plan was, but it seemed like a bad idea.

"Phoebe, I..." But she made the mistake of glancing at Mason again.

He was watching her with a faintly amused expression. She didn't care. She loved that he was still looking at her. Pathetic, ridiculous, silly. But true. His expression was hard to label. It wasn't the way he had been looking at Hailey, but she decided not to analyze that.

His eyes on her made her warm and a little jumpy, but not in a bad way. Jumpy, excited, short of breath, but her heart didn't skip or race. So it was all good. Very good.

Phoebe turned to Adrianne. "What time are we meeting to put the picnic stuff up tomorrow?"

They hadn't talked about that yet. "I don't know." Adrianne frowned, confused. "I thought..."

Phoebe turned back to Hailey. "See what I mean? She doesn't even know what's happening tomorrow."

Hailey sighed. "You need to learn to pace yourself," she said to Adrianne.

Adrianne really wanted to protest now. She didn't need to pace herself for drinking soda. And she always knew all the details to all the plans. She made most of the details and the plans. This was character defamation.

"Are you taking her home then?" Hailey asked Phoebe.

"Oh, I can't. My car's full of stuff for the softball game and picnic."

"Completely full?"

"Packed," Phoebe insisted.

Hailey sighed. "Drive her car."

"How will I get home?" Phoebe asked.

"Walk."

"It's like five miles."

"It's two. At most."

"I don't want to walk two miles in the dark."

Hailey rolled her eyes and reached for Adrianne's arm to pull her closer. "Fine." Though her tone suggested it really wasn't fine. "I'll take her. In a minute."

Phoebe frowned. "I think—"

"I'll take her home."

Hailey, Phoebe and Adrianne all stopped and looked at Mason as one. Adrianne quickly glanced at Phoebe who had a suspiciously pleased smile on her face. Her gaze swung to Hailey, who looked exasperated. Then she looked at Mason again.

He was watching her with a slight curve to his lip.

He didn't look like he minded the idea. He was already setting his glass down and straightening.

Phoebe looked at his half-full glass. "Have you been drinking?"

"Soda."

She beamed at him as if he'd announced she was Miss America. "Then that's a fantastic idea."

Phoebe pushed Adrianne forward and she had to step quickly to avoid Mason's toes. He steadied her with two warm, large palms on her upper arms. "Easy," he said quietly, staring down at her. His eyes went from her eyes to her lips and back to her eyes. "I've got you."

"Thanks," she said. It sounded breathless to her, but she couldn't help it.

"You can give me directions, I assume?" His smile hinted that he knew she was more than capable of telling him how to get her home.

"Seven twelve Crimson," Phoebe said, earning her another frown from Hailey.

"She could walk from here," Hailey inserted.

Adrianne felt her right knee buckle. Enough that Mason had to pull her up against him.

"Look at her," Phoebe said. "She can't walk home."

Adrianne knew exactly why her knee had given and she couldn't look at her friend or she'd start to laugh. This was junior high get-a-boy's-attention stuff.

"This is ridiculous," Hailey muttered. She pivoted on her stool. "There are a dozen guys here who would take her home. Hey, Dave!" she called.

"I'm taking her home," Mason said.

Adrianne was surprised by the firmness of his tone. He turned her and tucked her under his arm.

"It's fine," he said, less forcefully. "I was heading out anyway."

Hailey was quite obviously not happy. Adrianne carefully avoided making eye contact. Instead, she let herself lean into Mason, enjoying his strength and warmth.

What the hell? It wasn't like being up against him was going to last. He was only here for three days, and Hailey obviously had some kind of stake on him already.

Besides, Adrianne didn't want any kind of excitement or pulse-increasing activity. She was looking for a laidback, home every night, steady and simple farmer for the long term. So having Mason's hands on her was going to be short-lived. She might as well enjoy it for the moment.

"Let's go," he said near her ear and started for the door.

Adrianne wondered if she could get away with giving him the round-about directions to her house instead of going straight home.

As they stepped onto the wooden front porch of the Come Again, Mason said, "Hey, Adrianne, hold these a minute."

He flipped his car keys into the air and she reached out and snagged them smoothly. No problem.

Mason chuckled.

Oh.

"You definitely smell like butterscotch schnapps, but I'm not convinced you drank that much," he said.

"Um, we never said I drank it." She tossed the keys back to him and headed for the parking lot.

"Good point."

She headed for his car, the only one with Illinois plates in the lot. And the only Porsche in town. Or the county probably.

He hit the button on his key chain to unlock the doors—it was also probably the only car in the parking lot that was locked—but made no move to open the door.

Taking a deep breath, she turned to face him. He was standing really close to her. She pressed her back to the car, her palms against the warm metal of the passenger door.

"I need to ask you something," she said quickly before she could rethink it.

"Anything." He seemed to move closer.

"Did you offer me a ride because you would have offered anyone a ride or because it was me?" Internally, she cringed. Definitely junior high stuff.

It was a dumb question and she felt dumb asking—and even dumber letting the answer matter so much. But she really wanted to know. Because she was about to do something crazy and needed to know if there was even a slightly good reason.

"I would have given anyone a ride." Mason slipped his hands into his pockets and shifted his weight back onto his heels.

"Oh." Her heart dropped. She put her hand against her chest. "Okay."

He leaned in, hands still in pockets. "But I was really happy about it because it was you."

She wondered if she'd imagined the words for a moment, then she saw his grin and let herself be glad she'd asked.

Now for the crazy part.

"So you know that I haven't been drinking."

"I was pretty sure."

God, she loved that grin. She returned it. "So you will also know that anything I do or say is for reasons other than being under the influence."

"Okay."

She leaned forward, her hands still on the car door, rose on tiptoe and kissed him.

There were no hands, no contact other than lip to lip, but she felt her entire body catch fire.

She started to lean back away from the blaze, but Mason brought a hand up and cupped the back of her head, holding her in place.

This was—sensational.

They stepped forward at the same time, bringing them belly to belly. Or belly to belt buckle. And something very nice below his belt buckle.

The kiss deepened as he tipped her head to one side. Her hands went to his shoulders and she pulled herself up more flush against him.

Mason seemed to approve, because he growled in the back of his throat, grasped her thigh with his other hand, pulled it up to his hip and then stepped forward again so her back was against the side of the car.

With the firm surface behind her and her thigh in his big palm, Mason was able to press exactly where she most needed him.

They groaned together and Adrianne knew that this was going to get out of hand.

3

Though Mason felt his pulse hammering as he struggled to rein his desire in, their mouths moved together slowly, deeply and fully.

Her lips were perfect, her tongue was perfect, the sounds she made were perfect and how she smelled—like every one of his favorite things rolled into one and dipped in sugar—was absolutely perfect. And not a bit like butterscotch.

Several minutes—hell, it could have been a day or two—later, he pulled back. He stared down at her, loving that she looked dazed. The women he kissed enjoyed it, but he didn't exactly surprise them and wouldn't describe them as over-come by him. He dated women who dated a lot of men. He wasn't sure he brought anything new or unusual to the inter-actions.

Adrianne was acting, and looking, like she was stunned by him. Or by what was happening. Or how she was feeling. Or something.

Something he hoped wasn't inane like how nice the weather was tonight or that he drove a Porsche.

"No butterscotch," he said, pulling his thumb along her

lower lip, simply doing what he wanted to do, instead of thinking it out from every angle.

She shook her head. "No butterscotch."

"Too bad. I like butterscotch."

"How about cinnamon?"

"I really like cinnamon. Why?"

"I chewed cinnamon gum earlier."

He smiled. "Yeah?"

"I can prove it."

She pulled him in for another kiss.

She tasted good. Not specifically any flavor other than Adrianne. Which was better than anything he'd ever tasted.

She also felt good. She was short enough that tiptoes were necessary to really fit together, but her body seemed shaped perfectly for his. And vice versa.

When she pulled back, she smiled up at him. "See?"

"Delicious."

She licked her lips and he was ready to start all over again.

This was nuts. He felt a hunger. It was never like this with women. Things were very predictable in his dating world—as they were with everything in his world.

Drinks, dinner, dessert. That was the order in which his dating life progressed. Dessert was telltale for him. What his date ordered, how she ate it, how much she ate all told him how much she wanted him. He hadn't published his research, but it was ninety-five percent accurate.

He hadn't had dessert with Adrianne yet.

Then again, he never kissed women up against his car like he couldn't get enough of them.

He always got enough.

He knew the female body and the science and psychology of female sexuality better than anyone in his acquaintance. The same way he'd studied agriculture, geology, political science and business, he'd studied women, read about women, experimented with women until he understood everything and had the right formula.

The right formula meant the right—and predictable —outcome.

Adrianne was an anomaly.

Generally, he intensely disliked anomalies.

Looking down at her now, however, he realized he was going to make an exception in this case.

She was too short to fit where he wanted to be, so he did the logical thing and slid his hands to her butt, picked her up and set her on the hood of the car.

She instantly wrapped her legs around his waist, moaned and started unbuttoning his shirt.

"God, I want you," she panted. "This is crazy." She spread his shirt open, her gaze roaming over his shoulders, chest and stomach. "I want to taste every inch of you. I want to suck on your earlobes." She did, making Mason groan. "I want to lick your neck." She did that too. "I want to lick your chest." She wiggled against him to reach his left nipple, which she licked, making his erection pulse. "I want to suck on your fingers." Instead, she put her index finger against his mouth. Mason drew it past his lips, swirled his tongue over the pad and then sucked the length of her finger into his mouth. Her breath hissed out between her teeth. "Like that."

"I want to suck on a few things myself."

He slipped his hand under the soft, stretchy material of her top to cup one of her breasts and run his thumb over the silky cup of her bra that couldn't hide the hardened tip.

She pressed her hand over the back of his. "Yes."

When he felt her other hand at the front of his pants, he sucked in a sharp breath.

She moaned as she cupped him through his pants and he pressed into her hand.

She wanted him. Badly. He marveled at that even as a

strange thought occurred to him. His penis had never been touched by a female within the city limits of Sapphire Falls. He felt like laughing even as he fought against the intense urge to thrust fully into her grasp. The whole thing was thrilling—and arousing as hell.

He'd been wanted before. He didn't have self-esteem problems. But he hadn't been wanted like Adrianne clearly wanted him right now.

"Is it the Porsche making this feel so good?" she asked, breathless.

"I've had this car for two years and it's never felt like this."

She laughed and arched closer. "I have the most insane urge to get naked and spread out right here on the hood."

What little blood was left in his brain quickly re-routed south at that. "God, Adrianne."

The next thing he felt was the button on his pants give. "I want you naked. I want to feel every inch of you against every inch of me."

He rested his forehead against hers, trying to breathe. "Your talking is going to kill me."

"Sorry. I don't know what's going on. I never talk like this. I want to say even dirtier things for some reason. I want to use the word cock and fuck and—"

"Dead," he muttered. "I'm going to be dead. Happy. But dead."

"Sorry." She laughed. "I'll stop."

"I'll pay you to keep going."

"I really want to keep going."

He started to inch her top up, wanting—needing—to see as well as touch. "We could go—"

Suddenly a nylon jacket landed next to Adrianne on the hood of the car.

"I already told you that you have great tits, Ad. You don't have to prove it."

Mason whipped his head to the left as Matt Phillips strolled up to the car. "Get decent," he said quietly. "There's a crowd coming. I stalled as best I could."

Mason pulled his hand from Adrianne's top, then pulled her hand from his body and re-buttoned himself into modesty. Adrianne slipped into the shirt she had tied around her waist and Mason went to work on his shirt buttons.

"How'd you stall?" Adrianne asked Matt.

"How much did you see?" Mason asked, thinking that was the more important question.

"Enough to consider bringing a bucket of cold water instead of the jacket," Matt said with a chuckle. "Mike and Kevin were the ones on their way out so all I had to do was buy a round for the bar. They turned back around quick."

"You bought a round for the entire bar?" Adrianne asked. "There are probably sixty people in there."

Matt slapped Mason on the back. "I figured Mason would agree it was worth it."

Mason did indeed. He pulled his wallet from his back pocket and handed Matt several bills. "Thanks."

Matt slipped the money into his pocket without looking at it, then continued on toward the blue pickup three vehicles over from Mason's car, whistling as he went.

Mason turned back to Adrianne only to find she'd slid to the ground and was gathering her hair into a ponytail with a hair band he hadn't seen before.

"Where are you going?"

"Home," she said, her back to him and already several feet away. "Not really drunk remember?"

"I remember. Cinnamon only."

She glanced over her shoulder with a little smile. "It was nice to meet you, Mason Riley."

"It was..." he trailed off. That was all she had to say? "It was nearly orgasmic to meet you, Adrianne," he called.

She didn't turn back again, but he was sure he heard a snort of laughter before she disappeared behind two rows of cars.

He crossed his arms and leaned back against the side of his car. He waited until he saw her drive out of the parking lot and turn east. Then he headed for the bed and breakfast, happy for the first time almost ever that Sapphire Falls was small enough to ensure he would see her again. And again. And again.

———

"Adrianne, I need you to go the building site."

Adrianne had been expecting this call and she did feel a twinge of guilt when she heard Hailey's voice. Then she felt a thrill of excitement because she knew Hailey was going to ask her to meet Mason.

Then she felt the hot wash of embarrassment.

How was she going to face him? Good Lord, she'd thrown herself at him the night before. On the hood of his car no less.

She'd had her hand down his pants.

Her cheeks heated. She never did stuff like that. She'd had dirty dreams about it last night and she kept reliving the whole thing in her daydreams too. But she never did stuff like that and had no idea how to act when she saw him again.

Not seeing him again seemed a good option.

"What's going on?" Maybe she could handle the mayoral emergency. Heaven knew she handled plenty of things for Hailey every day. How hard could it be?

"Mrs. Langston is all riled up. There were apparently teenagers smoking in the park last night and she's demanding I come over and look for cigarette butts with her."

Thelma Langston lived across the street from the city park. She had constant complaints about it too, though she'd lived there for nearly forty years. Sometimes people let their dogs run loose and they came into her yard and pooped. Sometimes people had picnics and didn't pick up their garbage and then it blew into her yard. The smoking teenagers was a common complaint. She was convinced they were going to start a yard fire that was going to spread to her property and burn her to death as she slept—since, of course, the hoodlums were there in the middle of the night.

Yeah, Adrianne wasn't going near that situation.

Looked like she was going to face Mason Riley instead.

"How does she know there were teenagers?" She wanted to know how Phoebe had pulled this off. Hopefully, she hadn't recruited teenagers and bought them cigarettes.

"Someone called anonymously and told her."

Okay. Didn't that seem odd to Hailey? Or Mrs. Langston for that matter? "Why would someone tip her off?"

Hailey sighed. "She thinks it was someone concerned for her safety."

"Why didn't she call the cops?" She usually did. Of course, she also called the mayor's office to complain the next day as well, but she wasn't content to wait without doing something.

"This anonymous call didn't come until a little bit ago."

That should also seem suspicious. Who called to warn someone about something that had happened almost twelve hours earlier? But it was evidently working. Hailey was calling for backup, so Phoebe and Matt had pulled it off in spite of the holes in the setup.

"What do you need from me?" Adrianne was glad she thought to ask. She wasn't supposed to know that Hailey was meeting Mason this morning.

"Mason Riley is going to the build site to hear about our plans. I don't have a cell number for him and he's already left the bed and breakfast. Can you run out there and meet him?"

Geez, Matt had probably camped out across from the B & B so he'd know the exact moment to call Mrs. Langston so that Mason would have already left. Thank goodness, Mrs.

Langston could be counted on to get right on the phone to Hailey. And thank goodness Hailey generally ran ten to fifteen minutes late.

"Um." She shouldn't seem eager. But she couldn't say no. She never said no to Hailey. She was Adrianne's boss, and truthfully, Adrianne could do everything Hailey did except sign official documents, and that was simply because Hailey was the one who'd been elected and sworn in. "Sure, I guess."

"I thought he took you home last night."

Uh, oh. Hailey sounded suspicious. "Yeah, that's right."

"Your car was gone when I left the Come Again."

"Oh, yeah, I—" Shit. How was she going to explain that? "We were talking in the parking lot a little and some of the guys came out." That was all true. They'd been doing a lot more than talking, but they'd talked too. "And we got someone to drive my car home for me." Not true. But she hadn't given a name so Hailey couldn't check it out anyway.

"Oh, okay. I thought that was weird."

Adrianne breathed a sigh of relief. She wasn't going to press for more details. Details were what could kill you in a lie. It was hard to remember things that hadn't actually happened. Better to be vague.

Or to tell the truth.

Adrianne shook her head. She didn't like this. Lying wasn't good. And she wasn't totally sure why she felt the need to lie. Except that Phoebe and Matt were truly concerned about Mason and Hailey spending time together, and she trusted them.

And she needed her candy shop.

Besides, it was possible Hailey was truly attracted to Mason. He was a great guy. Amazing even. And Hailey had a proven track record of being interested in great guys. There wasn't a single loser on her list of exes. Hailey's attention to Mason might not just be about the money. If so, and if she got even an inkling about how Adrianne felt about him, she wouldn't like Adrianne hanging out with him. Which meant there would be no more kissing. And honestly, Adrianne was hoping for a little more of that before he left town.

So maybe she would have to be a little secretive with Hailey. She could live with that if it was for the good of the project, which meant it was ultimately for Hailey's own good. But she was going to try to keep from lying or sneaking. Much.

"What time do I need to be there?" she asked.

"Ten. And why don't you go over some basics? But I need to reschedule a time for him and me to sit down together. Will you see if you can arrange something? Maybe dinner?"

Dinner? Just the two of them?

"Are you going to be meeting with all the investors one on one?" she asked. "Because, you know, I'll need to make sure we can get it all into your schedule."

The only true must do on Hailey's schedule were the city council meetings, and those were only once a month, but Adrianne was the one everyone contacted for meetings, lunches and events that involved Hailey.

"Oh, no, I'll see them all at the investor dinner on Sunday."

"So Mason's the only one?" He did have the most money and she'd been serious when she'd told him that he'd give the whole thing a lot of credibility. With him on board, it would be easier to get the others to sign on. Maybe Hailey realized all of that and—

"I told you Mason's the only one of the bunch I haven't dated."

Yep, she sure had.

"So a date then?" Adrianne felt her chest tighten slightly and she rubbed the spot that always felt like someone had kicked her in the chest when she started to get emotional.

"I'm willing to do whatever it takes to make this project happen."

Yeah, poor Hailey having to date Mason. Her sacrifices were never ending.

"Do you think it's necessary to date him to get him to donate? Can't we show him the plans, impress him with our products, convince him it's a great idea? Shouldn't it be about business?"

Hailey laughed. "Of course. We'll do all of that too. But making sure he has a great time while he's here won't hurt, will it?"

Adrianne thought Mason seemed to be having a pretty good time so far. The memory of his hand on her breast shot through her mind and hot lightning seemed to flash through her body. Yeah, there had definitely been two of them there last night. In all her twenty-nine years of life she'd never made herself feel like that.

"Adrianne?"

She pulled herself back to the phone conversation. "Yeah?"

"So you'll meet him?"

"Sure. No problem." Because really, what was she going to say?

"And don't forget to set up a dinner for him and me. Tomorrow night would be good."

Tomorrow night was Saturday. Saturday was a great date night.

"Great," Adrianne answered, though she wasn't sure if she was referring to the pending date or the mess she found herself in the midst of.

———

M ason had been mentally preparing for seeing Hailey all morning. He wasn't worried exactly. She'd seen him last night and it had been rather obvious she liked what she saw. She'd asked him back to her house to go over the plans for the building project. He'd opened his mouth to reply, looked over to where Adrianne Scott was sitting and heard himself say, "I'd like to see the plans and the building site at the same time." That had led to them setting up this meeting outside at Milton Johnson's farm.

Technically, of course, it was Mason's farm. Which seemed strange. It was why he'd shown up a half hour early. He wanted a chance to look at the place for the first time since Milt had passed away and shocked and touched Mason by making him the heir to the property and everything on it.

Mason walked along the fence line at the back of what was officially the house's yard and where the rest of the land began. He knew every inch of the property from the pond to the pasture to the corn fields to the apple trees. He'd spent some of the happiest days of his life here. Out here, it didn't matter that he was different. Out here, he could be normal. He had to dig fence-post holes and put up barbed wire and detassel the corn the same way everyone else did. His immense intelligence didn't change any of that. He couldn't solve the problem of a loose shingle on the barn any other way than with his hands. Like a normal person.

Mason had known normal people—they'd been all around him playing football, hanging out in the commons at school, going out on Friday nights. He'd also known somehow from an early age, that he wasn't one of them. Even before he'd tested out of the fifth and sixth grades, he hadn't been interested in the things the other kids were.

Skipping two grades certainly hadn't helped. He'd left behind the few friends he did have. But fifth graders didn't have anything in common with seventh graders no matter their age or weirdness. And being two years behind his classmates in age and hormones hadn't made him more popular. Dances, girls and sneaking Playboy magazines and cigarettes simply didn't appeal. Which had made him even weirder.

Rather than sports or girls, he loved watching things grow. He'd watched birds hatch and fly away from nests in their trees. He'd watched corn go from seed to full-grown plant of the most beautiful green he'd ever seen to mature where it browned and dried and was ready for harvest. And then it all started over again.

Strangely, the interests that set him apart from his peers were also what made him feel normal. There was nothing as salt-of-the-earth as being a farmer, genius scientific mind or not.

He watched apples grow, corn grow, cows grow. It was amazing, and even as well as he could understand it, there was little he could do to influence it. Things took time to develop.

Or did they?

Some of the ideas he had gotten rich off of had started on this farm.

What ifs had taken root and grown in his imagination, fueled by his knowledge at first and his experimentation later.

Mason stooped and plucked some grass near a fence post he remembered repairing. He twirled a blade between his thumb and forefinger. As a kid, he'd studied things, as a teen he dived into the whys and hows and then in college it was like everything took on a magical quality. He'd met other people who were as curious and passionate as he was, he'd had labs and books and resources. He'd been able to finally do things. And he'd done it. All of it. Over and over until it was perfect.

He was now twenty-seven and on the verge of making an impact on the world. The growing project in Haiti only needed a couple of meetings and a few signatures and they'd be on their way to bringing more resilient and productive crops to some of the poorest areas on earth.

It was exciting, but the politics were exhausting. He wanted to do it and stop talking about it. Talking wasn't his forte. He was a thinker and a doer. Talking, explaining, debating, convincing and selling all tried his patience. To say the least. Doing it repeatedly irritated him to the point of alienating people. Like the Vice President of the United States. For instance.

Mason sighed as he turned to look at the farmhouse behind him.

This was technically the back of the house but Milt had built it so that his porch, complete with a swing, faced his west fields. Every night there were crops in his fields the older man sat watching as the sun set over them.

That porch swing had always been the epitome of home to Mason.

He was scheduled to meet with the Vice President of the United States next week. Newsweek wanted to do a story about their project. He had an entire team of scientists and students prepared to spend eight to twelve months in Haiti making this work.

And he was here wishing he had a porch swing.

"Good morning!"

Mason turned, knowing instantly that it wasn't Hailey greeting him. He felt himself smile as he saw Adrianne coming toward him. "Good morning."

She looked gorgeous. The blue sundress showed off smooth, lightly tanned skin and those perfect, delicious breasts he'd been treated to last night. The bodice of the dress would slide down even easier than the tank top had.

"I'm afraid you're stuck with me this morning," she said as she came to stand beside him. "Hailey had a last-minute emergency come up. Teenagers smoking in the park."

"I'm not the least bit disappointed," he told her honestly. She really was short. She couldn't have been more than five-foot-three. Her legs and arms were toned, her tummy flat, but she was curvy—she had hips and breasts that he truly loved.

"That's probably the nicest thing anyone's going to say to

me today." She lifted a hand to shade her eyes from the sun and smiled at him.

"Just in case, let me also tell you that you look beautiful."

Her hair was pulled back in a simple ponytail and she wore no jewelry and very light makeup. She looked like she could do a commercial for facial cleanser or herbal shampoo.

She was so different from the women he was used to spending time with. They were polished and put together—not an eyelash or thread out of place. They were beautiful, but he would have never gotten hot and heavy on the hood of his car with any of them. He wouldn't have wanted to wrinkle them.

In contrast, Adrianne looked sweet and wholesome and he really wanted to wrinkle her some more.

At his compliment, she grinned. "That's the nicest thing anyone will say all week."

"That's terrible. People should be telling you nice things all the time."

"Why are you honeying up to me? You're the one I'm supposed to be wowing with the building plans."

"Honeying up?" he repeated. "Isn't the term kissing up?"

She blushed.

All he said was kissing up and she blushed. He liked that. He hadn't really been worried that she'd forgotten the kiss from the night before, but this made him positive she'd been thinking about it.

"Same thing," she muttered, her gaze on the fence next to him instead of on him.

He moved closer. "I like anything with kissing in it better."

"Anyway," she said. "I'm supposed to be telling you about the building plans."

"Okay, what part of the property are you thinking about using?"

She laughed. "Right here. And a lot of the yard and extending into the fields."

Mason looked at her, not sure what the emotion was that he was feeling. The farm held great memories for him. Yes, it was a part of him. But he'd owned it for two years without visiting. He couldn't possibly be feeling protective of it. He couldn't really feel possessive. He didn't care if they knocked the house down and paved the yard.

Except that in that moment he did.

"We'll need to pave a road and put in parking too," she said.

Mason looked out from the rise that came up gently from the land around it, where Milt had built his house. It wasn't truly a hill by any definition. And it was three and a half miles from town. And it wasn't like they could slap some cement on and call it a road.

"Why right here?"

"Well, it's a hill…"

"Barely."

She shrugged. "It's more of a hill than anywhere else out here."

That was probably true. "Why does it have to be out here?"

"It's unused land that's big enough and not too far from the two major highways."

"But why do you want it outside of town?" That didn't make sense at all to him.

"That's part of the charm," she said, her eyes bright. "It's not only Sapphire Falls. We have potential business owners from Pierce and Dawson City too."

"It's not very accessible. Are you thinking about how to route traffic?"

She nodded. "Highway Three is busier than Forty-four. From Highway Three you have to go through Sapphire Falls to get here. This way people have to go through town. See what else we have to offer. Stop there too."

It was hard to resist that smile. Adrianne was clearly enthusiastic about the project. It was enough to make him continue talking about it to keep her smiling and talking with that bounce in her voice. But he had no intention of donating any money.

"What do the plans include exactly?"

And there was no way he was giving up the land. He was going to have to come up with some way of explaining that to Lauren. He'd get to work on that as soon as he came up with a way to explain it to himself.

He was having a hard time concentrating on anything, though, with the breeze continually blowing that strand of hair against Adrianne's lips. The lips that were moving as she talked but that kept throwing his thoughts back to the night before.

They were alone out here. He could have her dress off and her up against the maple tree in seconds.

Wow.

He shook his head. He never had this much trouble concentrating. He was picturing her naked while she was trying to make a business pitch. There was a snowball's chance in hell he was going to invest, but it was the professional, respectful thing to do to listen and ask questions.

Not picture her grasping that lower branch as he thrust up—

Yeah, that was the other problem. He never had that kind of sex. He'd never needed nor wanted to.

Until now.

She flipped a few pages up on her clipboard and then read off the potential businesses for this little shopping area. A card and stationery store, a furniture store, a candy shop, a sports bar, and a couple of still-open spots.

He frowned down at sheet she was reading from. "Tyler Bennett is opening a sports bar?" he asked.

She nodded. "Yes. Well, maybe," she amended. "He's agreed to be a part of it if we get the rest of it up and going."

Mason knew Tyler. Well, he knew of Tyler. Ty was the

youngest of the Bennett boys, but they were all rather infamous. Ty's older brother, Travis, had been in Mason and Hailey's class in high school. They were a family of team captains and homecoming kings and they all seemed to have pockets full of get-out-of-jail-free cards. It was hard not to know of them. No matter how hard someone tried not to.

"Why would Tyler Bennett open a sports bar?" Mason asked.

"He was a medalist in the Olympics."

Yep, even Mason Riley knew about Tyler's silver medal. "How does that qualify him to run a sports bar?" How did it qualify him to do anything other than run, bike and swim?

Adrianne gave him a little smile. "I'm assuming Ty's had his fair share of beer."

Not likely with the kind of training regimen the triathlons would require. Mason crossed his arms. "Uh huh. I've traveled on an airplane. Several times. Still pretty sure I shouldn't be flying the thing."

Adrianne winced slightly. "He'll bring a well-recognized name to the project. He has a...following."

"You think they'll all come to Sapphire Falls to drink his beer?"

Adrianne lifted one shoulder. "Even if not, Sapphire Hills will be mentioned whenever Tyler's mentioned in the media and he'll talk about it all over. And all the businesses are prepared for mail order."

Mason sighed. Mail order. Sure, that would solve every problem with this project.

"How does a sports bar fit into the vision for Sapphire Hills?" Mason asked. A collection of quaint locally owned shops and then a place where guys would gather to drink and yell at televisions? It didn't make sense.

Mason saw Adrianne grimace slightly and he knew that she

agreed it didn't quite fit. But she then proceeded to completely ignore his question.

"Here," Adrianne said, digging in her bag and pulling out a small white organdy bag. "Since we didn't know you were coming for sure, we didn't have this in your room at the bed and breakfast like we did for the others."

He fought a smile. Ignoring the ridiculousness didn't make it any less ridiculous. He took the bag and lifted it, looking through the gauzy fabric. "What's this?"

"Samples." She smiled. "There's some candy from the proposed candy shop, some of the specialty ground coffee from the coffee shop, a card like the ones Jennifer will create for her shop, and some photos of some of the furniture Greg wants to make in his store."

Mason opened the bag and withdrew a one-inch ball covered in chocolate. He held it up.

"That's a cake drop," she said, her eyes crinkling adorably at the corners. "Try it."

He bit into the sample and his eyebrows rose in appreciation. "Okay, that's pretty good," he said as he swallowed. It was perfect. He wasn't much for sweets, but the cake drop tasted like a perfect bite of the best red velvet cake and cream-cheese frosting he'd ever tasted.

"I'm glad you like it."

He liked her. The realization seemed to hit him out of the blue. Not that he'd disliked her for even a moment since meeting her, but it was clear the chemistry from the night before was very real and very present even in the morning light. Now, in addition to wanting her with a nearly staggering force, he also liked her.

"So Ty's place will be competing with Dottie's?" he asked briskly, trying to focus and a little pissed that he couldn't.

She looked startled by his sudden shortness. "A, um..." She cleared her throat. "No, not directly."

If he was going to say no, which he definitely was, he at least owed it to them to hear all the details first. "How is it not direct? Dottie serves food in town at the café. Ty will serve food out here. If people are already here, there's no reason for them to go back into town to Dottie's, right?"

He wasn't trying to antagonize Adrianne. But he was annoyed with her and couldn't seem to help it coming out. Annoyed that she was so tempting, so distracting, so able to make him not really want to talk about practical things like how much money he would waste on this project if he listened to her and looked into those big brown eyes.

"I haven't talked to Dottie about it," she finally answered. "But she hasn't said anything. She's friends with Tyler's mom, so I'm sure she knows about it."

"Maybe she'd like to provide food out here."

"Maybe."

"But that won't be okay with Ty, will it?"

"I don't know—"

"And there's not really anything to keep them here overnight."

"Here?"

"Sapphire Falls."

"Overnight? No." Adrianne frowned.

"So this won't benefit the bed and breakfast."

"No, but—"

"And you're an hour away from the city where there are shows and movies and concerts. So if someone wants to catch something like that on a weekend, either they won't come here or they'll leave early to make it."

She crossed her arms over her clipboard and frowned up at him. "Are you always so negative?"

"I'm always so logical. And honest." He was always logical—that's why this was driving him nuts. More specifically, why she was driving him nuts. None of this was logical. None of this made sense. There was attraction and then there was whatever this was.

"Hmm," was all she said.

That also drove him nuts. She was affected by him. He knew that. But she didn't seem bothered by it like he was. Did this happen to her so often that she was used to it?

Women were strange. It didn't matter how long or thoroughly he studied them—there were things that didn't make sense.

"You know a lot about this project."

She narrowed her eyes but nodded. "Anything you want to know."

He didn't like the idea overall, and usually he didn't care how someone would feel about that. In business, it was business, not personal. But somehow he sensed this was important to her and he didn't want to disappoint her.

Which meant this was even more of an anomaly. He found himself wanting to tread carefully so that he didn't hurt her feelings.

"Was it your idea?"

"Hailey wanted to do something during her term as mayor that was really big for the town, something that would really matter."

That didn't answer his question.

"This was all Hailey's idea?"

She waved her hand as if it wasn't important. "We've worked on it together from the beginning. It's hard to remember who came up with what exactly."

He could tell it was a purposefully vague answer. "So you came up with it."

"I didn't say that." But she wouldn't meet his eyes.

"You clearly like the idea."

Her head came up. "I do. I think it would be great for the town."

"So?" He watched her carefully.

"So Sapphire Falls deserves to have something great happen."

"Why?" He wasn't sure why he was pushing. He didn't want a tornado to destroy the town or anything, but he did want to know why this Chicago transplant cared so much about a place she'd only lived in for a short time. A town that he didn't have a lot of warm and fuzzy feelings for.

"This town is full of good people, living good lives, taking care of their families and friends and neighbors. If they have a dream, why can't we try to make it come true?"

Wow. Okay. "They're not that different from any other little town."

She seemed to pause to think about that. "Well, they're different from the towns and people I know." Then she took a deep breath. "And now they're my town."

"Why do you care so much?" he asked. "You haven't been here long."

She looked up at him with a thoughtful expression. "Home isn't about time," she finally said. "It's about where you feel good and can be yourself."

"Ah, well, that would explain why I don't feel at home here." He didn't mean to sound bitter. He'd been himself here, but it hadn't made him want to build them stuff.

She tipped her head and looked up at him, not with pity or censure, but with understanding. "Home is also the place that has what you need. Maybe you didn't need anything here."

Maybe. But that was now quickly becoming not the case. There was something he was beginning to really need right here in the middle of Sapphire Falls.

He looked into her eyes and sighed. "This is quite inconvenient."

Her eyebrows rose. "What's inconvenient? This meeting? I thought that Hailey—"

"The fact that I can't concentrate on anything."

"Anything like—"

"The business proposal, the details of the plan, why it's a bad idea."

She looked surprised. "You think it's a bad idea?"

"Yes."

"Why?"

"It's..." He sighed and rubbed the middle of his forehead. This was ridiculous. "For a number of reasons I can't quite put into a plausible argument right now. Which is the inconvenient part."

"I'm sorry." She didn't sound sorry. She sounded ticked off. "I didn't realize that I was getting in your way of...something." She recapped her pen and started to turn.

He grabbed her elbow as she started to step away. "Adrianne."

She stopped but didn't face him.

"You're in the way of me thinking clearly and acting logically."

She twisted to look up at him. "You're not acting logically?"

"No. And it's about to get worse."

"What do you mean?"

"I'm going to kiss you, probably even more than that given half the chance, rather than tell you all of the reasons that this building plan doesn't make sense and would be a bad investment for me and anyone else."

She blinked several times, the tension in her body relaxing under his hand. "You want to kiss me?"

"Even if I hadn't had a taste of you last night."

She sucked in a quick breath and turned to completely face him. "Kissing can be logical."

"Oh?" He pulled her closer and her thighs bumped his.

"It seems logical given the chemistry between us."

He could go with that argument. Hell, he didn't remember

what didn't make sense about it right now anyway. He leaned in slowly. Last night in the parking lot had been crazy, out of control, nuts. This was still nuts, but at least it was intentional. He could handle things much better when they were intentional.

Adrianne slid her fingers into his hair, pulling him close. Her clipboard fell to the ground as he put his hands on her hips. He loved her hips. She wasn't skinny. She had places he could hold onto and squeeze. She was soft and curvy and sweet. He brought her against him and touched his lips to hers.

He wanted to go slow. He wanted to be thorough. She was a variance in what he knew. That brought out the researcher in him. He needed to examine her effect on him fully.

He breathed in, wanting to remember her scent. He concentrated on memorizing the feel of her lips, the feel of the soft cotton dress under his palms, the heat of her skin through the cotton. He even noted the feel of the sun on the back of his neck, that there was a light breeze and that the dirt shifted slightly under his right shoe. This is good, he thought as he lifted his head and tipped the opposite direction to taste her again. He was beginning to gather data—

Which all went to hell when she sighed and opened her mouth.

She flicked her tongue out along his bottom lip, pressed her breasts to his ribs and arched closer.

Screw data.

Mason licked her lip in return, then stroked in along her tongue, the hot, wet slickness erotic and new. She tasted faintly of mint, smelled like honey and felt like...nothing he'd ever felt before.

Which didn't faze him at the moment. Because she was moaning and pressing closer. He slipped the strap of her dress off her shoulder and cupped her breast. The hot skin and firm tip against his palm pulled him back from his fog of want and he glanced down. No bra. Bare breast. And nice bright sunlight.

He lifted his eyes to hers as he ran his thumb over her hard nipple and she gasped, watching his face.

It wasn't like breasts were brand new. It wasn't like pleasuring a woman was brand new. But that look was new. That look Adrianne was now giving him—that was new.

He was a scientist. He liked to see how things worked, how things responded to stimuli. He felt the slow grin he gave her just before he tugged on her nipple.

"Holy...Mason." Her eyes slid shut and she arched her breast closer.

"Like that? Or this?" He rolled the tip between his thumb and finger.

She gripped his forearm. "I, um..." She hadn't opened her eyes and she licked her lips. "Yes."

God, he loved cause and effect.

He ran his thumb over the nipple again, letting his gaze slide over her. She was gorgeous. Generous breasts, full, soft, except for the tip. He bent and licked her nipple, causing her to make a funny high-pitched sound at the back of her throat.

The dark parking lot last night hadn't given him enough of a look. But her scent and sound were permanently imprinted on his well-above-average memory. The sight of her along with the taste, sound, scent...everything, combined into a hot swirl of lust that filled his groin and his head.

"Mason," she groaned as he sucked harder.

The next thought in his head was absolutely the last thing he would have expected.

Hydrogen.

He needed to adjust the hydrogen levels.

That was the answer.

Right in the middle of making out with the sexiest anomaly

he'd ever experienced, he had the answer to the problem with the soil he'd been working on for two weeks.

Which went to show that this whole situation was crazy.

He needed a piece of paper and a pen.

Adrianne's scent drifted to up him and he knew he couldn't stop and make notes now. She'd cover up, she'd pull away, he would lose the moment with her. But now he had the solution. He stared at Adrianne, her eyes shut, her breast in his hand, her lips parted, breathing hard—for him. It was like the emotions she caused in him had freed his imagination, inspiring the answer. She was like a muse.

"Adrianne, I need your pen," he murmured near her ear.

He had to keep touching her, but he had to get this down. There was only one option.

"My...pen?"

She started to open her eyes, but he rolled her nipple again and kissed her long and deep.

She relaxed with a sigh and he bent and picked up the pen where it lay next to her abandoned clipboard. He took her hand from his shoulder, straightened her arm and turned her palm up. Perfect.

"This might tickle." He put the pen against the sensitive skin of her inner forearm and formed the first few letters and numbers that would work as shorthand notes for him when he was able to write it out fully later.

"What are you doing?" She didn't try to pull away, tipping her head to try to read his scribbles.

"Taking notes."

"On how to make me moan?" she asked with a sexy little smile that almost made him forget there even was such a thing as hydrogen.

But the hydrogen levels were a huge key. Something he should have thought of before, but he'd thought they had all the levels...

The breeze stirred her hair, flipping a strand against her lips again and he stared at them. He wanted to feel them against his, and then his neck, his chest, his—

"Mason?"

He shook his head.

Jesus. This was impossible. He couldn't concentrate on work because of her, but he couldn't concentrate on her because equations and ideas kept popping up.

"Can I..." She was going to think he was insane.

"What?"

"I have to make these notes or I'll lose them," he said honestly. "But I don't want to let go of you."

"So write them down," she said simply.

"I don't have any..."

"It'll wash off." She flipped her hair over her shoulder and pulled the other strap of her dress down to reveal a lot more skin. A lot more writing area.

"Really?"

"I don't want you to lose anything," she said with a smile.

His hand shook a little—unbelievably—as he put the pen back against her arm. But as soon as he made the first notation, it flowed. A lot of it. Ideas kept coming, one on top of the next. The words covered her inner forearm and he had to go past her elbow to the sweet skin of her upper arm. He continued until he'd reached the top curve of her shoulder.

Then the soft curves below made his pen pause. He glanced to her face and froze. She was watching him with—well, he wasn't absolutely sure but it seemed to be...fascination.

"You okay?" he asked.

"Overwhelmed," she said quietly.

"Overwhelmed that I'm writing on you?"

Her lips curved into a smile and she shook her head. "Overwhelmed by you. All of this..." she looked down at her arm, then back to him, "...is so—"

"Weird," he supplied. It wasn't like she'd be the first woman to notice he wasn't like most men. He'd never stopped and written notes during a date and certainly not on his date, but he did occasionally slip with a strange term or topic. This by far topped that in the weird department.

But Adrianne shook her head again. "These are equations right?"

He nodded. "Things I've been working on in the lab. Things that weren't coming together before and now, inexplicably, they are."

"Your mind is...amazing. You're standing here in front of me, looking like a regular guy, but inside your head things are happening that are going to turn into products and techniques and...stuff I don't even know how to describe...that are going to help the world. You are writing things on my arm that are going to turn into actual things that people are going to use and..." She trailed off, sincerely looking lost as to how put it into words.

Mason couldn't come up with anything adequate either. He stared at her, wondering if it made sense that he wanted her even more now. She thought he was amazing and he was being not-quite-but-almost as weird as he got.

Yeah, it made sense that he didn't think he would ever get enough of her.

She knew what he did for a living—thanks to the profiles she'd done—so she knew a little of what she was talking about. If she could be amazed by him writing on her, then a lot of what he did wouldn't bother her.

He studied the notes about the things he needed to retest and a new soil combination that would surely fix the pH problems. He couldn't believe how incredibly erotic Adrianne looked with scientific notations on her skin. That was definitely weird. But these notations were what would propel his latest project forward and, as she'd said, help the world. It was the first step toward a lot of other bigger steps that would take some time and negotiations, but yes, eventually these notations would turn into something that meant crops for people in places where there were no crops now. It was his passion, and seeing it represented on the skin of the woman he felt this other crazy, out-of-control passion for really was...amazing.

Work and non-work had always been stringently divided for him. Now they were not only combined but they were combined in a sensual way that made him almost certain that if it weren't for his desire for Adrianne, he might not have ever found the right equation.

"Ever had sex on a farm?" he asked, tossing the pen aside and reaching for her.

Never ever would he have thought of having sex on the ground at Milt's farm. Now it seemed like the best idea ever. He was a farmer. Down deep in his soul, at the heart of what he knew and loved, was farming. It made sense to have the most erotic encounter of his life in the place that felt the most like home.

She chuckled even though she was breathing hard. "Sounds like a fetish."

"It's simply dirt and grass, sunshine and fresh air," he said, drawing her dress up in one hand. "It'll be good for you."

"I do like dirty sex."

Her hands went to the bottom of his shirt and started tugging as her cell phone rang.

"Do. Not. Answer. That." He had her skirt to her waist. Her panties matched the blue dress.

He really liked the color blue.

She sighed. "I have to. It's Phoebe."

"How do you know?" He was on his way to his knees. Her dress bunched at her hips, pulled down from the top, gathered up from the bottom. He needed to know if she tasted as sweet everywhere.

"It's her ringtone."

He didn't recognize the tune, but that didn't surprise him. He followed almost no pop culture and current music was only one thing he had very little clue about.

"Ignore her." He still hadn't dropped her skirt, appreciating the not-all-that-long but silky smooth expanse of leg.

"Can't." She took a deep breath and let go of him. She pulled her dress straps back up.

He looked up at her. She stared down at him. He ran his open palm down the back of her bare leg from the curve of her butt to her ankle. "You sure?"

She swallowed hard. "Can you...um...hold that thought?"

He stayed on one knee, running his hand up and down the leg that he wanted wrapped around his waist. "I'm not likely to forget about this any time soon."

She swallowed again and bent to dig in the purse she'd dropped next to her at some point. "Phoebe, this isn't really a good... Okay, what?" She paused to listen. "Shit. Okay."

That didn't sound so good.

Still, he really wanted to hook a finger under the edge of her panties, pull them down and make her forget about whatever was going on.

She hung up the phone. "We have to stop." She stepped back out of his reach. "Seriously."

"We're two single consenting adults and we're not bothering anyone."

She stepped back as he reached out and he ended up tipping forward onto both knees.

"Oh, we're about to be bothering someone." She sighed. "Quite a bit, I'd guess. Hailey's on her way out here."

Reality returned just like that.

Hailey Conner.

It worked like a bucket of ice water dumped over his head.

He was in Sapphire Falls. On his knees in front of a woman. How appropriate.

He stretched to his feet. "I'll hold the thought a little longer than I'd planned."

She smiled but definitely looked disappointed. "Sorry."

"It's fine." It was good, in fact. This woman had him doing, saying, thinking things that made no sense. He didn't like that. Things had to make sense. Things had to be predictable. So far, Adrianne Scott had been anything but.

So this was good.

Ironic even.

Hailey Conner was saving him from making an ass of himself over a woman.

4

"I, um..." Adrianne ran a hand through her hair and smoothed the skirt of her dress. Then she sighed. "This sucks."

He chuckled. It did. In lots of ways. "We're waiting here for Hailey then?"

"It's Sapphire Falls. It's not like it's going to take her long to get here."

"We could leave and..." He hoped she was filling in the blanks the same way he was.

She shrugged. "Very tempting. But Hailey is...persistent."

"Self-absorption and wanting to get her way isn't the same thing as being persistent."

The right corner of her mouth curled up. "That's not nice." But she didn't deny that Hailey was self-absorbed. "Being persistent means you care about something."

He studied her face. "What do you get persistent about, Adrianne?" What mattered to her? What did she care about?

"Oh, persistence used to be my middle name," she said. "Seemed like I was persistent about everything for a long time."

"And now?" He was fascinated by her and he wanted to get deeper and deeper—in lots of ways.

She gave him a smile, then tipped her head back, spread her arms and took a deep breath. "Now I found a place where I can get exactly what I want."

The smooth length of her pale throat made his mouth dry. "What do you want?" His voice was gruff.

She met his eyes again. "Peace, quiet, fresh air and a good night's sleep."

"That's pretty basic stuff."

She nodded. "Strange how hard they can be to find."

He thought about his life and had to admit she had a point. But in her expression, he saw something that he realized he rarely saw in people—contentment.

It looked good on her.

So did his pen marks.

"What is Hailey going to think of that?" he asked, gesturing at the ink on her skin.

Adrianne looked down at it, as if she'd forgotten it was there. "Oh, um, right." She looked back up at him. "That might be hard to explain."

"I need those notes. I'll have to copy them."

She looked at him for a few seconds and then said, "Do you want to go back to my house? Then I can shower when you're done."

Her house. A shower... Mason's mind ran with the invitation. Then sobered.

Right. She was going to have to wash all of that off. "I'm sorry, Adrianne. That was dumb. It might..."

She stepped close. "It's okay, Mason. We were caught up in a moment. Crazy things happen in moments like that. Don't worry about it."

She was right. Nothing was hurt. It had been an inexplicable mix of passion and emotion. His brain synapses had been firing so quickly it was no wonder something had been shaken loose.

"I can come over. Sure, that would work."

They'd take it from there. But at least inside a house was less crazy than the middle of the field where they hoped to build Sapphire Hills.

A horn honking signaled they were no longer alone.

"Like I said, it doesn't take long to get from anywhere to anywhere else around here," Adrianne said with a small smile.

"Hailey?"

"Likely."

They started toward the front of the big house together. Hailey stepped out of her Lexus a moment later. "Hi!"

Her attention immediately went to Adrianne's appearance, but her first words were not what Mason expected.

"You're wearing a dress?"

Adrianne looked down at herself. "Looks like it."

"You don't wear dresses." Hailey seemed very confused.

"I don't wear dresses much," Adrianne corrected, but her cheeks grew red.

"Are you going to church?" Hailey asked.

"No."

Mason felt a smile spread on his face. Adrianne had dressed up for him. Thanks to Lauren, he knew that mattered. Then he focused on Hailey.

Holy cow, some things never changed.

Hailey Conner was a gorgeous, sexy woman. The night before, he'd been stunned by how little she'd changed in appearance over the years. Today, she was decked out in a blood-red suit, three-inch red heels and makeup that would make a runway model jealous. Her long blond hair hung loose and sexy.

She turned heads, there was no doubt about it, and regardless of how much time had passed or how much he had changed, or how he still hadn't forgiven her for being a complete and total bitch to him, Mason had to admit that she was beautiful.

She carried herself with a confident air that clearly said that she knew how great she looked and was pleased to have everyone else notice too.

But he knew she hadn't dressed up to see him.

"And what's all over your arm?" Hailey asked, grabbing Adrianne's hand.

"Mason needed—"

"I was showing Adrianne some of the soil formulas and chemical balances we need to perfect in order for our seeds to withstand—"

"Why?" Hailey asked without letting Mason finish.

"I was interested in what he does." Adrianne was looking at him as she spoke. "It's not every day you get to hang out with a genius who's making the world a better place. I should have asked more questions," she added.

Mason had the distinct impression that she was saying that for him.

"We can—"

"You better get it all washed off. We have the softball game this afternoon." Hailey turned to Mason. "You're on my team, okay?"

Mason considered himself quite good at any number of things. A few sports were even on the list—golf, racquetball, running. Softball was not one of them, however. "I'll come watch, but I don't think I'll play," he said.

"You have to play or our teams won't be even," Hailey told him. She put a hand on a hip that was tight and trim.

He glanced at Adrianne with her soft curves and hips—

"Don't worry, I'll hold your hand if you need me to," Hailey said.

At one time, that offer would have made his palms sweat. Now he was trying to think of how to get out of it.

But there was very likely no use in arguing. Hailey Conner had always gotten her way—especially from males. It wasn't worth the effort.

"I need to get these notes from Adrianne before she washes them off," he said, changing the subject. "We were heading to her house."

"Oh, well, that's silly. Here." Hailey pulled a notebook out of her purse and handed it to Mason. "Copy your notes right here. Then we can let Adrianne get cleaned up and I can take you to lunch."

"That's okay," Adrianne said quickly. "I don't need to go."

Hailey quirked an eyebrow. "You're not going to wash that off?"

"I'll..." Adrianne glanced down at herself, then back to Hailey. "I guess—"

"You have to wash it off," Hailey said with an eye roll. "It's not like you can walk around with long sleeves on. It's almost ninety."

Adrianne gave in with a sigh. "You're right."

Mason flipped open the notebook and took the pen Adrianne held out. The same pen he'd used to mark her. He'd written fairly small so he had to get closer to Adrianne to read his notes. "Thanks for letting me do this. This formula could be a big deal," he said quietly as he wrote.

"I'm enthralled," Adrianne said. "Watching this idea come to you like that and knowing that my arm holds the secret to some big agricultural revelation in another country is pretty exciting."

She was pretty exciting.

"You really did do homework on me." She had to have gathered a lot of details—and read them—to know that he'd worked on projects for crops in other countries.

"Homework for what?" Hailey asked.

"His profile," Adrianne said without looking at her. "All the info about his company and everything he's been asked to do."

Hailey had evidently not read his profile.

Mason thought maybe he should be more surprised, or even disappointed, about that. But he wasn't either.

The last of the notes ended well above the dip of her dress, but Mason had seen the glorious curves underneath the blue cotton and his mouth got dry as he finished copying the formula from along her shoulder.

"Thanks again," he said to her.

"Sure. I'll see you at the softball game." She bent and grabbed her clipboard, then was gone without a look back.

Mason watched her go, thinking that he should be grateful she was gone, he was no longer on his knees and he was about to have lunch with the girl he'd had a crush on for five years of his life. At one time, he would have given anything to have Hailey Conner's attention—her positive attention. He'd experienced her attention in a big way one time. That had been more than enough.

Which was probably part of why he didn't want to have lunch with her.

But it seemed that a bigger part of it was driving away in a blue sundress and black ballpoint-pen ink.

There had been nothing predictable about this trip at all.

He didn't like unpredictable, dammit.

———

"This is great!"

"No, Phoebe, this is definitely not great." Adrianne hauled the big box of softball supplies out of the back seat of Phoebe's car. "I almost had sex with him right there in the great outdoors."

"Well, where would you expect a genius farmer to have sex?" Phoebe grabbed the bats from Adrianne's trunk.

"Really?" Adrianne asked. "You think he takes women out into cornfields all the time?"

Phoebe laughed. "Probably not. He lives in Chicago after all. So you almost had sex with him. Outside. Big deal. I think it's great."

"What's great about it?" Adrianne asked, starting toward the field.

Some of the guys were already there and would help them set everything up, but Adrianne couldn't help but think that this was how things always went with Hailey. She'd come up with a kernel of an idea and then expect Adrianne to iron out the details and make the damned thing happen. Like this game. Hailey had wanted to have an event that could be put between the other festivities on Friday that would involve all the investors and the alumni group gathered. It had to be fun, a place where there was something to do but everyone could still talk. Something that might be sentimental for some of them, bringing out their sense of home and affection for Sapphire Falls and loosening their wallets a bit.

Adrianne had talked with Phoebe and Matt and they'd told her how Sapphire Falls used to have a big co-ed softball tournament every fourth of July.

It wasn't the fourth of July, but since the tradition had died out sometime over the past ten years, Adrianne thought it was the perfect fit for Hailey's event requirements.

And now Adrianne was hauling bases and catcher's gear to the field on a sunny, ninety-two-degree day, working up a nice sweat forty minutes after showering, her hair already falling out of the ponytail she'd pulled back when she realized she wouldn't have time to do anything more with her hair.

While Hailey had lunch with Mason.

The whole letting-Hailey-have-the-spotlight thing was starting to suck a little.

Phoebe put the bats and bag of softballs next to the bench in the closest dugout and turned to take some of the stuff from Adrianne's arms. "What's great about it is that Mason Riley, the biggest dork in school, the never-had-a-date-in-high-school guy, is now getting it on with the hottest girl in Sapphire Falls. Good for him."

Adrianne felt sick. "You think they're getting it on?"

Phoebe faced her. "They? I meant you and Mason. Who's he with?"

"Hailey. They're having lunch. Supposedly."

"How did that happen?"

"They left together from the farm." Adrianne checked her watch. "Of course, there's plenty of time to eat, have hot, sweaty sex and still make it here in time for the game."

"Dammit," Phoebe muttered, pulling her cell phone from her pocket. She dialed and then leveled a stare at Adrianne. "What part of 'keep them apart' doesn't make sense to you?"

"I tried but—"

"Matt, it's me," Phoebe interrupted as she spoke into the phone. "Mason's with Hailey having lunch." She paused to listen and then said, "Check there first, but drive by her house too." She hung up and looked at Adrianne. "Seriously. Keep them apart. Period."

"She's my boss. He's a guest. He's practically a stranger to me. I can't control—"

"I'm thinking you have more control over him than you know."

"What do you mean?"

"You're the hottest girl in Sapphire Falls. And he's getting frisky with you. And you like it. This is great."

Adrianne felt her eyes go wide. "I'm the hottest girl? What

the hell are you talking about? You've met Hailey Conner right?"

Phoebe waved that away. "Yeah, yeah. She's Hailey, always will be. But she's always been here. And she's dated pretty much all the eligible men. You're new. You don't date guys from here—which drives them crazy but also intrigues them. Hailey's out there with her...stuff. You're much more under-stated. You make them all nuts."

Some of the guys came over to gather the equipment so Adrianne kept her mouth shut and gave them smiles and casual greetings. As soon as they moved off, she said to Phoebe, "You're nuts."

Phoebe held out her phone. "Call Matt. Ask him. It's true. Hailey shows it all off in her skirts and heels, with her hair and her lips and her boobs. You go around in jeans and T-shirts and tennis shoes, ponytails, no makeup. You're more of a mystery. They haven't known you since kindergarten—which makes some of us much less of a mystery. They don't know your grandmother who can tell them every embarrassing story about you they don't already know."

"But—"

"You're the girl next door. And you're sweet," Phoebe went on when Adrianne tried to interrupt. "You're nice. You're genuine. Guys like that. These are good guys from a nice town. While they do tend to think with their penises more than they should, deep down they all want a nice girl. Like you."

Adrianne stared at her friend. Then felt a little dizzy. "No," she groaned. "No, no, no."

She didn't want any of that.

Her look, her attitude, her lifestyle were all simply a product of doing the opposite of what she'd done for years. She was downsizing, simplifying, uncomplicating her life.

Sapphire Falls was her haven. This was where she could be herself, where she could relax.

Dammit. How could she relax now that she knew what the guys were thinking?

She didn't date guys from here because she didn't want a relationship with anyone from here. Dating a guy from a small town like this was more than dating just the guy, or even his family. It was like dating the whole town. Everyone would be involved, invested, full of opinions, judgments and advice.

No way did she want that kind of pressure.

"Anyway," Phoebe said, seemingly unconcerned by Adrianne's distress. "I think it's great that Mason gets to show the other guys around here what he's got."

"He's not going to show them anything. It's not like he's going to be bragging in the locker room."

Phoebe laughed. "They'll notice, Ad, trust me. And he hasn't even been here for a whole day. This is gonna be great for him."

Adrianne sighed. Terrific. "I think I need to stay away from Mason Riley."

"No," Phoebe said quickly. "No, you can't. We have to keep him and Hailey apart and you might be the only one who can really keep him interested in something else."

"He's that interested in her?" Adrianne asked, feeling her stomach dip again.

"I don't know." Phoebe shrugged. "He used to be and I'm not willing to risk it now. I wanted you to be the one to tell him about the project, but now it looks like there's even more reason for him to spend time with you."

"You don't think that we—and when I say we I mean you—are overreacting here a little?"

Phoebe shook her head. "No way. This is important. The future of your candy shop is on the line here." She looked at Adrianne contemplatively. "Why don't you relax and have fun? He's obviously got you a little riled up. Enjoy it. It's only a few days."

That was exactly the problem. She was riled up and she hated that. Being riled up, worked up, wound up—she avoided all of that. She was in Sapphire Falls for the very fact that things were laidback, even-keel, even boring here.

And it was only for a few days. Then he'd be gone. It wasn't worth it.

"My heart can't take this stuff."

Phoebe sighed. "Sweetie, your heart...thing was two years ago."

"It was a heart attack," Adrianne said. "Not a thing."

Her doctor, thank God, put up with her neuroses and reassured her regularly she was doing everything right. But he did want her to stop obsessing. Which she obsessed about a little.

"You're perfectly healthy now. You've stopped smoking, drinking, cut down on caffeine, reduced your stress, changed your diet, you work out...honey, you're fine," Phoebe said. She wasn't Adrianne's doctor, but Phoebe made Adrianne repeat her doctor's advice whenever she got worked up. Or Phoebe would repeat it to her. "At least fine enough to spend some time with a hot guy who looks at you like I look at Snickers bars."

Adrianne smiled at that. "Maybe. But I do not want drama with Hailey. If she thinks I'm moving in on a guy she wants—"

"Hailey shouldn't always get what she wants. It's already made her a brat. Help her not become a total bitch. Get in her way."

"I'm not sure a two-day fling with a guy I may never see again is worth the risk." She rubbed the spot on her chest over her heart. Dammit. She didn't want a guy who made her heart flutter just by thinking about having a fling with him.

Phoebe looked at her for a long moment. Then her eyes flickered to something over Adrianne's left shoulder. Her mouth stretched into a slow, knowing smile. "Tell me that he's not worth the risk after you spend the next two days with him."

Phoebe left Adrianne standing there and she slowly turned

with apprehension. Sure enough, Mason was striding toward her.

She forgot how to swallow. He was in a black T-shirt that stretched across his broad chest and shoulders, and gray cotton athletic shorts that showed powerful muscles and tanned skin.

Her heart raced and she pressed her fingers over the pounding.

There was no way around that really. Simply seeing him caused that reaction, and she couldn't very well duck and hide every time she saw him coming over the next forty-eight hours. But she could avoid kissing him. Probably.

"This is a really bad idea," he said as he got close. He was frowning.

Yeah, well, she had a whole list of really bad ideas. "You're going to have to be more specific."

"This game. I don't play softball, Adrianne."

"Oh, this is for fun. No pressure. Not even that much exertion."

"No, I really don't play softball. Like I've never swung a bat."

She frowned. "How is that possible? You never had to play Wiffle ball in PE class?"

"If I did, I've blocked out the memory because it was so awful."

She chuckled. What a drama queen. "Okay, here." She handed him a bat. "Show me."

"Show you that I don't know how to swing a bat?"

"Have you ever seen a baseball game? On TV? Anything?"

"Of course."

"Then use that genius brain and try to imitate what you saw them do."

He took a very awkward-looking batting stance, lifted the bat and swung.

She did not laugh. But looking into his face, she was sure he knew she wanted to. "Okay, you're right, that's not great."

"Thanks so much for the confirmation." He looked seriously pissed.

"It's not a big deal."

"Look, Adrianne, I don't really care what these people think of me. Honestly. But I'll be damned if I'm going to make an ass of myself."

"Okay, okay, hang on."

Hailey wanted him to play, and she'd find a way of dragging him into the game. And possibly make an ass of him.

Adrianne didn't want that to happen either. Whether or not he put her at risk for another heart attack with the way he made her feel, she liked him. Sincerely.

"Here's what we'll do," she said, a plan coming to her. "We'll get on opposite teams. I'm going to pitch. When you're up to bat, I'll walk you."

He stood staring at her.

"Do you know what a walk is in baseball?" she asked.

"Adrianne, I know things like phenolic compounds are composed of one or more aromatic benzene rings with one or more hydroxyl groups."

"Right. Okay. If a pitcher throws four balls before he throws three strikes, the batter gets a walk—to automatically go to first base. A ball is when the ball is thrown outside of the strike zone and the batter doesn't swing."

"I know what a ball is."

"Thought I'd be sure." She fought another smile. Not because he didn't know much about baseball, but because he didn't want to know, seemed exasperated by the idea of needing to know and would possibly never use the knowledge again. And he was okay with telling her he didn't know anything about it. "So I'll pitch four balls. You stand there and don't swing. Then you'll get on first and no one will know you don't play."

He looked skeptical.

"Do you know what happens after you're on first?"

"I go to second."

"You run to second. And not until the next batter gets a hit or gets walked."

"Then to third?" he said dryly.

She grinned. "You're catching on."

"Which brings up another problem. I'll have to play in the field too. And have no clue."

"Hmm, I'll make Matt be the other coach. Then he can put you in right field. Probably the lowest chance of having to do anything. Basically, if it gets hit out there, run after it, pick it up and throw it to the closest person."

He sighed. "This is going to be so much fun."

She patted his arm—his warm, strong, thick arm—and said, "It's one game. It'll be fine."

Thirty minutes later, Adrianne wasn't so sure it would be fine. Her blood pressure was definitely up anyway. Hailey had finally shown up, dressed in a tight tank top, short shorts and full hair and makeup. Adrianne rolled her eyes. At least she'd known better than to wear heels.

Hailey had successfully put herself on Mason's team and was using that as an excuse to give him a pep talk while he was on deck waiting to bat. Adrianne was having a hard time concentrating on throwing the ball even near the plate while her peripheral vision was filled with Hailey pressing up against Mason, her hand stroking suggestively up and down the bat he held, stretching up on tiptoe to whisper something—surely quite instructional—in his ear. Adrianne ended up lobbing one to Stephanie Wilson who hit it to their short stop, landing her safely on first base.

Then Mason was up.

Someone had to yell at him to get his attention. Adrianne turned to watch as Mason removed his hand from Hailey's hip, said something to her that caused her to smile and slap him on the butt as he headed for the plate.

When he stepped into the batter's box and turned to face Adrianne with his clumsy batter's stance, she narrowed her eyes. He was flirting with Hailey? Touching her? After what had happened between him and Adrianne at the farm not two hours ago?

She'd promised to help him get on first base without having to swing. And she would.

She threw the first pitch straight across the plate.

As instructed, he stood there and didn't swing though it was a strike.

"It's okay, Mason," Hailey called, clapping her hands. "You can do it."

Mason gave Adrianne a questioning look. She gave him a little shrug in return. Then she wound up again.

This time the ball also went exactly where she intended. It hit Mason directly in the shoulder.

He gave Adrianne a seriously? look. Adrianne gave him another shrug. Then Wade Hiser, who was acting as umpire, instructed Mason he could take his base. But before he could jog down the baseline, Hailey rushed to his side. She rubbed her hand over his shoulder, saying something Adrianne couldn't hear from the mound. She turned away, catching Phoebe's eye from third base. Adrianne ignored the knowing smile her friend gave her.

The game continued with Mason easily getting batted home, a score that was quite clearly Jason Stein's accomplishment with his double into center field, but Hailey acted as if Mason was the star player, gushing over him. And rubbing him. Again.

Adrianne was tempted to hit Hailey with the ball when she was up, but instead settled for striking her out. At least that way she didn't have the chance to run the bases—especially since it was obvious she hadn't worn a bra under the spaghetti-strapped tank top.

The second time Mason was up, Adrianne avoided eye contact and walked him.

He didn't get up to bat again.

After the game, he found her. Only because she had to load all the equipment back into Phoebe's car—without any help from Hailey who was taking all the credit for a great event.

Strangely, she felt someone come up behind her and knew it was him even before he spoke.

"You hit me."

She didn't look at him. "It was another way to get you on base without making you swing the bat."

"A more painful way, but I did get to first."

"Hell, you got to first base standing in the on deck circle with Hailey," she muttered, slamming the car door.

When she finally faced him, he gave her a little half-smile. "No need to be jealous. I got to second and was well on my way to third with you on the farm."

She crossed her arms, not wanting to be affected but completely powerless to keep her body from reacting instantly to the memory his words conjured. "You got thrown out by Hailey before you even got a foot off of the bag."

He chuckled as he reached for her, pulling her hips against his. "If my foot was still on the bag, how could I get thrown out?" He leaned in and kissed her neck. "I'm safely on second and have my eyes firmly on third."

It was startling, but the silly baseball analogy—well, and his lips—made her melt. "You sound like you know what you're talking about."

"I looked some stuff up before the game."

"Some stuff? Like what?"

"Terminology, rules, stuff like that."

"The rules? To softball?"

"Yep."

He read up on the rules before coming. "And you remember them all?"

"Genius, remember?"

"Right." She couldn't help it. She started to laugh.

"What?" he asked, with his own big grin.

"Seems that a genius would have thought to duck when a ball was coming at him."

He opened his mouth but apparently had no answer. Which made her laugh harder.

"Hey, Adrianne!"

Dammit. Hailey. And dammit, Mason stepped back a little as Hailey came toward them.

"Yeah?" She couldn't quite muster a smile, but she couldn't blatantly ignore her boss.

"I need to talk to you." Hailey arrived slightly out of breath. She had a big smile for Mason. And got way in his personal space. "Good game, Mason."

"Thanks. It was fun."

Adrianne gritted her teeth. "What do you need, Hailey?"

"Oh, I need to run something past you. Can I borrow her for a minute, Mason?"

"You bet. I'm going to head to the B&B and shower. I'll see you ladies later."

He gave Adrianne a little wink and she felt her tummy trip.

"That is so great," Hailey said as he walked away.

The view of him from behind was definitely great. But Adrianne didn't appreciate Hailey noticing.

"What is it, Hailey?" she asked, stepping in front of the other woman in an immature and ineffective attempt to block her view of Mason's ass.

"I wanted to touch base with you. It seems that you and Mason are getting along great."

Adrianne peered closely at her pseudo-friend and boss.

Was she being sarcastic? Fishing? Catty? "Yes, we're getting along fine."

"That is so great." Hailey's attention finally bounced back to Adrianne's face.

"It is?"

"Definitely. I love that he has a friend here. And the guys seem to be getting along with him too. They really accepted him during the game. It's one final nail in the coffin."

"We have a coffin for Mason?" Adrianne asked.

"It's a figure of speech," Hailey told her.

"We have a figurative coffin for Mason?"

"What we have is the perfect situation for Mason to feel completely welcome and accepted here. Which will make him happy. Which will make him more apt to donate to the project." Hailey looked quite pleased with herself.

"You were worried he'd be unhappy?"

"Ad, I told you he was a geek. He was really not...in. Like really. He didn't have a ton of friends, never had a girlfriend."

"And now?" She was feeling way too defensive here. She wasn't Mason's champion, or his BFF, or his girlfriend. They'd just met. She didn't know the history. For all she knew, he'd been a jerk in high school.

"Look at him." Hailey gestured in the direction Mason had gone. "He can give any of the guys here a run for their money."

"He was always a genius, right?"

"Sure. But he wasn't..."

Adrianne cocked an eyebrow waiting for what she knew was about to come.

"...hot or rich."

Right. She wanted to slap Hailey. Seriously. This was Shallow Bitch 101. How could Hailey not hear what she was saying and how could she not be embarrassed?

"Do you realize how that sounds?" Adrianne asked.

"Yes, yes, I know." Hailey sighed. "We were in high school, Ad. We were not very nice to him."

"You kissed him at one point." Adrianne wanted to know that story for sure.

"And I wasn't very nice to him before or after that."

Adrianne waited. Then she realized that Hailey wasn't saying more about it. Okay, so it was going to take a couple of margaritas. But she was going to hear how this went down.

"So now your plan is to be sure he feels accepted, liked and generous?" she surmised.

"Exactly. Mason obviously likes you. So you'll be in charge of making sure he's included in all the events and get-togethers. I'll tell Drew and Mike and all the guys to be really nice. And I'll make sure that he feels fully appreciated from a female perspective."

That got Adrianne's full attention. "What does that mean?"

"Mason always had a crush on me. I'll flirt with him, make out a little, all that stuff. That will be the icing on the cake."

"Make out a little? All that stuff?" Adrianne repeated, hoping her voice sounded funny only to her.

"Or whatever. It's not like it will be a hardship." Hailey grinned. "I'm a big enough person to admit that I was wrong to overlook Mason Riley."

Adrianne's stomach hurt. First, how had Hailey seen her with Mason and not gotten the vibe that maybe Mason was already feeling appreciated? And second, how come Adrianne got to be Mason's social director but Hailey got to be his playboy bunny? That wasn't fair.

And Hailey was going to hurt him. It wasn't like she was looking for even a long-term affair. Phoebe had hinted that Hailey had really messed with Mason at one time. This could not be a repeat.

For one thing, if Mason found out Hailey's attention was only a ploy to get a donation, there was no way in hell they'd see any of his money. For another, Adrianne liked him. It wasn't only jealousy that made her want to keep Hailey away from him—though that was one definite reason for wanting Hailey as far from Mason as possible—it was also that she liked him, as a person. He didn't deserve to be used. And if Hailey had told Drew and Mike to be nice so that he'd write a check, then they'd be in on it too. All behind Mason's back, faking it, or at least having ulterior motives. Really not good.

She couldn't tell Mason what was going on though. What was she going to say, "Hey, Mason, by the way, Hailey's only paying attention to you because you have money now." That would definitely not help their cause.

She was going to have to make sure he didn't find out. And that Hailey didn't have a chance to make things worse.

"Make sure he's at the poker game tonight," Hailey said.

"No problem." The poker game was happening at Drew's house but obviously Mason was now on the guest list. And Adrianne would be there to be sure that no one did or said anything that might hurt him. Or their cause. In that order.

She dialed Phoebe as soon as she was safely in her car heading away from Hailey.

"Mission Keep Hailey Away From Mason is a go," she said. "I'm totally in. In fact, I'm captain of the freakin' team."

5

The poker game was a Tuesday night tradition, but Hailey had talked Drew into hosting a game on Friday for the alumni group. The guys had played poker on Saturday nights in high school and she'd felt it would be another way to get them all together and feeling nostalgic.

The invitation had garnered enough interest that there were two tables of players tonight, one in Drew's kitchen and one set up in the living room. Drew wasn't married and didn't currently have a girlfriend, so Hailey had offered to clean the house, help provide snacks and act as hostess. Which meant that Phoebe and another friend, Jill, had cleaned while Adrianne cooked. The four women were supposed to play waitresses together, but the three were secretly plotting how to get back at Hailey as they worked.

"Guess it's just you and me," Phoebe said, bringing a bag of ice in from Drew's deep freeze in the garage.

"What's that mean?" Adrianne asked with a scowl. She didn't mind making appetizers. She didn't mind entertaining. She didn't mind dusting—even if it was a bachelor's house and they'd had to bring their own dusting spray. But she hadn't seen Hailey yet and if she wasn't coming...

"Hailey's not feeling well and I told Jill to take off, that we could handle it."

Adrianne had been planning on sending Jill home anyway. She had two little kids and it was ridiculous that Hailey had talked her into coming in the first place. "What's wrong with Hailey?"

Phoebe waved her hand. "Oh, some allergic reaction."

Adrianne paused in mixing the salmon dip and looked at her friend. "What did you do?"

"Me?" Phoebe looked offended. Or tried to. "Matt did it," she finally admitted.

Adrianne groaned. "What did he do?" It occurred to her after she asked that it might be easier if she didn't know.

"A little cat hair in her face powder."

Adrianne thought about that, but it didn't make sense. "Why?"

"She's allergic to cats."

Adrianne sighed. "That's mean."

"Her eyes will water and she'll sneeze a few times. She'll live," Phoebe said, clearly unconcerned.

Adrianne frowned suspiciously. "Then why isn't she here?"

"Relax. She's a little puffy and bloodshot. A few blotches. It's fine. It will settle down by—about the time the game's over."

"Convenient," Adrianne muttered.

Men started showing up in clusters, and Adrianne felt her chest getting tighter and tighter, anticipating Mason's arrival. Every time the door opened or a knock sounded, she jumped a little. But it was never him. And her growing disappointment was ridiculous. Maybe he didn't play poker. Actually, once she thought about it, she was pretty sure Mason didn't play poker.

Maybe he was in his room at the B&B working. Maybe he

was working some magic with the formulas he'd figured out and scribbled on her arm that morning.

With that thought, her whole body got tingly and she felt the need to do jumping jacks or run a lap around the house to get rid of some of the energy she felt coursing through her.

That made the most sense though. Surely Mason Riley, world-renowned agricultural specialist, would rather be working than playing cards.

Adrianne had just taken the spinach and artichoke dip out of the oven and finished arranging the pita bread triangles— knowing full well that the guys would have been fine with chips and bean dip—when the doorbell rang and she heard Drew call, "Come on in, Mason, it's open!" through the screen door.

Her whole body reacted to the sound of his name.

Crazy.

A moment later, Mason was escorted into the kitchen and to a seat at the table with Drew and the other regular players. Mason probably didn't realize it, Adrianne thought, but being given a seat at that table meant he was a VIP.

They made eye contact across the room. She was at the kitchen island behind the breakfast bar and he was near the patio door, but they looked at each other at the same moment and she felt it clear to her toes.

He gave her a warm smile and she was stupidly glad he was here instead of working in his room. The world would be a better place if he was working in his room. But her world was a better place at the moment because he was here.

She'd feel guilty about that later.

She headed for the table with drinks. Beer for all the guys but Mason. She'd known them all long enough to know that was their drink of choice and it didn't matter what kind as long as it wasn't light. "What can I get you, Mason?"

She wondered if that sounded suggestive to him. It did to her and she was the one who'd said it.

"Anything I want?" he asked.

That also sounded suggestive. It was probably just her.

"I'll do my best."

"Butterscotch schnapps?"

She straightened from setting Tim's beer down and looked at Mason, warmth curling through her. Okay, it wasn't just her. "Or maybe something cinnamon flavored?" she asked. She had gum in her purse. He simply had to say the word.

"Very tempting," he answered.

No kidding.

"What the hell are you talking about?" Drew asked her. "I've got beer and soda. No sissy schnapps." He glanced at Mason. "No offense."

"You don't know what you're missing," Mason told him, taking his chair.

"I've got tequila if you want to do shots," Drew offered. "But I better warn you, this poker thing is fun but serious. You lose, you lose. No blaming it on the liquor."

"Got it," Mason said with a nod. He looked up at Adrianne, humor in his eyes. "Guess I'd better stick to soda. For now anyway."

She grinned and headed for the fridge. She knew the poker games went late, but they did end at some point. At some point, Mason would be done here—and maybe in the mood for schnapps.

Adrianne didn't even have to try to linger near Mason's table over the next half hour. Phoebe was focusing on the table in the living room, leaving Adrianne to see to the needs in the kitchen.

Their plates were refilled before they asked and their drinks never got completely empty.

She felt Mason watching her every move. Every time she looked at him, he seemed to sense it and look up as well. She was sure it was her imagination, but it seemed that every time their gazes locked, there was more heat as well. It was driving her crazy. So she figured it was only fair he feel a little crazy too.

Every time she got close to him, she made a point of touching him. At first, she made contact with her hip against his upper arm. The next time, she put a hand on his shoulder as she set the popcorn bowl down. The next time, she chose his side of the table and leaned in to put the nachos in the middle, making sure her breast pressed into his shoulder blade—and making sure to pause long enough for him to know what it was that was pressed into his shoulder blade.

As she lingered, she took note of the actual poker game for the first time that night. She had played with these guys before, and while the games were usually more of a break from home and a chance to hear themselves talk, the guys always played for real money. It was one of the unwritten rules. If you didn't have the cash to put up, don't show up. There were definitely winners and losers here.

As Tim dipped into the nacho chips, Adrianne noticed the distribution of the other chips around the table. One thing was quite clear. Mason was losing big.

She grabbed Drew's empty bottle and replaced it with another while she listened to the bidding going around. Mason met and raised on his turn. When she grabbed another can of soda for him, she peeked at his cards.

He had nothing.

She felt his eyes on her face and looked to find him watching her. Maybe he was as distracted as she was. If so, it was costing him—seriously.

Hmm.

She listened for a few more minutes and it took her only half that time to figure out that Mason was either losing on purpose or had no idea what he was doing.

She heard a phone ring in the other room and an idea occurred to her.

Her purse was in the bedroom and she slipped down the hall without being noticed and quickly dialed Drew's home number from her cell—thankfully, he was too cheap to have caller ID. It rang three times and she heard chairs move on the kitchen floor.

"I'm heading for the can," Tim called.

Adrianne hung up and waited for Tim to shut the bathroom door before she headed back for the kitchen. The phone call had succeeded in breaking up the game for a bit and Adrianne found Mason and motioned him to the corner of the kitchen that had no food or drink and therefore no other people. "Can you reach that pitcher for me?" she asked, loud enough for everyone to hear, pointing to the cupboard above the fridge.

He stretched up, the position pulling his shirt tight across his stomach and chest. "Which one?"

"You know, if you're losing on purpose to make them happy, you need to not lose quite so badly. It would be more convincing to win at least a hand or two," she said, pointing to the blue pitcher. "And you don't want them to know you're letting them win. That will piss them off."

"What do you need the pitcher for?"

She took it from him and set it to one side. "I don't. I needed to talk to you. Because I don't think you're losing on purpose. Am I right?"

"I don't really care that I'm losing."

"Answer the question, Mason."

"No, I'm not losing on purpose."

"So you actually suck."

Mason opened his mouth, but seemed to reconsider whatever he'd been about to say. "Yes. I actually suck. At poker, anyway."

"Here, will you put this back up there?" She handed him the pitcher. "Have you ever played?"

"No."

Adrianne glanced at him and fought a smile at the disgruntled look on his face. "Never?"

"Never wanted to." He stretched to replace the pitcher.

"Then why are you playing tonight?"

He shrugged. "They asked."

She rolled her eyes but also understood. Mason had never been included in group stuff with the guys in his class in Sapphire Falls. The invitation to do something with them now had likely been too tempting.

"Okay. But you're going broke," she pointed out.

"I don't mind losing the money," he said.

"Well, you're losing respect too." Adrianne pointed to a clear glass pitcher. "Grab me that one."

"I'm losing respect?"

"They won't let you play anymore if you keep this up. They like to win and they like to brag, but beating the worst poker player in the history of the world isn't much to brag about."

Mason reached for the pitcher, saying nothing.

She took it from him. "Okay, so I'm going to help you win a couple. Or all of them if you want to."

"How?"

"We'll cheat."

He lifted an eyebrow.

"Oh, come on," she said. "Drew and Roy would both cheat you in a heartbeat given the chance. And you've basically handed them over a hundred dollars of your money by now. This is you getting your own money back."

He looked amused as he took the pitcher and put it back in the cupboard without being asked.

"You ready for the plan?" she asked.

"There's a plan?"

"If we're going to cheat effectively without them catching us, we need a plan," she said. "But it has to be simple."

"The gist, I would imagine, is that you're going to walk

around behind the guys, pretending to wait on all of us while looking at their cards."

She smiled. "You really are a genius."

Mason laughed and Adrianne felt a warmth curl through her that made her want to make him laugh again.

"We'll need signals I suppose," he said.

She nodded, grinning like an idiot. This sounded like fun. She was counting on Mason's superior memory and ability to process things quickly. "I'll press my lips together to take one card, yawn for two and cough for three." She pointed to the silver studs in her earlobes. "If I touch one it means raise."

Mason rolled his eyes.

"If I drop something it means fold."

"What if you drop something accidentally?" he asked.

"I won't. I'm very graceful," she returned with a little sass that made him smile wider and made her grin right back. "I'll touch the shoulder of the guy with the best hand."

"I'd rather lose all my money than have you get too friendly with any of the other guys," Mason said.

From his tone, Adrianne thought maybe he was only partially kidding. The idea that he might get jealous made her want to climb up on his lap and reassure him that he was the one she wanted.

"You'd better get back to your game," she said, trying to keep from kissing him.

"Here, you better end up with one after all of this in case someone's taking notes." He pulled a yellow plastic pitcher from the cupboard and handed it to her.

What the hell did Drew need with all these pitchers?

"I look forward to our partnership," he said, making partnership sound sexual.

He gave her a wink and sauntered back toward the table.

Adrianne waited two minutes and followed with the pitcher full of Drew's tequila and orange juice and a stack of cups.

As she made her way around the table with the drinks, she avoided eye contact with Mason but she did pay attention to his hand of cards, and everyone else's.

She gave Mason two signals, one to take two cards and then to raise. She rested her hand on his shoulder as she leaned in to pick up some empty glasses from the middle of the table, telling him that he now held the highest hand in spite of Drew's bluffing. She let her hand stay for a moment, enjoying the warmth and strength of him, considering it a perk of the favor she was doing for him.

Mason won the hand, and she hid her smile so as not to tip the rest of the men off to their ruse. They were surprised enough that he'd won.

Adrianne allowed Mason to lose the next hand so no one would get suspicious and ignored the frown he gave her.

The next hand, after laying down new coasters at each man's elbow, whether they needed a new one or not, she signaled for Mason to take two cards. He did, discarding the obvious two from his hand.

She'd only checked Roy and Brad Peterson's hands when Drew asked, "Hey Mason, have you tried Adrianne's candy?"

Adrianne froze and she slowly turned to face Mason. Since everything sounded sexual tonight, that certainly did.

Mason pressed his lips together as he met her eyes, clearly trying to smother a smile.

"Yeah, I've had a taste," Mason answered.

So she wasn't the only one taking that the wrong way.

She turned away, trying to look busy with the cracker box. And not pant.

"I think I'd definitely like more though," he said.

"It's the best," Tim said, tossing a couple of cards into the middle of the table. "Everyone says so."

She rolled her eyes and dropped a plastic cup on the floor. Mason should definitely fold.

"Lots of people have had a taste then?" Mason asked.

She blushed. Only she and Mason knew what they were talking about. Drew and Tim were talking about actual candy. But it didn't matter. She couldn't help her reaction to the combination of Mason, her and tasting in the same thought process.

It also didn't matter that not many people had been involved with her or her candy—real or analogous—since she'd come to Sapphire Falls.

"Oh, sure a few. Not as many as will once she gets her shop at Sapphire Hills."

Mason paused in the midst of folding the cards together in his hand. "Her shop?"

Oh, yeah. Mason didn't know one of the proposed shops was hers. It wasn't like she'd not told him on purpose but...okay, it was.

Had he not seen her naked breasts she would have felt more comfortable asking him for money. Had she not climbed all over him, nearly orgasmed on his car hood that first night, she might have felt better about trying to sell him on something personal to her. She wasn't all that comfortable selling him on anything at this point. Her role, as she saw it, was to give him general information about Sapphire Hills and keep him company in Hailey's absence. She wasn't going to be the one specifically asking him for anything that had even a little bit to do with her shop since sticking her tongue down his throat within two hours of meeting him.

She didn't want him to think the two things were connected.

One glance at his face confirmed that was exactly what he was thinking anyway.

"She's been cooking and feeding us since she moved to town, but her candy is by far the best thing she's got." Drew took a swig of beer and must have thought about how that sounded. "Well, not the best thing she's got in general. She's also got great legs and... well, anyway, she's got a lot to offer," he said with a wink at her.

"Hey, Adrianne, remember the candy you made for Karen's graduation party?" Tim asked. "You should totally have those in the shop. Those rock."

"Thanks, guys," she murmured, her eyes on Mason.

Why did the pit of her stomach suddenly feel heavy? Like something bad had happened?

"I'm all in."

She stared at him. He was all in? He was betting on that sorry hand? He should have folded long ago. He was going to lose everything.

And obviously he knew it and didn't care. He was staring right back at her as he pushed his chips across the table. All of his chips. Then he lay his cards down. His sucky, couldn't-win-at-Old-Maid cards.

Tim hooted and chuckled as he pulled the huge pile of chips toward him. Mason pushed back from the table. "I'm heading out."

"You're leaving?" Adrianne asked, starting toward him without thinking about it.

"I have some other things I should do tonight," he said.

She wished that sounded sexual. Because it didn't. At all. It sounded kind of ominous in fact. She wondered if fighting with and dumping her were on his to-do list for tonight. Then she wondered if it was technically dumping when they'd known each other twenty-four hours.

"I'll drive you," she said.

"He's been drinking soda all night," Drew pointed out as he shuffled.

"You don't know what I've been putting in his soda," she returned.

No one argued, including Mason. She hoped that meant

that he wanted to talk. Or kiss. Kissing would be even better. And easier.

But as she followed him to the front door, she doubted kissing was on the agenda.

———

The candy shop was hers.

Of course it was.

Fuck.

The candy shop that couldn't be built without his money and land. The money and land that he definitely didn't want to give.

One of the shops was hers.

He hadn't seen that coming.

He really hated when things didn't go predictably.

"I didn't make out with you to get your money." She was slightly out of breath since she had to jog to keep up with him as he stormed down Drew's front steps and long driveway to his car.

"But you definitely knew who I was when you made out with me." He didn't look at her. When she'd offered to drive him home, his traitorous body and heart had been in full agreement—his imagination jumping to all the candy he still needed to sample.

But now he realized that of course she'd offered to go home with him.

"Why was I invited tonight?" he asked, whirling on her. They were right beside his car and it was so similar to the position they'd been in the night before that he had to make himself draw a deep breath.

"The guys wanted you to play poker," she said.

"I never played poker with them in high school. It doesn't

make any sense that they'd invite me tonight unless the purpose was very specific."

"We want you to feel included, yes. We want all the alumni, particularly the investors, to feel welcome and have a good time." She met his eyes directly. "It's not a secret that treating you well is partly about our hopes that you'll invest."

"And you know better than anyone, including Hailey, how much I have to offer," he said, his gut churning.

"I wrote your profile. I know what you're worth, roughly," she admitted.

"So makes sense that you would put so much effort toward treating me well and making sure I have a good time." God, that did make sense. He should have known. He should have questioned her motives from the beginning. He knew what was motivating everyone else in Sapphire Falls, but even after finding out she was on the committee and knew a lot about the project, he'd stupidly gotten caught up in the crazy chemistry, the draw that had him still wanting her even if she didn't really want him.

"Mason, I know how this looks but..." She seemed to be struggling for words. "Look, I don't know what this is between us. I've never felt this so quickly for someone before. But it's real. It had nothing to do with Sapphire Hills."

"I'm not supporting the building project."

She didn't even blink. "Because you can't trust me?"

"Because it's really important to me that when I give you the best orgasm of your life you know it's all about me, not about a damned check."

She sucked in a sharp breath and he saw her eyes widen. He wanted to think it was desire.

"If I just wanted your frickin' money, I could have been nice and polite. This is far beyond nice and polite." She grabbed the front of his shirt, jerked him forward and proceeded to kiss him hot and long and wet.

When she pushed him back, they were both breathing hard.

"I intend to keep kissing you," she informed him. "And I still want Sapphire Hills to happen. And I want you to have a good time here. So those things might all seem to collide at times. But I intend to keep kissing you, and when I do, you're going to know that it's just because I want to kiss you." Then she turned on her heel and headed back for the house.

He stared after her. Yeah, well, he intended to keep kissing her too.

Regardless of any frustration or irritation, he couldn't leave her alone now, and the next time his mouth was on her body, they were both going to know that what she was feeling was about him and what he could do to her. No matter what his bank account said.

She wasn't going to use their chemistry to get anything out of him or as some kind of payback for what he could give.

As he drove the dark, winding country road back to town from Drew's, he was reminded of another night eleven years ago.

God, women and Sapphire Falls just didn't work out well for him.

It had been spring, only a week before graduation, and he'd been driving home from Milt's farm. It had been dark, almost too dark to see the figure walking alongside the highway leading back into town. But she'd been wearing a white top that had shone in his headlights and it had taken him no time to recognize the way she walked.

Hailey had been walking home. She and her then boyfriend, Mark Andrews, had gotten into a fight, she'd told him to pull over so she could get out, and he'd done it.

She'd been walking for about a mile when Mason pulled over.

She'd been crying.

He could still remember the way that had tightened his chest. That and the way she looked at him. Like he was her hero.

He'd taken her home and she'd asked him to come in. Her parents were still out for the evening and she was shook up from the fight with Mark and walking alone in the dark. So he'd stayed.

And she'd kissed him. She'd also taken off her shirt. He'd seen Hailey Conner's naked breasts. They'd made out heavily until they heard her parents' car. He was sure, even years later, that if her parents hadn't interrupted, he would have had sex with Hailey Conner—the most popular girl in school.

Her parents had been grateful to him for bringing her home and staying with her so she wasn't alone. Hailey had walked him to his car and thanked him for being such a great guy. And she'd kissed him again.

It stood to reason then, that he'd assumed he would be greeted warmly the next time she saw him.

Not so.

Mason's hands tightened on the steering wheel and he scowled at the road in front of him.

He should have let her walk.

He never should have kissed her.

He should have hiked up her skirt and done her on her mother's dining room table.

That sounded good, but he'd known better. What he never should have done was trust her. He should have questioned her motives. Should have wondered why she was all over him after years of ignoring him.

It had been about what he could do for her—take her home, get her away from the scary dark highway, and make her feel wanted when her boyfriend was being an ass.

Now Adrianne thought he could do something for her too.

Mason sighed and tried to relax his shoulders. What he

should have done was avoid Hailey like the plague after that night.

Instead, he'd optimistically approached her at school the next day. With her friends around. And kissed her on the cheek.

And she'd humiliated him.

So what he should do tomorrow was avoid Adrianne like the plague.

Of course, the chances of that were somewhere around a billion to one.

And he'd very likely regret it as much as he had eleven years ago.

————

Adrianne stirred the pot on the stove, mixing butter, corn syrup and sugar—the beginnings of her homemade caramels. She had to keep checking the recipe though. Which was unprecedented for her. She'd made these caramels a hundred times. But she was thinking about Mason, his kisses, how angry he'd been last night and how much she wanted him to know that she wasn't doing any of this because of his money.

Except that she kind of was.

Not really. Not the kissing and stuff. But she'd been hanging out with him to preserve the chances of him donating.

Dammit.

This was getting complicated. And stressful. Completely opposite of what she wanted.

Her phone rang and she grabbed it, hoping it was Mason.

"Hello?"

"The guys are taking him golfing."

"Hi, Hailey," Adrianne said dryly. No greeting returned, not that she'd expected it.

"They're picking him up in half an hour."

She frowned. So what? Why did she need to be aware of every move Mason made? It was bad enough she couldn't stop thinking of him on her own. Having everyone constantly alerting her of every detail of his schedule wasn't helping.

"And?" she asked.

"And I think you should prep them."

"Prep them?" she repeated. "What's that mean?"

"You've spent some time with him now."

Yeah, because Hailey had messed with him in high school and Phoebe and Matt had talked her into being the buffer. Which had led to her spending time with him, which had led to her liking and wanting him, which was complicated because she had originally spent time with him for reasons other than wanting to and...

Frankly, it was exhausting.

"Yeah, I've spent time with him, so?"

"So you need to tell the guys what to talk to him about."

"They should..." She thought of Drew and Tim and Steve. "Probably not talk to him at all."

"I know. But this was Drew's idea, and I appreciate him trying to help out, and apparently Mason said yes so they can't cancel now."

Adrianne thought back to the night before. It was possible that Drew had asked Mason because he wanted to. It didn't necessarily have to be about the donation and the project. She thought maybe Drew, and maybe the other guys, liked Mason and wanted to get to know him better. And maybe Mason thought so too.

Which meant she couldn't let him golf with them.

Not because they might screw up the donation, but because he was enjoying being one of the guys for a change. And if those guys screwed that up she'd have to kill them.

She wasn't meddling now because of the money.

She wanted to protect Mason from having any more bad

experiences in Sapphire Falls. Part of her even wanted him to like Sapphire Falls.

"What do they have in common? What do they know that he would also know?" Adrianne asked.

"You."

Before she could answer, her smoke alarm erupted and she whirled to find her pan of butter and sugar smoking.

"Shit!" She pulled the pan from the burner, dumped it in the sink and started fanning the air under the smoke alarm with a towel. Finally, the beeping stopped.

"What do you mean me?" she finally asked.

"You're something that they all know. They could talk about you."

"Oh, hell, no," Adrianne said. There was no way she was going to let Drew or Tim talk about her to Mason.

"Then you better think of something else. Fast."

She frowned but knew right away what she should do. Distraction and evasion had worked to keep Mason away from Hailey. Surely the same would work for Drew.

"I've got it covered," she told Hailey.

"Okay, I'm counting on you."

Terrific.

Adrianne headed for her basement after disconnecting. She stood staring at the hose that connected to the back of her washing machine. The cold-water hose.

Dammit.

She dialed Drew's number before she touched anything.

He answered on the second ring.

"Oh, my God, Drew!" she exclaimed, putting the right amount of panic into her voice. "There's water all over my laundry room. Help!"

"Adrianne? Where's the water coming from?"

"I don't know. Please get over here."

"Okay, okay, I'm on my way."

Adrianne smiled as they disconnected. The other guys wouldn't golf without Drew. Taking a deep breath and wincing as she did it, she turned the water on and then pulled the hose free from the machine.

Watching water run over her floor made her want to cry, so she headed back upstairs.

This thing with Mason kept getting messier and messier. Literally.

Of course, it didn't take long for Drew to fix the problem, but he was kind enough to stay around and help her clean up. It took far too long to salvage his game, but he wasn't upset.

In fact, Drew was a pretty nice guy.

A guy that could have been a good friend for Mason.

Dammit.

She wanted to find Mason but she also felt like she should leave him alone. He was mad at her, she'd hurt his feelings, she'd made him doubt her. She felt like she should wait for him to come to her.

She was going to try to do that.

She'd see how long she could hold out.

———

Mason might not have been the most popular guy in school, but even he had attended the Sapphire Falls Annual Festival. Everyone within a ninety-mile radius had. Bringing a Ferris wheel and corn dogs to a town without any entertainment beyond school programs and recreational sports was a sure-fire recipe for good attendance.

Walking the sidewalk from the bed and breakfast toward the town square, Mason felt nostalgic. Not necessarily for his own memories of the festival, but for the memories he wished he had. More than one girl had been kissed for the first time on the Ferris wheel at the festival. It had turned into a kind of tradition. If the girl had already been kissed by the time she went with you to the festival, then the next step was taking her to the haunted house. Scary encounters in the dark made girls press close, and the multiple dark corners in the old Herschfield House—which was always used as the haunted house on Halloween and for the festival—were very conducive to getting on to other firsts. Finally, if all of that was old hat, then there was the fireworks show. It had become tradition that if you had a girlfriend, you took her to the top of Klein's Hill, the hill in the middle of the field where the fireworks were lit. Blankets were spread out and things moved beyond what the Herschfield House had seen.

Not that everything about being a teenager centered around physical boy-girl interactions but...oh, who was he kidding? Of course everything centered around that.

Especially at festival time.

Part of Mason's problem in high school had been that he was two years younger than the other boys. They were more developed, more confident and, yes, more hormonal than he had been. And part of the problem had been that Mason...had been a geek.

He knew it. He remembered it well. He'd known it even then and had honestly not done much to change that impression. His life was less dramatic, less angst-ridden, less distracted than that of his peers. And he'd been smart enough to recognize that as a good thing. Mostly.

At least when he hadn't been thinking how much he'd like to be normal and do normal things—like make out on a Saturday night. Or any night.

His one and only high school make out experience had been with Hailey, which had been very not normal.

Now, as he approached the square and the lights and the sounds and the smells of the festival, he thought about how he'd really like to get Adrianne Scott on the Ferris wheel. Yes, he'd already kissed her—and done at least a few of the things that went on in the haunted house—but he wouldn't mind doing it all again. And heading for Klein's Hill later.

Or, since he was an adult with a large credit limit capable of putting him in the best room in town, back to the bed and breakfast.

He was going to be here for two more days. It would be a fling at best. But it had the potential to be the best two days he'd ever spent in Sapphire Falls.

As he stepped onto the sidewalk that ran the east edge of the town square, Mason immediately spotted Adrianne. She stood near the fountain in the center of the square talking to two teenage girls.

She gestured with her hands, then frowned and shook her head. The girls replied and Adrianne threw her head back and laughed. He couldn't even hear it, yet it caught him in the gut the way it had when he'd bid three hundred dollars on a few dances with her.

She was so...real. She hadn't told him about the candy shop, but looking at her now, he couldn't believe it was for devious reasons. Her reactions to things were freely broadcast, from her enjoyment of a joke to her frustration over the opposing team's homerun in a softball game.

He really liked that. He could tell what she was thinking and feeling. That was very refreshing after spending time with politicians and especially nice after his past experiences in Sapphire Falls. He appreciated straightforward cause and effect. If Adrianne felt something, she showed it.

He took a step in her direction.

"Mason, there you are!"

Suddenly, he was surrounded by guys. The guys. Drew led the group, but Steve, Tim and Jake were all there too. The group that Mason had never been a part of.

Until last night. He'd been at the table for the poker game

and then today they'd invited him to golf. The game had been cancelled, but he'd been invited.

He'd be lying if he said he hadn't been looking forward to it. He could hold his own in golf.

"Hey."

"Sorry about the golf game today, man," Drew said. "Had to go bail Adrianne out. Couldn't wait."

"Adrianne?" He couldn't believe the way his heart sped up at the sound of her name.

"Her washing machine sprang a leak and she had a little flooding."

"Is she okay?" he asked.

"Definitely. No problem. We got it all fixed and cleaned up."

It was completely irrational, but Mason really hated that Drew had been called and able to help Adrianne with her problem. Especially considering that he wouldn't have had the first idea how to fix the plumbing problem. Still, he wanted to be the one she called. For everything.

"So what are you up to nowadays, Mason? You're in Chicago right?" Jake asked.

"Yes, Chicago. I'm involved in a number of projects with my research firm. Mostly agricultural research." If he expanded on that, he would not only sound like the geek he'd always been, but he'd bore the guys to death. But he had no idea what else to say. He had nothing in common with these men.

"Adrianne told me you've been to the White House," Drew said, glancing at the others.

So Adrianne had been talking about him? She'd definitely done her homework on him, which still surprised him, but it surprised him even more that she was sharing her knowledge. Or had she been prepping them for conversation with him? To make him feel included? He didn't really think she was physically involved with him because of his potential donation, but he couldn't help it if her motives for other things were suspect.

But...nah...but then again...it was convenient that her plumbing problem had come up in time to interrupt the golf game.

And she'd been making a habit of saving him from awkward situations with both softball and poker.

Dammit.

That woman needed to get a hobby beyond protecting him. Like sleeping with him.

Mason nodded, tucking his hands into his pockets and forcing himself to think through what he was going to say before speaking. Lauren had taught him that. In small social groups like this, if he talked off the cuff he often used terminology and went off on tangents that confused his audience. His usual talk was fine when he was lecturing in front of a bunch of other scientists or when he was in the lab, but talking to guys he'd gone to high school with took some tweaking.

"Yeah, I've been there a few times. I was a part of a special advisory group."

"For the president?" Jake asked.

"Yes, indirectly. We worked with the Secretary of Agriculture and Secretary of State."

"Did you meet the president?" Jake asked.

Mason nodded. "A few times." They hadn't really gotten along though. The president wanted a quick fix to smooth relations with foreign countries. He'd wanted to use the advisory group to spur ideas for foreign countries that needed to diversify their crop production. Unfortunately, things like that took longer than the president liked.

Still, Mason's ideas had worked, so they were tentative friends.

"That's cool." Drew gave him a sincere grin.

Mason smiled in return, if less warmly. "I agree." What he did really was cool. It was just that most people didn't even know about it, not to mention understand it or respect it. He did enjoy his work and believe it was important, but he hated the politics. Intensely. Having people who knew nothing about what he did tell him what he should do made him want to yell. Which he did on occasion. He also swore from time to time. Even at important people.

"What's involved in agricultural research anyway?" Steve asked. "I'm farming with my brother now. Sounds like something I'd be interested in."

Steve had been the quarterback. The leader of the male in-crowd. He'd even passed biology and chemistry. With help.

"The most recent project is working on more resilient seed for a number of crops. They can go into the ground sooner and be harvested faster."

Steve frowned. "Why would we need to plant sooner? It's not like you can change the weather and that's what decides when we get in the fields."

He couldn't change the weather, so he was changing the plants' reactions to it.

"It's for countries where the growing seasons are short enough—due to rain or cold seasons—to prohibit some crops from being viable."

"So you're working for other countries?"

"Yes."

"Which ones?"

"Various."

"If they grow their own stuff, they won't need our crops."

Mason frowned. It wasn't a new argument, but the fact that these were the most words the Sapphire Falls quarterback had ever said to him rubbed him wrong. "Most of the countries we're working with have severe food shortages."

That wasn't how it had started with the White House. It had been initiated as a foreign-relations plan, but when they'd resisted working with the poorer countries—who didn't have anything to really offer the US—Mason and Lauren had taken the plans and expanded it on their own to the countries most in need of food crops.

"They need our crops," Steve said.

"They need all the food they can get," Mason said. "But if they can grow their own, they'll be less dependent—"

"And the demand for our crops goes down."

Mason sighed. He understood the farmer's concern, he really did. Steve wasn't entirely wrong, but the global truth was that these countries had years to go before they were self-sufficient, if that ever truly happened. There were so many factors. It wasn't as easy as handing more resilient seeds to a bunch of average Joes and having them throw them in the ground.

But it was a start. He and Lauren had the luxury at this point of having made enough contacts that they truly could do more than develop the seeds.

But they had to have the seeds before they could move forward. And they were nearly there.

"I understand where you're coming from, Steve, but—"

"Oh, you work for the government. You don't care. You're not out getting your hands dirty like the rest of us."

That also wasn't entirely true. Mason loved nothing more than digging in the dirt. He didn't do it daily, but their greenhouse was his favorite place, and he always led the planting projects personally. Like he was planning to do in Haiti in a few months. He'd be there personally to put the seeds in the ground. His hands would definitely get dirty.

There was no use trying to convince Steve of that, however. He was going to think what he was going to think. And Mason could honestly say he didn't care what Steve thought of him.

"It's difficult between flying from Chicago to the Middle East and Greece and Africa and sitting in on conference calls with kings and presidents," Mason said.

"Oh, wow, you guys, did you see who's in the dunk tank?"

Suddenly Adrianne was beside him, oozing enthusiasm, her eyes wide, her smile wider.

"Who?" Drew seemed relieved by Adrianne's interruption.

Mason had to hide a smile. Likely Drew had been told to make sure the boys played nice with Mason and he was worried about getting into trouble with Hailey. Mason wasn't sure what kind of punishment Hailey might dole out, but he did know that she wasn't as sweet as she seemed.

"Kelsey Kramer," Adrianne said. "And she's wearing a white shirt."

"Anybody dunked her yet?" Drew asked.

"Nope. But Jason Conrad is up next."

"Okay, well I'm feeling the need for a little walk across the square," Drew said, clapping Steve on the shoulder and turning the man in the direction of the dunk tank. "Who's with me?"

The others seemed to agree that a wet white T-shirt on somebody named Kelsey was more interesting than Mason's job—kings or not—and headed off with Drew. Leaving him alone with Adrianne.

"Who's Jason Conrad?" Mason asked, watching the other men cross the park.

"The all-star pitcher from the state championship baseball team." Adrianne didn't look at him either.

"And Kelsey Kramer?"

"Hot new kindergarten teacher."

"A kindergarten teacher is in the dunk tank in a white T-shirt?"

"No. But by the time they realize that, you and I will be gone."

6

Adrianne turned and started toward the Ferris wheel.

The Ferris wheel where he'd very much like to kiss her. At least.

"You lied? I was thinking about how much I appreciate your openness," Mason said as they walked.

"Oh, I was quite genuine in my desire to get rid of the guys," she said.

He chuckled. "Afraid I was going to punch Steve in the face?"

"Afraid you were going to hurt his brain by challenging it to think outside of his backyard and beyond his own direct compensation to something truly significant on a worldwide, humanitarian scale."

Mason wasn't quite sure what to say to that. Adrianne Scott seemed to really understand—or at least grasp and admire— what he did. That was so unusual and satisfying that he knew he took longer than he should have to answer.

The universal truth was that it was hard to stay mad at a woman you wanted to cover in chocolate syrup. Or powdered sugar, he thought as they passed the funnel cake stand. It was how wives got their way so often.

He stopped. "We'll be gone?"

She turned and came back to him. She tipped her head back to look up at him. "Traditionally, you should be the one insisting we talk about last night, especially after that kiss I laid on you. But since you were a bit of a dork with the girls in high school, I'm giving you a pass on this one. We're going somewhere to talk. I insist."

He fought the smile that pulled at his lips. Only Lauren knew him and liked him enough to dare tease him. He liked that Adrianne felt comfortable doing it too. "And here you are saving me again."

"Saving you?"

"The softball game, poker game, golf...and now this. You're always saving me from my nerdiness."

She frowned. "How did you know about the golf?"

Ah, he'd been right. "Incredibly high IQ, remember?"

She gave a half smile. "Right."

"I'm good at golf, Adrianne."

"I was more concerned about the conversation. And you proved me right, by the way, with your little discussion with Steve."

Mason grimaced. Maybe she had a point. "I don't do well being questioned. It...irritates me."

"Yeah, I'll remember that." She didn't sound intimidated at all.

He liked that about her too.

"Admit it, you just can't leave me alone," he said, moving in closer.

He knew now that he couldn't leave her alone either. And the Ferris wheel might not cut it.

S he was never going to be able to leave Mason alone, she realized as she looked up into his eyes. The man had the strangest effect on her. She'd seen him talking to the guys and by his posture—and she'd known him for what? A little more than twenty-four hours—knew that he was tense and the conversation wasn't going well.

Yes, she'd been assigned to make sure he was accepted and comfortable and happy, but that wasn't what propelled her across the street and up the sidewalk. She'd been watching for him for almost an hour, and when she finally saw him she couldn't stay away.

Once she had his full attention with no interruptions, she should ask him more about the building project and why he didn't like it and work on convincing him that he should like it. She was a star in sales and marketing after all.

But she wasn't going to do that.

She wanted him to know that she was with him simply because she couldn't help it.

Something over his right shoulder caught her eye and she glanced at it. At her to be more specific. Hailey had arrived. In her stupid high heels and another short skirt. Had her clothes always been so skimpy or had she gone shopping?

It didn't matter. Adrianne wasn't ready or willing to share Mason.

"Dammit." She quickly looked around, then grabbed his hand and pulled him across the street and through the wrought-iron archway over the sidewalk leading to Herschfield House. The haunted house for the weekend.

"Where are we going?" he asked, following her without hesitation, which she appreciated.

"Somewhere we won't be found." She pulled him around the side of the house and then through the door leading to the kitchen.

"I think we're supposed to go in the front." He sounded amused.

"I helped set this damned thing up," she told him as they walked. "If I can't duck in a side door, somebody's gonna get yelled at."

"You helped set the haunted house up?"

Once through the side door, instead of stepping through the cobwebs into the room where they were going to be threatened by a chainsaw-wielding Dracula, Adrianne turned right and tugged Mason along with her behind the black curtain that separated the victims from the actors who needed to periodically jump out or grab people as they walked by.

She ducked the elbow of a man with a plastic ax lodged in his head and dodged the two zombies heading for the front of the house.

"I helped set everything up for the festival except the rides and games that the carnival company brought in. I did the craft fair, the quilt show, the pie shop, the beer garden...and this." She pulled him with her up the back staircase to the second floor.

"Why do they have a haunted house at the town festival anyway?" Mason asked. "I've always wondered."

She'd thought it was strange too, but Hailey had insisted it was a tradition that would not end during her reign. Hailey didn't call it a reign but Adrianne knew that's how she thought of it. "It's fun."

"To be scared?"

"Yeah."

"Then this doesn't make sense."

"What do you mean?"

"You know this is fake, right? No one would let a bunch of people walk through a house with a real ax murderer in it. So it's not really scary."

She chuckled. "Right, but you suspend disbelief during the experience."

"Why?"

She rolled her eyes but grinned. In the candle-lit hallway, he couldn't see her anyway. "Because it makes it fun."

"So you're fooling yourself into thinking it's fun."

"I...guess."

Adrianne stepped into the first bedroom on the left with Mason right behind her. When she stopped, he bumped into her and steadied them both with his hands on her waist. And he didn't let go. Or move back. In fact, he seemed to press closer. At least part of him pressed closer. She felt his breath along the side of her neck and then he trailed his lips along her skin.

She sighed. God, that felt good.

The sound of a chainsaw and a chorus of screams interrupted the fantasy she had going of his mouth continuing on down.

"Crap." She stepped out of his hold, closed the door and then locked it. "We can hang out in here for a while."

"We're hiding."

"Yes." From the whole town, the whole world, for at least a week if she could arrange it. "So you've never been in a haunted house before?"

"No."

"Why not? It's been a part of the festival for years. Wasn't it here when you lived here?"

The distant sound of screams drifted up the stairs.

"Yes. But I have trouble with the whole suspension of disbelief thing."

"Right." A smart guy like him was probably too logical for something like fantasy. Which was a bit of a bummer considering some of the impure thoughts she'd had going lately.

"And a very hard time with fooling myself into anything."

"Especially something fun," she said dryly. Maybe she could show him how fun fantasy and imagination could be.

There was no bed nearby, but they could make do.

Herschfield House had once been an actual residence but now served as a sort of town museum. Sort of. This room for instance, held clothing and furniture that people felt were historic. For the most part, it was just old, but it was true that some of it easily dated back to the 1930s. The ladies of the Museum Guild—many of whom had donated a lot of the clothes and furniture—kept the rooms clean and somewhat organized. Like the room of historic dishes or the room of historic books—old yearbooks, cookbooks and scrap books.

The first-floor living area was used for events like Mother's Day tea, bridal and baby showers and club meetings—book clubs, Garden Club, Sewing Club—and of course, the Haunted House at Halloween and festival time. It was the oldest house in town, was right on Main Street and was huge with a multitude of rooms that lent itself perfectly to a haunting.

"Why not have fun for real?" He moved to the far side of the room and grabbed the cushions off an old couch. He propped them up against the wall by the windows, then took a seat, stretching his legs out in front of him.

"Like what?" She'd love to know what Mason Riley thought was fun.

"Whatever's fun for you. What do you like to do?"

She tried to gauge if he was being suggestive, but it was hard to tell. She sat next to him and positioned herself like he had. "I like to…"

Why was it such a hard question? It wasn't that she never had fun, but she…stayed home a lot. It didn't feel un-fun, but it wasn't the interesting trips or late nights at clubs and parties and shows that she used to have. "I love movies. I read a lot. I…" Go to bed early. Grocery shop with an obsession for food labels. "How about you?"

She felt him lean more fully into his pillows. "Honestly? I have to make myself go out. Or more specifically, my partner, Lauren, has to make me go out. I work too much."

"Your partner?"

He nodded with a smile that had her feeling a little jealous of Lauren. It was clear that Mason had a lot of feelings for the other woman.

"She's also my best friend," Mason said.

"Tell me about her." Adrianne knew she shouldn't sound so possessive.

"She's awesome. Everything we've done, we've done together."

"She's a genius too?"

"Not literally, but she's incredibly bright. She's the leading authority on water and soil conservation in the United States."

Yeah, but could she make candy? Adrianne rolled her eyes at herself. She made candy, she was the assistant to a small town mayor, because they'd been sorority sisters. What did she have that would interest a guy like Mason?

"So you work together and socialize together? Does that get complicated?" she asked, meaning, of course, have you ever slept together?

"No. I'm her charity case. I make her feel good about herself."

"Charity case?" Adrianne asked. As if feeding third-world countries wasn't enough?

"Yeah, she keeps me on the normal side of the spectrum. Whenever I start to drift in the nerd direction, she pulls me back." He smiled. "Kind of like how you rescue me when I'm in a situation that's going to make me look bad."

That got her attention even as she grimaced. She wasn't sure if he appreciated that or not. But she couldn't seem to help herself.

"You think of yourself as a nerd?" she asked.

"I am a nerd, Adrianne. I'd rather read scientific journals than novels. I'd rather play with my plants than go to a nightclub."

"Your passion is science. And you're doing things most people can't even imagine not to mention do. There's nothing at all wrong with that, or you, Mason."

He looked surprised by her vehemence. She was too. But she meant all of it.

"Wow, why couldn't you have gone to my high school?" he asked with a little grin.

She smiled and settled back against the cushion again, having realized her passion about his normalcy had made her sit up straight. "I'm sorry to say that I was probably not as enlightened about what makes a man truly attractive at that age."

"You were a cheerleader, class president, homecoming queen?" he asked.

She sighed. "Yes."

He laughed. "No need to sound embarrassed. That's normal stuff. What everyone wants. Even nerds. At least on some level."

At those words, she felt a twinge near her heart. Different from the others Mason had been causing. This felt like—she wanted to hug him rather than ravish him. The desire to ravish was under the surface for sure, but she would have been okay with simply hugging. For now.

"You didn't feel normal?"

"Never here. Well...rarely."

She wanted to know more about those rare times, but he wasn't sharing more at the moment and she hesitated to push.

"You would have liked to golf with the guys today?" she asked.

"I would like to think that I'm to the point where I can have a normal conversation with normal guys."

"Why do you care about talking with those guys?" Part of

her really hated that Mason had never felt normal, but she also hated that he was measuring normalcy by Drew, Tim and Steve.

"I can talk to anyone else. Mostly. I have to think through what I'm going to say, but I generally hang out with people I have something in common with, so it's easier."

She grinned. "You see these guys as a challenge then."

He grinned back. "Something like that."

She really liked him. She wanted him to feel normal, accepted, appreciated.

"Maybe they'll invite you to go golfing again," she said.

He looked at her. "Do not tell them to invite me to go golfing, Adrianne."

Okay, so he was kind of on to her and the whole plan to make him happy. "Okay, I won't say anything to them about golfing."

"Adrianne." His voice was deep and full of warning.

She looked up at him.

"Don't tell the guys to invite me to do anything with them."

Dammit. She'd been thinking they could invite him for more cards. Or fishing. Or beer. That pretty much summed up the men's social activities in Sapphire Falls.

"Fine, I won't say anything."

"Thank you."

"So when you make yourself go out, what do you do?" she asked, knowing it wasn't playing cards, fishing or drinking beer in someone's backyard.

"Shows, dinner, parties."

With women, she was sure. He lived in Chicago and rubbed elbows with some very interesting people. The high-class parties and weekend getaways she'd experienced were probably nothing compared to what he was invited to.

"I like comedy," she said. "There was a club in Chicago I used to love: Picadilly's."

"Never been there."

"No? You should go."

"So, it's like jokes and stuff?"

She smiled. "Right." She could only imagine his reaction to the raunchy, politically incorrect stuff he would hear at Picadilly's.

They sat quietly, listening to the muffled screams and pounding going on below them.

"Did you hear about the cat that ate the ball of yarn?" Mason asked.

"No." She was already smiling. Mason Riley was telling her a joke.

"It had mittens."

There was a long pause and then she burst out laughing. Holy crap, he'd told her a joke and it was...corny, dumb and something she could tell a Sunday-school classroom. She loved it.

"Did you hear about the skeleton that walked into a bar?" she asked in return.

"No."

She could hear the smile in his voice. "He ordered a beer... and a mop."

Another long pause, and then Mason chuckled. "Nice."

"I can do corny jokes all night long."

They lapsed into silence again for nearly a minute.

"You didn't like Chicago then?" Mason finally asked.

"No, I love Chicago. I needed...a break."

She wasn't going to tell him all about her heart. She wanted to, but that would be too much. They barely knew each other really. And he was still maybe a little mad, or at least suspicious. He didn't need her dumping on him or sounding like a freak, as she knew she often did when it came to her heart stuff. She smiled. She and Mason had a lot in common. They were both...quirky.

"I had a really high-paced, high-stress job and I wanted a change. I knew the travel and strange routines were not good for me. When the chance came up to move to a small, quiet, slow-paced place like this, I jumped." She sighed. "And I love it here. There are no sales quotas and high-pressure meetings. There's no politics, no hidden agendas. I sleep in. I eat food out of my own garden. I kick back. I'm healthier than I've ever been."

"You like Sapphire Falls better than Chicago?" He sounded completely disbelieving.

She understood. Three years ago, she wouldn't have believed it either. But she knew exactly what it was that made her love the small town.

"I was popular," she said. "I was on the inside. I was that girl, seemed to have a lot of friends. But people were always putting on an act. I went to parties and had money but didn't really ever have fun because I couldn't fully relax. I was always first in everything and always came out on top, but I never felt satisfied."

And all of it had almost killed her.

"So I gave it all up and came to a place as opposite from all of that as I could find."

"That's an understatement," Mason muttered.

She shook her head. As much as she wanted everyone to genuinely like him, she also wanted him to like Sapphire Falls. Because she loved it.

"Did you know that Steve raises extra-sweet corn so that he can supply all the little old ladies at church all summer? And Mrs. Langston feeds stray cats? And Phoebe works after school teaching some of the adults Spanish? And Drew voluntarily drives the snowplow in town because he's got insomnia and is the first person awake?" She stopped and took a deep breath. "I could go on."

"I didn't know any of those things," Mason admitted.

"Are you surprised?" She truly wanted to know.

Mason paused and then said, "Not really, I guess."

"These are good people who let me be who I am," Adrianne said. "I would never judge any of them because they're way better than me. I'm glad they let me be a part of this town."

They were quiet for nearly two minutes. "You don't miss the city at all then?" Mason asked.

She could honestly shake her head. "Except for the shopping, no."

"You ever come for a weekend shopping spree?"

She looked over at him. Was he hinting at something? "I haven't for a long time. But I think I'd like to." She paused and waited. Then she chuckled. "I don't know if it's the dork thing again or what, but now would be a great time to say we could go to Picadilly's if I come to town. And so you know, I'd say yes."

"Damn."

She sat up. "Damn?"

"Yeah, I..." He started patting his pockets. "Something...I need to take some notes."

Memories from the farm—it seemed like a week ago—hit her all at once and she had to catch her breath and clear her throat. "Oh, okay."

She leaned over to search her purse for a pen as Mason pulled one from his pants pocket along with a little notebook.

Darn it anyway.

No, she wasn't going to lose out to him being better prepared this time. She wanted him. She wanted him to know it —and to do something about it.

"You know, I'd love to be a part of saving the world. I want to do my part." She stretched back as he turned toward her.

"What do you—"

She slid her legs out straight, inched up the hem of her shorts and stretched her arms overhead. "Plenty of note-taking surface. If you need it."

It was the most bizarre seduction/flirtation/whatever that she'd ever been a part of, but it fit. And it seemed to be working. Mason's gaze flared with heat and he licked his lips as he took in all of the bare skin she was offering.

"Believe it or not, I almost never get stuck like I have been for the past few weeks, and ideas don't generally jump out at me in the midst of other normal conversations," he said.

"How do your ideas usually come to you?"

"While working in the lab, or as a tangent from something else I'm doing, or when I'm brainstorming with Lauren or the team."

"Never out of the blue?"

"Rarely. Maybe if I'm alone, reading something or on a run, but never when I'm doing something else. I promise you that I was focused on you and what we were talking about."

She rolled to her side and reached out a hand, laying it on his arm. "We were telling dumb jokes and chatting. I'm not offended."

"But I was focused on you. Completely. Like I was at the farm. These ideas...it's like..."

She raised an eyebrow and waited.

He sighed. "It's like you shake something loose for me."

She laughed. "That doesn't sound complimentary, but if it means that it's helping you then I'm good with it."

He shook his head, smiling ruefully. "It's a good thing. But it's not very...romantic."

"You're trying to be romantic with me?" Sure, they'd kissed —almost a hell of a lot more than that—but romantic made it sound more serious.

"I'm not that good at it," he admitted.

She scooted closer. "That's not what I meant. Mason, I..." Want to take my clothes off every time I see you. That would certainly reassure him that he was good at something.

"We're off script here so I'm not sure what's next."

She didn't know what that meant, but he did look a little confused. "Off script?" she asked.

"Things are usually very predictable with me. I'm usually in control, smooth, sure of what the next step is, but with you it's all been—crazy, off the charts, erratic."

She could tell that bothered him, but she really liked it.

"Even getting mad at you last night was new for me, unusual. I don't want to be used—"

"Oh, Mason, I'm sorry—"

"No. I mean, the reason I was mad was legit, but I don't get upset with the women I date. I don't usually care that much, I guess. If we don't agree on something, we finish dinner and don't get together again. I only get upset about work."

She could tell that meant something. Her heart skipped and she decided to give him some assurance.

"Mason, every time we're together, I find myself smiling more and wanting to get naked more than I have in a really, really, really long time with a guy. Nothing else matters. I can tell you what the next step is, but if you roll over here, I'll show you. Which will be way more fun."

He gave an aroused groan. "I'm already having more fun than I can remember."

Oh, she really liked that.

"So come here."

He did. He turned and stretched out beside her, bracing himself on his left elbow, pen poised in his right hand. "I need to take some notes, before I forget."

"I'm guessing you haven't forgotten something in...ever," she said with a smile.

"I haven't been distracted by you before."

He smiled too, but his eyes held a heat that made her tingle.

"Then you better start writing." She inched the bottom of her shirt up to the bottom of her bra. "Because I'd like to get even more distracting. Soon."

He took a shaky breath. Then the only sound in the room was the click of his pen. The tip touched the skin over her ribs and she felt her stomach quiver. He seemed intent on his task, but she noticed that he was definitely breathing faster. She felt like she was holding her breath and her heart thundered, but she didn't feel the panicky tightness she usually got when that happened. This felt good.

He wrote notes across her stomach from left ribcage to right about an inch below the underwire of her bra. Then he started again, left to right above her belly button. Then below it.

He cleared his throat and finally looked up at her. "I need a little more room."

Without a word, still holding his gaze, she lifted her hips. Watching her face, he popped the snap at the top of her shorts, lowered the zipper and then sat up slightly to hook a finger in the waistband on both sides and slide the shorts down to mid-thigh.

Her panties dipped low in front, giving him a few more inches of skin, and his attention dropped from her face to the black silk. He traced the top edge of the panties with the pad of his index finger.

Then he chuckled.

She felt herself smile, though she had no idea why. "Thought of another joke?"

His finger kept moving between the elastic edge and her skin and she felt her entire body growing warmer from that one touch.

"I was thinking of all the books, all the researching...and it's all deserting me at the moment. I can't think of a single thing right now except that I want to touch you all over."

She moved her legs restlessly. "Touching me all over sounds like a great plan. No offense, Mason, but I'm caring a little less about your plant research projects right at the moment."

He chuckled again and dipped his finger deeper, skimming

lightly over her soft curls. "Not plant research, Adrianne. You. Women. Sex."

The word sex from him made her stomach flip. Which was stupid. It seemed rather obvious that they were heading in that direction, but that confirmation made her want it.

"What do you mean? You've been researching women?"

"Of course." He gave her a grin. "Studying and analyzing is my natural reaction to things that fascinate me that I don't fully understand. Women and female sexuality certainly fall into that category."

It was funny. He'd been a nerd in high school by all counts, but that grin and the matter-of-fact statement about studying women and sex were full of confidence.

"How do you study female sexuality?" she asked, eyes narrowed as a thought occurred to her—how many women had Mason Riley been with since leaving Sapphire Falls?

"Like I study everything else—books, observation, interviews. Experiments."

Her eyes widened. "You're kidding, right?"

"I've used all of those methods."

He had to be kidding. "How?"

"There are hundreds of books written on the subject. One I like in particular is Lou Paget's How to Give Her Absolute Pleasure."

Adrianne didn't know who Lou Paget was or how he knew all about absolute pleasure, but Mason didn't seem to be kidding.

"And the observation? Are we talking porn here?"

He grinned. "Some of that. But the mechanics of sex aren't hard to understand. It's the flirting and seduction that I needed to understand. So I observed men and women interacting in bars, restaurants, the office, anywhere I could to figure out what worked, what didn't, what made women respond, how to tell if she was responding."

"How do you tell?"

"With you, it's your mouth."

Her lips tingled and she pressed them together.

"Like that," he said. "When you're aroused, you press them together, you lick them."

She did then without thinking.

He chuckled. "Drives me crazy. Then there are the other signs too—you breathe faster, your pupils dilate, your cheeks get a little pink."

"I didn't realize I was giving so much away," she said softly.

"It's natural. I see the effect I have on you and it makes me want to do even more."

She swallowed. "Oh?"

"As nature intended."

Right. Scientist. Nothing magical or special—just pheromones and the like.

His finger was still in the waistband of her panties, but it wasn't moving. She tipped her head. "What about the interviews?"

"I've talked to dozens of women about what they like, what they want from men..."

"Are they naked while you do this?"

He raised an eyebrow and she was sure he noticed the jealous note in her voice, but he didn't comment on it.

"Not usually," he said. "Often they were fully dressed and drinking coffee."

"You bought random women coffee and asked them about sex?"

"I knew all of these women in some capacity and had reason to believe they would be comfortable talking with me. You'd be surprised—women love to have a man who will listen to them and wants to know what they want. Sometimes it was a planned meeting, sometimes it was casual conversation."

She wouldn't be surprised. He had a point. Most women

wouldn't likely have that conversation with a total stranger, but if they got to know Mason she could see them being willing to spill. He was a researcher. She could imagine the sincere, intent way he'd look at them, the straightforward way he'd ask the questions.

"And then of course...the experimentation?" she asked.

"Well..." He trailed off with a wicked grin.

She rolled her eyes but found while the jealousy was still there, she was curious what he'd learned.

"So this is all very academic for you."

He leaned in and moved his finger along her tummy again. "It's also very fun."

She recalled what he'd said earlier. "But this feels different with me?"

"I can't remember anything specifically from the books," he admitted. "I want to look at you and feel you and taste you. And do whatever it takes to make you moan. Period."

Right after she sucked in a quick breath as heat poured over her, she laughed. He really seemed at a loss. "You don't have to use special techniques, Mason."

"I'm not good without a plan," he said.

"I'll give you a plan," she said. "Put your mouth on me."

His eyes darkened and his voice dropped to a husky tone. "Where?"

"Anywhere." She meant it. She was more turned on from this crazy conversation than she ever had been. He couldn't do it wrong, she was sure of it.

"I'm not giving any money to that damned building project."

"Okay."

"You still want me? This?"

"More than anything I've ever wanted in my life."

And without anything more than a simple nod, he lowered his head and kissed her stomach, then kissed her again, adding a little lick of his tongue. She sucked in a sharp breath, her eyes sliding closed. Yep, she'd been right—he couldn't do this wrong.

"Now the plan is to keep doing that. All over. Wherever you want."

He chuckled, his mouth still against her stomach. "I feel much better now."

They were both on their way to feeling really damn good, but she couldn't tell him that because he'd wiggled her shorts down and off her legs before she could form a syllable.

When he'd tossed them away, he crawled up, sliding his body along hers until they were face-to-face. "This is somewhere I really love to put my mouth."

And he kissed her. It was a slow meeting of their lips, a lift, a change in angle and a reapplication of the sweet pressure. At first. Until he parted his lips over hers and she willingly opened. The kiss grew longer, hotter, wetter, and he stroked his tongue in along hers.

She couldn't keep her hands to herself. She ran her palms up and down his back before gripping his butt and pulling him closer. He pressed against her, but it was more against her hip than where she really needed him. She wiggled against him, turning toward him and lifting her leg to drape over his hip.

The position spread her thighs and Mason, being a genius and all, took advantage of that. He smoothed one hand down her side, stopping to rub the center of his palm over the rock-hard tip of her breast before running it over her ribs, waist and hip. Finally, he cupped her butt, pressed her a little closer and slid his middle finger under the curve of her buttock and along the edge of her panties.

"Mason," she groaned when he didn't continue on. "Keep going."

"I thought the plan was to put my mouth wherever I wanted," he said gruffly.

Oh, yeah. "Right. Have to stick with the plan," she said quickly.

He laughed—she loved that deep rumble in his chest—and he lifted his head. "Some techniques are coming back to me."

"There are...techniques to this?"

"There are techniques to everything. But the important part is making sure that it's working for you. They don't all work for every woman you know."

No, she didn't really know. She and her girlfriends had never spent a lot of time talking about which oral sex techniques they each preferred. "I'll take your word for it."

"So I really want you to let me know how things are going. I like to play with cause and effect."

There was that cocky-in-spite-of-being-a-science-geek grin again. "I'll let you know," she said dryly.

He was still holding her left buttock in his hand and he gave her a squeeze. "I'm thinking I'll be able to tell with you easier than most."

That was an...interesting...comment. "Oh?"

"You're very expressive."

"With you I am," she said with a little sigh. "It's like I can't keep from saying or doing what I'm feeling."

"It's a good thing," he assured her. "I like results."

His grin was wicked and sexy, and she felt a heavy warmth settle low.

"I'm all for results myself."

The hand that had been holding her butt slid up, and he hooked his fingers in the back of her panties and pulled them down as he moved her leg off his hip so he could get rid of them entirely.

Then he rolled her to her back, rubbing his hand back and forth over her stomach as he looked at her naked from the waist down.

"You'll smudge your notes," she said breathlessly.

"The real notes are above this. I kept writing because I didn't want to stop."

She lifted her head. Sure enough, the notes above where her panties would have rested were simply the alphabet. She laughed. "Genius move."

He gave her a wink. "It comes in handy." He ran his hand down along her bare thigh. "We can try any position you want."

She of course had a vague idea of what other positions might work, but she hadn't used any others for this. This was a fairly rare occurrence for her.

"You're the expert," she told him.

He took a deep breath. "Several things are coming back to me." He moved and urged her knees apart so he could kneel between them.

Adrianne supposed she should feel very exposed, but instead she felt ready. He bent her knees, pushed her knees toward her chest and spread her thighs in one smooth move.

She was wide open to him and she felt...hot. She would have typically expected to feel vulnerable, maybe even shocked by how specific he was about the positioning, but the look on his face made her want to cause it again and again, whatever it took.

"God, you're gorgeous,"

He studied her, his gaze moving over her body, including her breasts, her face, her hair and, of course, the heart of where she needed him.

"You like nipple stimulation," he said.

She licked her dry lips and nodded. She sure did.

"Take your bra off."

She reached behind her, unhooked and peeled it and her shirt up, exposing her breasts.

"Play with your nipples while I do this."

She moved her fingers to her right breast, rubbed over the tip and rolled it between her thumb and forefinger. She added the left breast too when she saw the effect on Mason. "Is that good for you?" she asked.

"That is so far beyond good I don't have a word."

She saw what he meant about cause and effect.

Then he really showed her. He put his finger right at her entrance, feeling the beginning of her heat and wetness. He slid it up and down, stopping short of her clit.

"Most women orgasm easiest and hardest with clitoral stimulation."

She was definitely in that camp. "That's what works best for me," she said when she found her voice.

"Good to know," he muttered and lowered his head.

The first touch of his tongue made her back arch and she moaned. When he moved his fingers to spread her as open as she could get, she caught her breath. When he licked, dragging his tongue over her slowly and sweetly, with perfect friction and pressure, she felt like crying.

"How is that?" he murmured after a few minutes. "More pressure? Less?" He slid a finger into her, then out and added another finger.

"I'll tell you this," she gasped. "If you stop doing that, I'll hunt you down and..."

He sucked on her, pressing his tongue against her clit while also drawing on her. The fastest orgasm she'd ever had crashed over her and she cried out his name.

She couldn't move of her own accord after that. He set her legs down and stretched them out before he slid up next to her and pulled her into his chest.

"Wow," he said against her head. There was a long pause before he said, "I'm really good."

There was a beat of silence and then Adrianne started giggling. She curled into him, her face against his chest, letting the feel and sound of his chuckle and the little flashes of heat that still sparkled along her nerve endings wash over her. Amazing. He was amazing.

She said it out loud too.

"That's one of the things I like best about you," he said. "How much you like me."

He said it with a light tone, stroking his hand over her hair, but she sensed a kernel of truth, or vulnerability, or something in his voice.

She wiggled closer.

They lay like that for several minutes. Finally, noise from downstairs filtered up and Adrianne realized they couldn't stay —not all night like she wanted to.

But he did need to transcribe this latest set of notes.

"Come to my house with me," she said, propping her chin on his chest. "You can use my computer to do something with these notes. Then we can explore more cause and effect."

He grinned down at her. "Had I known how great a visit to Sapphire Falls could be, I would have come back a lot sooner."

Right. A visit. Just a visit. That would end. In a couple of days.

She didn't let her smile falter, but dammit—he wasn't staying. She knew that. Wasn't surprised by it. Was surprised more that she'd sort of forgotten. But it was good. She was willing to risk a few hard heartbeats for a couple of days—well, she didn't seem to be able to help it anyway—but she wanted a quiet, peaceful, easy life. Mason lived in Chicago. The place she'd escaped. He flew all over the world, slept in hotels, ate strange food, had pressure and odd hours and a hectic schedule. He was important. His work was important.

She didn't want any of that.

She wanted to make candy in a tiny Midwestern town where teenagers smoking in the park was the biggest excitement.

So this was a fling. Mason would leave and it would all be good.

She was going to enjoy it while he was here. Once-in-a-life-time events were like that—meant to be thoroughly enjoyed and remembered forever.

Oh, and she had to keep him away from Hailey because she truly, honestly liked him and didn't want him to be used or hurt.

"Seven twelve Crimson, right?" he asked, shifting away so she could sit.

She pulled her fingers through her hair and was glad she barely wore makeup—no lipstick to smudge. "How did you know that?" All of the east-west streets in Sapphire Falls were named after colors. The founders had, apparently, thought that was quite clever. She found it odd and funny, another quirk of a small town she truly did love.

"Phoebe told me at the bar. It's Mrs. Hanson's place," Mason said, watching her pull her panties and shorts back on.

Wow, he really did have a great memory. She started to say that yes, she'd bought it from Mrs. Hanson's daughter, but she looked at him watching her, saw the heat in his gaze, remembered how he'd bent his head and taken her hot and fast to heaven, and she couldn't not take him to her house and...take him.

Holy crap. No one had ever had this effect on her. But for the first time in two years, she didn't care that her heart was racing and she couldn't slow it down. If this was how she was going to go, she was going to be the angel with the biggest grin in Heaven.

She had two nights until he left town. She wasn't going to spend even an extra minute worrying.

She grabbed Mason's hand. "Let's go."

They made their way down the stairs and out the side door undetected—until they rounded the front of the house.

"There you are!"

Hailey.

"Drew said he saw you two come in here. Lord, you've been in there forever."

Crap, shit, damn, son of a bitch. Adrianne tugged her shirt down, hoping to cover the ink on her stomach. Hailey would be far more than curious or even suspicious.

"Hi, Hailey," Adrianne said sweetly. "What's up?"

"I'm taking Mason on a Ferris wheel ride," Hailey said, looping her arm through his. "We need to talk about the project."

"Thanks, Hailey, but I can't," Mason said quickly. "Adrianne needs to get home. I want to be sure she gets there safely."

"This is Sapphire Falls," Hailey said. "The only risk is that she might get roped into helping serve ice cream over at the 4-H tent."

"I really do feel like I need to go home," Adrianne said. "I need to lie down."

Hailey looked at her like she was crazy. "It's not even six o'clock."

"I know but—"

"She's been working really hard on all the festival stuff," Mason added.

Adrianne felt even warmer toward him and it had nothing to do with his magical tongue. "Thanks, Mason."

"Are you sick?" Hailey demanded.

"I do feel a bit of a pain coming on," Adrianne said wryly.

"Okay, that's no big deal," Hailey said, even sweeter than Adrianne. "Go ahead. We'll see you tomorrow."

"I really don't want her going alone," Mason said.

Adrianne had to stifle her giggle. She'd really prefer Mason to be with her in her bed tonight too. And the orgasm she planned to have later would be better with him there.

Hailey sighed. "Fine." Then she raised an arm and bellowed, "Drew, come here!"

Drew headed for them from the group he'd been chatting with. "Yeah?"

"Walk Adrianne home, will ya? She's not feeling good and I need to keep Mason."

Drew looked at Adrianne. "What's wrong?"

"Um...feeling a little sick to my stomach actually," she said, glancing at Hailey pressing up against Mason.

"'Kay, you ready?"

Drew was a nice guy. He'd walk her home, make sure she was okay. If she needed him to. Which she obviously didn't.

Though she did feel feverish when she looked at Mason's mouth and thought about what he'd been doing with it ten minutes before.

"Hey, you want this?" She reached into her bag and pulled out a pack of gum, showing it to Mason.

"Um, well, I have a really good taste in my mouth right now..."

Adrianne was sure her cheeks were bright pink. She threw the pack of gum at him to shut him up. It hit his chest and he caught it with one hand, looking at her with heat in his eyes all over again.

"Better use it." She glanced pointedly at Hailey. They were going to be sitting very close together in the Ferris wheel anyway and she was sure Hailey would narrow the space and get into Mason's face as much as she could. She might even try for a kiss. Adrianne knew about the kissing-on-the-Ferris-wheel-at-festival tradition.

She looked at Mason again. He probably hadn't participated in that tradition when in school.

Dammit.

She didn't want him doing it for the first time with Hailey. Or any time with Hailey for that matter. She'd like to think that after what had happened inside Herschfield House he wouldn't dream of it, but this was Hailey. She had an effect on men, and Mason used to have a huge thing for her. It probably wouldn't take much for Hailey to get a kiss. Or give one. It was very realistic to think that Hailey would take what she wanted.

Dammit.

"Let's go Mason. They're saving a seat for us." Hailey started to tug him in the direction of the Ferris wheel.

"Can't do it," he said, physically extracting her. "I need to take Adrianne home."

To everyone else it probably didn't sound suggestive, but Adrianne felt the heat build in her stomach and spread downward. She knew exactly which needs he was talking about.

M ason had been resisting the urge to tell Hailey to shut up, but his patience was growing thin.

"I'm pretty sure Adrianne can find her way home with Drew," Hailey said with a little laugh.

"I don't care," he said bluntly. "I'm taking her home. I can see you tomorrow."

He wouldn't normally let her get to him, frankly, but he only had a couple more days in Sapphire Falls and he wasn't sure forty-eight hours was enough to do everything with Adrianne that he wanted to do—even if they didn't pause for food or sleep. If he closed his eyes right this second, he would be able to conjure every detail of Adrianne's body, her taste, her smell.

"The project is going to mean so much to the town, Mason. I want to be sure you have all the details."

Truthfully, Hailey smelled great too. She was the type of woman to smell great. And she was definitely beautiful.

But it didn't matter anymore.

It was the strangest thing. He'd spent three years of high school believing that she was the essence of the female gender. Now he couldn't care less. It wasn't only the fact that she'd been the source of the single worst high school memory he had. It wasn't about anger or revenge.

It also wasn't just about Adrianne Scott, though she definitely figured in.

Adrianne was...the only woman he ever wanted to make love to again. And the fact that he'd decided that before making love to her—and within the span of forty-eight hours—was alarming. But he never second-guessed himself.

He didn't have to. It wasn't that every single theory he ever had was right or that every factor in everything he did was spot on every time—that was part of science, experimentation, exploration. Trying to get it right was the fun part, the challenge. But eventually his hunches always turned into something. Eventually it all worked out.

Exploring things with Adrianne was going to be a pleasure. For them both.

But this lack of attraction to Hailey was also simple growth.

He'd been out in the world. He'd met other women. He'd had relationships—good and bad. Hailey Conner didn't do it for him anymore.

"I'm happy to listen, Hailey, but I already told you, I'm not sure it's the right direction to go."

And he was giving her one hour. Tops.

"But you don't—" Hailey started.

"I'll meet with you tomorrow," he said firmly.

Hailey didn't look pleased. It was rare that someone didn't go along with her, especially a male someone. "Fine. Tomorrow. I'm holding you to that. We'll do lunch at my house."

He almost laughed. Hailey Conner was inviting him over to her house. Alone with her. Only the two of them.

She knew that this would feel familiar to him.

The sense of déjà vu was even stronger as he realized that Hailey truly thought this would be like last time, her bedroom, her seductive smile, her slowly undressing...

Good thing he was too damned smart to fall for something like that again. And way too interested in someone else's bedroom.

"No. I'll only have time for coffee." He intended to be very busy—and naked—for most of the hours he had left in town with Adrianne.

Hailey narrowed her eyes. "Wait a minute." She turned her attention to Adrianne. "We're supposed to be having dinner tonight. Aren't we?"

"Oh, um—"

Mason turned to look at Adrianne, feeling the tension in her body.

"You and Hailey are having dinner?" he asked, knowing that wasn't what Hailey was talking about.

"No." Adrianne said, not looking at him. "You and Hailey."

He glanced at Hailey, who looked very pleased with herself.

"We are?"

"Yes. Adrianne set it up for us."

"You did?" he asked with a frown. What the hell?

"Yes. Yesterday." She looked up at him, but her expression was hard to read. She looked irritated but resigned.

"Well, something's come up. I won't be able to make dinner. Right, Adrianne?" he said. She wanted to be with him, she did. He knew it. This had to be more important than the fricking building project.

"We have reservations," Hailey said, looping her arm through his. "Adrianne had to sweet talk Mrs. Cooper to get us in. With the festival and everything, they're very busy."

Mason waited. He was going to trust Adrianne. He was going to let her decide how this went. He knew she didn't like drama, he knew she liked the path of least resistance, but he also trusted that she wanted him more than she wanted things to be easy.

She'd been protecting him, saving him, whether he needed it or not. She would save him from this, from dinner with Hailey, from Hailey.

He saw her take a deep breath and knew this was tough for her.

"Hailey, Mason's coming with me," Adrianne finally said.

Hailey's eyebrows rose. "Excuse me?"

Adrianne met her boss's eyes. "Mason's coming home with me tonight. You'll have to save your conversation for coffee tomorrow." She took another deep breath. "And don't schedule coffee too early."

Then she took his hand, pulled him away from Hailey and started in the direction of Crimson Street.

7
_____

Seven twelve Crimson was a typical old two-story with a wide porch that ran the length of the front of the house. There were a lot of potted plants hanging and sitting on the railing, a couple of tables and the floor of the porch. There was a swing and a welcome mat. The perfect picture of a home and a far cry from the condo he lived in. He had a doorman, no room for plants or a welcome mat and no yard.

Of course, he wasn't there much so it didn't really matter. But looking at the evidence that Adrianne liked to grow things made him think that having his own plants—rather than the ones in the greenhouse at work that were poked, prodded and manipulated constantly—just for the joy of having them might be really nice.

And then there was the three hundred and sixty acre farm he owned. Now there was some space for growing things.

The farm had a really great house too, with a huge porch that would be perfect for a welcome mat and hanging flower baskets. A house that could really be a home. And why not? It had been home to Milt and his large, happy family for more than fifty years. Mason had always felt at home there.

His thoughts were interrupted by Adrianne unlocking the front door.

Neither of them said anything as he followed her across the threshold and shut the door behind him.

Before he could speak or reach for her, she walked to the desk and then turned, holding out a pen and notebook. Without a word, he crossed to her and took them. She stepped back and stripped her shirt off.

Heat surged through him and he felt his erection swell.

She wore a simple white silky bra, but he could see her nipples pressing against the cups as if beckoning him.

He knew he had to get the notes down now or never. He flipped the top of the notebook open and began scribbling.

Adrianne reached behind her and unhooked her bra, letting the straps slide down her arms before tossing it away.

He swallowed hard and paused in his writing, taking in the sight of her full breasts and the pink centers.

"Keep writing," she urged.

He glanced, somehow, from her nipples to the notes on the smooth skin of her stomach. He relived the texture and taste of it under his tongue.

"Mason, keep writing."

He realized his eyes had closed so he took a deep breath and did what she said, somehow making the notes on the paper legible.

Thankfully, it had been a relatively short note and two equations.

As he scribbled, she undid the button and zipper on her shorts and let them drop, leaving her only in the black panties. He swore softly, having to cross out some numbers and start again.

She laughed and moved toward him. "Keep writing."

He stared at the paper in front of him, concentrating on getting the note down about checking the oxidation rates.

She reached for his belt, undoing the buckle as he completed the notation. Then he tossed the notebook and pen to where her bra lay on the floor as she slid his belt free of the loops. He undid the button and zipper as she ran her hands under the bottom of his shirt, then slid them up, palms against his stomach, chest and shoulders, taking the shirt with her. He whipped it off and tossed it.

"Adrianne," he groaned when she pressed her lips against his chest. His hands went to her head to hold her there.

She licked and kissed her way across his chest and up to his right shoulder. When her lips and tongue met the side of his neck and she sucked slightly, he dropped his hands to her butt and lifted her up against his hard shaft.

"That's it. Where's the bed?" he demanded.

She wrapped her legs around him. "Too far. I'm burning up, Mason. Please."

"You want it right here? Like this?" A shudder of lust shook him. Sex was generally like everything else in his life—planned out, done with purpose and about results. Not that it wasn't great. It really was. He was a huge fan. And the women appreciated the results as well. But it was never out of control. Mason didn't do out of control.

Except that he kind of did. Evidently.

"Yes, now," she groaned as her breasts rubbed against his bare chest.

He bent and took her mouth in a hungry kiss. There was nothing purposeful about it—it was simply because he couldn't not taste her.

He was going to take Adrianne Scott absolutely any way she wanted, however she wanted.

"Desk? Wall? Floor?" He managed the series of one-syllable questions as he let his hands slide lower on her ass, his middle fingers slipping under the edges of her panties and up against hot, wet woman.

He'd never done it against a wall or on a desk, or even on the floor for that matter, but all he really cared about was getting inside of her. From there it would all be fine.

She gasped. "Couch."

He knew the kitchen was to the right, so he turned left. He found the couch and sank down onto it with her straddling his lap. Intending to lay her back, he shifted her slightly, but before he could turn, she reached for and freed his straining erection.

The feel of her hands on him, bare skin to bare skin made him freeze and drag in a long gulp of air. "Adrianne."

"Oh, I like how this makes you sound." She encircled his aching flesh with her hand and slid up and down the length.

He tightened his hands on her hips but he couldn't move otherwise. The sensation of her stroking him was so intense he wanted to shout but couldn't find the air.

"I love how this feels. How you make me feel. How I want to do everything with you," she said, continuing to move her hand up and down on him. She pressed her lips to the base of his throat. "I want to ride you. I want you on top and behind."

He groaned and she sucked his earlobe into her mouth.

"And I want to eat ice cream with you," she went on. "And watch TV and dance and tell jokes...it's crazy and it's the most unexpected thing, but I love it."

Her words nearly overwhelmed him. He'd been with women who talked during sex before, but this was different. There was true emotion in her words, not explicit talk to turn him—or her—on. She wasn't telling him what she liked or wanted, she was telling him how she felt, how he made her feel, and it was powerful. In typical Adrianne fashion, she was giving him the real her, the nitty gritty, unembellished.

"That you're here with me like this, that you want me, that you're letting me do this—" she stroked him again with the perfect pressure, making his eyes cross with lust, "—is so awesome."

There it was again. That feeling that she really thought he was special, that this was special, that she liked him so much. It was more of an aphrodisiac than anything.

"I need to be inside you, Ad," he said gruffly. "Lie back."

"No, like this." She lifted herself slightly and he felt her hand leave him and then return to roll a condom in place. She did it with remarkable dexterity, and he knew he didn't want to know how she'd gotten so good at that. Then she pulled her panties to one side and sank back down...taking him deep within her.

The feeling of sliding home, into the sweetest, hottest thing he'd ever felt, was almost too much. He gripped her hips, holding her in place, gritting his teeth. This was where he was supposed to be. The thought was stunning and he needed a moment, a second, to grasp some control so that he could do this right. But the urge to lift his hips, thrust hard and deep, was so compelling that his buttocks flexed in spite of his attempt at restraint.

Adrianne moaned from even that small motion. She leaned forward, dropping her forehead to his shoulder.

The movement made them both groan.

He seemed to fill her completely, stretch her to the point of exquisite pleasure, a perfect fit.

"Yes, Mason, please move. Do something. I need this. Make this...craving go away."

He knew exactly what she meant. "Okay, honey, hang on tight." He lifted his hips, thinking there was no room to slide any deeper. But he'd been wrong. To be sure, he pulled out and thrust again.

Adrianne put her hands on his shoulders and started to move with him, lifting herself up and down, meeting his thrusts.

He watched her as she moved. Her head tipped back, her

back arched, her lips were parted and she lifted her hands to cup her breasts.

"I can help there." He leaned in and took her nipple in his mouth, sucking gently at first and then harder as her tempo picked up.

"Mason," she groaned.

His name on her lips like that, with that needy, almost desperate sound, made him want to do it to her again and again, over and over, for days, weeks, years on end.

"Ad, you're so...God, you're...everything," he said gruffly, surging upward as she came down.

She held his head in both hands and kissed him, hot, wet, wild. Then she tore her mouth free and cried out as she came.

He definitely wanted to hear and see that for the rest of his life.

The realization, combined with her look of ecstasy he was very proud to have created was enough to push him over the edge. He felt the heat and pressure build and burst into her. The only woman he ever wanted to be with again.

She leaned into him, resting her forehead on his shoulder again, neither of them moving. Their breathing quieted, their heart rates came back down and still they stayed as they were.

"Holy crap," she finally said against his chest.

He laughed and smoothed a hand over her hair. "Poetic, Ad."

She lifted her head and gave him a grin. "Sorry. But wow."

He cocked an eyebrow. "Yeah?"

"I mean...that sounds dumb and it's not like I was a virgin but—"

He squeezed her butt. "You can skip the part where you tell me about all the other guys, okay?"

She tipped her head to one side. "Really? It really bothers you that I've been with other men?"

Mason swallowed. How could he tell her all he was feeling?

It made absolutely no sense. For him to feel possessive and like she belonged with him, to him, that he looked at her and thought mine, that he wanted to be there for every birthday and Christmas and when she was sick and every time she smiled or cried or orgasmed—well, it was crazy. They barely knew one another, had spent only a few hours together and it was illogical to feel the things he was feeling.

Illogical was difficult for him. Things that didn't have proof and something he couldn't explain made him suspicious.

But here, with her, it was true.

He felt like he'd been late in getting to her and it was incredibly unfair that he'd missed out on so much with her.

"Adrianne, I think there's something I need to tell you."

She looked concerned. "That doesn't sound good."

He was counting on her to think that what he was about to say—because he couldn't not say it—was not good. Was, in fact, insane. He knew that the connection, this chemistry, this craziness wasn't one-sided, but maybe Adrianne would be more rational about it and would insist that it was too fast and too incredible. She might be able to convince him that it wasn't real, that it was a combination of physical attraction, nostalgia being home again and the fact that it was a fling—fun and unimportant in the overall scheme of things.

She pulled the blanket from the back of the couch and wrapped it around her, sliding off his lap. "Do I need to be dressed for this conversation?" she asked.

If he had his way, she'd never be dressed again. "You're not going to be dressed for the next several hours, honey."

She seemed relieved at that. She grabbed a tissue box from the end table and handed it to him. He took care of the condom and pulled his underwear and pants back together but didn't fasten them. He turned to face her. She was leaning against the arm of the couch, the blanket tucked under her arms.

"Adrianne, I think you should know that—"

"You're leaving," she said. Then she sighed. "I know. It's not like I thought you were going to stay here with me forever."

Stay here with me forever. The words hit him directly in the chest.

It was what he wanted.

He had a farm here that he loved. He wanted to plant and grow and dig in the dirt. He wanted to go to the annual festival and have a welcome mat and...Adrianne.

He stared at her. Fuck. How had this happened in two days? How was this even possible? He didn't want to go back to Chicago?

But he didn't even have to think about it. He didn't. He believed in what they did there, but he didn't have to be in Chicago to do it. He could be anywhere. He could oversee experiments anywhere, he could conduct team meetings virtually, he communicated with many members of their team via computer anyway, and he could fly out of the Omaha airport. There was no reason he had to be in Chicago instead of Sapphire Falls.

And there were a few really good reasons to be in Sapphire Falls instead of Chicago.

"I want to stay," he said simply.

Her smile slowly shrank and her eyes got wide. "What?" she whispered.

"I want to stay." He lifted a shoulder. "Sapphire Falls is, surprisingly, more appealing than anything in Chicago."

"You want to stay...for a few more days?" she asked.

If he wasn't mistaken, she sounded almost hopeful. He frowned. "You only want a few more days?"

She stared at him, the blanket gripped in her fist against her chest.

"I want a hell of a lot more than that, Adrianne. I want to have sex with you in every position possible, but I want more than that."

"What are..." She stopped and cleared her throat. "Like what?"

"Everything."

"Everything?" she repeated, her voice nearly a squeak.

"I'm falling in love with you," he said. "I know it. I love that you get me. I love that you're so genuine and accepting—not just of me but of everyone. You try to make Hailey look good even when she's being selfish and flaky. You smile at Drew even when he's being annoying. You make gourmet candy for all the guys even though they have no appreciation for anything gourmet. You don't try to change anyone. You let them be who they are."

He shifted so that he could lean closer to her, let her see the truth in his eyes. "You're so happy and content. You've figured out what you want and you've found it. I want to be near your... energy. I want that real, open satisfaction that you've found."

The only place he'd ever felt even close to that had been in Haiti and on the farm here in Sapphire Falls. And now with Adrianne.

It was ironic that his sanctuary was in the midst of the last place he thought he ever wanted to be. Part of his haven was this woman who loved this town and was in the middle of everything that happened here.

Sapphire Falls was different with Adrianne here.

For instance, he'd gotten to make out in Herschfield House. He even kind of liked poker.

"So I'm staying," he said resolutely.

She swallowed. "Whoa."

He waited for a few seconds. "That's it? Whoa?"

"We hardly know each other."

"I'm not saying it makes sense."

"But I—"

"We'll get to know each other," he said, cutting her off. "Because I'm staying and I don't want to wake up without you.

Unless there's a really good reason for us not to be together, you better be okay with sleeping naked."

. He'd said it firmly, with a frown, but she looked turned on. And completely shocked.

But slowly her mouth spread into a smile. "I sleep in a silk nightie with no underwear. Will that work?"

He shook his head, still frowning even as relief spread through him. "Nope. You'll have to lose the nightie."

"Okay, okay," she said with mock exasperation. "If you're going to insist."

"Oh, I'm going to insist." He shifted, moving so he could cover her body with his. "I'm also going to insist on you getting rid of that blanket and spreading your sweet legs for me again right now, because I need you, Ad. I really need you."

———

In the middle of the night, they lay spooning on the couch, Mason behind her sleeping, his arms around her and the blanket over them both. In spite of being well spent physically, Adrianne was wide awake, her mind reeling.

Holy crap.

Not poetic, but fitting.

Mason wanted to stay. In Sapphire Falls.

She pulled in a long, slow breath and pressed her hand over the familiar spot on her chest.

This was crazy. Completely, utterly insane.

He made her heart pound with the things he did, said, who he was. But worse, now he said he wanted to stay.

Nothing had made her heart pound like that idea did.

And the fact that she wanted him to.

Because the discomfort in her chest now was only the beginning.

Because it would never work. He couldn't leave Chicago and

everything he had and did there to move to Sapphire Falls. Sapphire Falls had nothing for Mason. Okay, he thought part of what he wanted was her, but that couldn't be true. This kind of stuff didn't really happen in the real world. People didn't meet, fall in love and live happily ever after in the span of two days.

He was drunk on the nostalgia of home, the feeling of fitting in, the idea of getting the girl.

She understood and part of her was thrilled to be a part of that for him. She liked him, so she was glad his homecoming was good.

But she was to the point now where his leaving was really going to hurt. And that was before he'd tempted her with the idea of his staying.

She felt his lips moving over the back of her bare shoulder and his thickening erection pressing into her butt. A shiver went through her as her whole body heated. She had never wanted sex like this. Right now, after three orgasms she still felt needy, like there was a hunger that hadn't been satisfied yet, an itch that desperately needed scratched.

She was going to itch for the rest of her life after he went back to Chicago.

"Hold still," he whispered against the back of her hair.

He ran a large palm down the side of her hip and thigh and brought her leg up and back to drape over his hip behind her. He slid his fingers forward then, stroking over her stomach, lower, pressing against her mound, circling her clit and slipping into the hot wetness that seemed to be constant for him.

Two fingers slid deep and she gasped as his thumb stroked over her clit at the same time.

"Mason," she choked.

"I'll never get enough of you," he murmured, kissing her hair, her shoulder.

She knew the feeling. But she couldn't think like that.

Hearing him say it was almost painful. She needed to keep him from talking, from saying all the things she yearned to hear—like how they could work it out, how they could be together, how his hands would be the only ones to ever touch her like this again.

"Mason, I want—"

He thrust his fingers deeper and she forgot that she wanted anything else.

"Reach a condom," he urged.

He'd brought several she'd learned, so she reached for the pants that lay on the floor between the couch and coffee table and pulled one out. "I can't reach to put it on you." He had her firmly pinned right where she was.

"I've got it."

He slipped his fingers from her, which made her want to whimper from the loss. Stupid. Dangerous. Bad.

A moment later, he lifted her thigh farther and she felt the tip of him at her entrance. Instinctively, she arched her back and he pressed forward, sliding fully, thickly into her.

They moaned together.

His hand returned to her, stroking her clit as he moved behind her. She had less leverage in this position, but Mason was doing fine, pumping deep, long and slow.

She was quickly breathing hard, feeling the coil of desire wind tighter, as if she was reaching for something just beyond her, something that only Mason could provide.

"I love you, Ad," he said gruffly as he thrust deep.

And she shattered.

Her orgasm, her heart, her resistance.

"You're what?" Lauren demanded as Mason dodged two kids on bikes on the sidewalk on his way from Adrianne's to the café. It was a beautiful morning.

"Staying in Sapphire Falls. I'm in love." He said it with a big grin even though she couldn't see it over the phone.

"You've got to be fucking kidding me," Lauren muttered.

He grimaced as he heard a crash on Lauren's end of the phone and the expletive that followed. "What are you doing?"

"Dropping a pan of brownies on my ceramic tile floor."

"You okay?"

"Oh, sure, I'm great. I send you off to a reunion you didn't even want to go to so I could have a romantic weekend with Alex. And you end up in love and I get dumped. And I now have to go to the store for more brownie mix. Because I am going to eat brownies. But I'm definitely great."

Lauren never ate sweets. Unless she was upset. Generally, she was upset about something that happened in the lab or with their contracts and he could easily get her through that.

Damn. "You and Alex broke up?"

"Yes, she dumped me. Because my idea of having a life outside of work wasn't enough. She didn't want to be part of my life. She wanted to be my whole life."

Mason wasn't sure what to say here. He was the best friend, so he knew it was his job to say something comforting, but Lauren was always the one to break up with her boy- and girl-friends. That generally required taking her out for a drink and telling her she was right to do it. This was new territory. He couldn't remember a time she'd been dumped.

"I thought this weekend...the point..." He really didn't know what to say.

"The point was to show Alex I cared about our relationship, that I was willing to give her some time, focus on her, make her a priority. But as soon as I said something about Haiti, she freaked. She wanted me to give everything up. She wanted me to get a normal job."

Mason frowned. "A normal job like what?"

Lauren sighed. "Hell if I know. A science teacher, I guess, or a researcher in a lab where I can go home at five o'clock and have Christmas off."

It was quite clear Alex had no idea what she was talking about. Dr. Lauren Davis couldn't work a normal job. There were plenty of talented people who could do those normal jobs extremely well. Lauren needed to do more than that. She was needed for innovative things, things that those science teachers would be talking to their students about, things that didn't follow a clock or a calendar...things like they did together.

"That's ridiculous," Mason said.

"But it's reality," she returned. "Most people don't understand what we do, and they sure aren't going to understand how much we do it. If we want to be in love with normal people we have to have more normal lives."

He could hear scraping sounds that indicated Lauren was cleaning up her brownie mess while she talked to him.

"I don't think that's true," Mason argued. "Adrianne—"

"This is your fault anyway."

"My fault?" Mason repeated. "I left town when you asked me to so you could be with her."

"I mean all this craziness that I'm choosing over her. We can't stop now. The stuff we're doing at work is bigger than both of us, thanks to you being brilliant and stuff."

"Have you been drinking?" he asked.

"No, dammit." She took a deep breath. "Okay, I put some vodka in my orange juice this morning. But that's not why I'm saying this. Mason, we're supposed to be in Haiti in two weeks for the preliminary visit. We're supposed to be in DC next week. I dumped Alex for this."

He heard a thump on her end of the phone.

"I thought Alex dumped you."

"Alex dumped me because I said I was going to Haiti instead of staying here with her. So you are not staying in Sapphire Falls."

"This is different. Adrianne is—"

"I get it," Lauren said. "I do. She's hot, right?"

"Yes. She's..." Mason trailed off, at a loss for the perfect way to describe Adrianne. Beautiful wasn't enough. The way he felt about her was so much more than how she looked.

"I know," Lauren said. "The lips, the breasts, her smell, her skin, her hair...I get it. But that heat that fast doesn't make sense. What about compatibility? What about what we—you—have in common? How can I—you—keep her interested when I —I mean you—are sitting on the couch watching Dancing with the Stars and all you can think is how much you could be getting done at work instead?"

Mason's knew his mouth was hanging open in shock. Lauren didn't rant and rave like that. She sounded...crazy. She sounded...

"Are you crying?" he demanded.

She distinctly sniffed. "No."

He really had no idea what to say now. Lauren didn't cry. She yelled sometimes. She slammed doors. She ate brownies. But she never cried. And she'd never been crazy about anyone like she was about Alex. Alex was different. With Alex, Lauren had been distracted, spontaneous...different. It had been fast and hot and crazy.

Like him and Adrianne.

He sighed. "Maybe you should just watch the show, Lauren. If that's what she wants, do it."

"I'm still not there though. I'm still thinking about other things."

"Then maybe," he said carefully. "She wasn't the right one." He hesitated with what he was about to say. "Adrianne gets it."

"Gets what?"

"What we do. Why we do it." He paused. "Who I am." Lauren didn't answer right away.

"Does she?" she finally asked.

"Yes. And she likes it. Admires it." She let him write work notes on her.

"Ah." Lauren's tone had totally changed. "She likes you."

"She likes me," he agreed.

He knew that Lauren understood what he was talking about and didn't feel pathetic about it. She was almost the only one who could really know him without him feeling vulnerable. Almost the only one. There was another woman, a short blond with the sweetest mouth, who he was more than willing to have as close as possible.

"Of course she likes you."

"Don't say it like that."

Lauren sighed.

Lauren knew women liked him. But not the real him. He was great at putting on the act. He was suave, polished, sexy, sure of himself. As far as they were concerned. But they didn't really know him. When conversation turned to fertilizer and irrigation, most lost interest, if they didn't just outright think he was weird. So he kept it superficial. They talked about social issues, politics, his travels, their work.

But Adrianne knew him. Knew about him, even some of his past here in Sapphire Falls. And liked him. Wanted him.

He'd left her sleeping this morning. She was probably going to be sore when she got up this morning, he thought with a grin. He'd been unable to keep from waking her every few hours throughout the night. At least when she wasn't wakening him.

They'd made love repeatedly in several variations, each more incredible and better than the last. Especially after he told her he loved her. She hadn't repeated it, but he could feel it —stronger every time.

"You'll see," Mason said gently. "It's going to be fine."

"This is all my fault," Lauren said. Something clattered on her end of the phone. "I made you go to Sapphire Falls. I made you so attractive that Adrianne couldn't resist. I told you that something had to be more important than work. But don't listen to me, Mason. Because of Alex, I've been distracted and leaving work early instead of focusing on the stuff for Haiti. And now she's gone and all of that is wasted time. But none of the time we've spent on Haiti is wasted. Those people need us. Those people will appreciate us. They deserve us. Hot girls who make us think about nipple clamps and bubble baths and being in love forever and ever do not deserve us."

Mason's eyes were wide. He wasn't sure what he was more stunned by—Lauren's continued ranting, his mental picture of Alex and nipple clamps, or the fact that his best friend really believed that Adrianne was bad for him.

Damn.

None of that was good.

"Lauren, calm down. Everything is going to be fine—"

"Are you coming home?"

"I'll have to make a trip eventually. I'll have to figure this DC meeting out."

He thought about suggesting Lauren go without him. But the truth was she couldn't. She could explain everything, present everything, make the case. But the vice president was upset with Mason. Mason had to deliver the presentation and make nice. Not that he exactly cared if the vice president liked him or was happy with him, but it would undoubtedly make things easier in the future when he and Lauren wanted to work overseas. They could do what they wanted without the vice president's blessing, but it would be easier with it.

Dammit.

"I was thinking we could do a conference call—"

"Oh, sure. A conference call. Why didn't I think of that?" Lauren asked with sudden brightness. "I think that's a fantastic plan."

"You do?"

"Hell no. That idea sucks."

"Why? They'll get the info they need. I'll even apologize to Vice President Forrester."

"You're seriously telling me that you're going to ask the Vice President of the United States to have a conference call with you so you can stay in Hicksville for a fling."

"She's not a fling," he said stubbornly. "She's the one. You'll like her. She's—"

"A distraction you, we, don't need."

He arrived at the café. "I have a meeting. I have to go." He could have told her the guys had invited him to coffee, but she would have thought he was making it up.

"Mason," Lauren said quickly. "I don't lie to you, right?"

"Right," he said with some reservation.

"Then believe me when I say that if you are not on a flight to Chicago by tomorrow morning, I will do whatever I have to do to save you from yourself."

That didn't sound good at all.

"I don't—" he started.

"Do not make me come to Sapphire Falls."

"I'll have to call you later."

"Sure, you do that," she said. "Whenever you get a minute. No big deal. I'll go ahead and do all of our work for the DC meeting without you and—"

He hung up.

He'd never, ever hung up on Lauren before. But she was pushy and bossy and had been dumped and was blaming him —at least indirectly—so there wasn't really anything good to come out of further conversation at the moment.

A minute later, he had to silence his phone as he stepped into the diner. Lauren could leave all her thoughts and opinions about all of it on his voice mail. Which he was sure she would.

"Mason!"

Drew's enthusiastic greeting made him smile in spite of himself. Maybe they were all faking it to make him feel good. But maybe they found him interesting. He was going to stay carefully away from the topic of his work and concentrate on things they cared about—the Sapphire Falls high school football team, the University of Nebraska's football team and the Kansas City Chiefs football team.

All things he'd spent time researching on Adrianne's computer that morning.

"'Morning." He took the chair across from Tim. "I see the Huskers have a great new running back from Texas."

8

"This is so great."

Adrianne dropped her head onto her hands. "No, Phoebe, this is not great."

"How is you falling in love with a great guy not great?"

Adrianne's head whipped up. "What?"

Phoebe grinned and lifted the takeout coffee cup she'd brought with her knowing, she claimed, that Adrianne would be too tired to get up and make anything. She'd brought Adrianne tea too.

She was tired. No doubt about it. And sore. But if she were given the chance to repeat the night, she wouldn't change a thing. Except for Mason's declaration of staying in town. And she wouldn't have wasted even the time she had sleeping. He was leaving Monday—he was—and she wanted to spend as much time with him as possible until then.

Until she had to swear him off with the carrot cake and drinking and staying up too late and her Blackberry and...all the other things that she'd loved and been addicted to.

"You've never been in love before?" Phoebe asked, reaching for one of the sugar packets she'd brought along as well.

"I've..." Adrianne thought about it. Besides one college boyfriend, she couldn't honestly say she'd been in love. And that had been first love, kid stuff. Certainly, she'd never felt the way she did about Mason.

With a groan, she dropped her head back to her hands. "This is terrible."

Now not only did she know he couldn't stay, and she was going to be sad to see him go, it really was going to break her heart.

Dammit.

"How did this happen?"

"He came to town, you danced with him and the rest is the story you'll tell your grandkids."

"Stop it." Adrianne lifted her head again. "Seriously. This can't happen."

"It already did."

"Then I have to keep it from...continuing. Even if he has some feelings for me, he can't stay."

Phoebe didn't look convinced.

Adrianne tried harder. "He's wrapped up in everything, being a part of the crowd, the phenomenal sex, the idea that the in crowd wants him for something. It won't last. It's not real."

Phoebe added another sugar packet and stirred her coffee. "I probably shouldn't say anything. I'll make you mad. Again."

"If you're referring to what you said about me not being willing to fight for him, then yes, please don't say anything," Adrianne said. Phoebe was right. That was the sucky part. She didn't want to have to fight. She was tired of fighting. She didn't want to have to try. She wanted easy, simple, angst-free.

"I'm thinking that if the guy you're in love with isn't enough to make you want to take a risk then I don't know what will be. I worry about you."

Adrianne swallowed against the lump in her throat. "I'm fine."

"Well, at least you're getting laid. That's more than I can say."

That simple reminder was enough to make liquid heat rush through Adrianne's body.

Phoebe must have seen something in her face because she whistled. "Wow, it must have been good."

It had been. It had been enough to ruin her forever for other men. It had been enough to make her want to beg him to stay.

"It was…" Her cell phone beeped, signaling a text message and she hoped it was Mason, then she hoped it wasn't. This was complicated.

But it didn't matter, because it was Hailey. "S.O.S. He said no to Drew too."

"Frick," she muttered.

"What's up?"

"Hailey. Mason was invited to coffee with the guys this morning. He insisted he was fine to go alone, that it was social. Obviously, Hailey talked Drew into asking Mason for the money too. He turned him down."

Phoebe snorted. "She's pretty dense, isn't she?"

"I suppose she has to try every angle."

"Oh, I love it," Phoebe assured her. "The harder Hailey tries, the more fun it has to be for Mason to say no."

"You think he's saying no for fun?" That didn't feel right.

"Hey, if he doesn't want some revenge, he's a better person than I am."

Adrianne frowned. "Revenge? Mason doesn't really strike me as the vengeful type, Phoebe."

"But you don't know what Hailey did to him. I think even the Pope would be less than forgiving."

"What did she do?" Adrianne didn't think she really wanted to know.

Before she could think of an appropriate answer to text to Hailey, her phone rang. It was Hailey. "We have to do something, Adrianne. I have to do the presentation to all the other investors in an hour. What should we do with Mason?"

Adrianne had several ideas. None of which included a we.

"I was thinking maybe he could hang out with me. I'm going to be making all the candy for the reception. Maybe it would be good for him to hang out with me and see some behind the scenes of one of the potential businesses." She was making this up as she went along, but that sounded pretty good.

Phoebe's grin and thumbs up said she agreed.

"Oh, that's perfect," Hailey said. "He'll see up close and personal what a great idea it is."

Well, if her boss was going to insist she spend time with Mason, she was going to have to, wasn't she? "Sure. Sounds great."

"Okay." Hailey didn't say anything else, but she also didn't disconnect.

"Hailey?" Adrianne prompted.

"I'm sorry about the Ferris wheel and insisting on dinner with Mason," Hailey finally said in a rush. "I didn't know you had a real thing for Mason. I know no guy has spent the night with you since you've lived here, so I know he must really mean something to you. I'm sorry I didn't...notice. I thought we were friends but...maybe I'm not a very good friend."

Adrianne sat in shock. Hailey Conner had just apologized to her. Was there a full moon or something?

"Adrianne?"

She shook herself. "Yeah?"

"So, I, um...still have to try to get him to invest but I will back off on the..."

"Cleavage?" Adrianne supplied.

Hailey actually gave a soft laugh. "Yes. The cleavage. And everything."

"That would be great."

"I could help you with your cleavage a little though," Hailey offered.

Adrianne's call waiting beeped and she glanced quickly at the incoming number. It was Mason.

"I'm good, thanks. Bye." Adrianne quickly hung up on Hailey and picked up Mason's call. "Want to hang out today?"

"With you, yes. With anyone else, no."

She grinned. "Good answer."

"Want to go to the farm with me? I want to check a few things out about the house."

"I need to make candy today. A ton of it."

"Do it at the farm. The kitchen is great. Huge."

A huge kitchen was a sure way to tempt her. As if she needed more temptation than just being with Mason. Her kitchen was great for making a meal or two a day, even a batch of candy here and there, but big batches got complicated. "The stove and stuff works?"

"Never shut anything off," Mason admitted. "Kept thinking I might sell it and seemed best to keep the heat and everything working."

"Sounds perfect. I'll meet you there." She disconnected, making a grocery list in her head as she grabbed her purse and started to stand. She paused when she noticed Phoebe watching her with an amused expression.

"What?"

"I think making candy is a great euphemism for sex," Phoebe said.

"We're not going to..." Adrianne trailed off as she realized that was probably a lie. "I'm going to make candy. Too."

Phoebe's laughter accompanied her out of the kitchen.

———

Adrianne was properly impressed by the farm's kitchen. It was perfect. Perfect for candy making, perfect for cooking huge family dinners, perfect for hosting barbecues with friends. Perfect.

She sighed and knew it sounded wistful.

She wanted a kitchen like this. She also wanted to make candy, cook huge family dinners and host barbecues for friends.

Mason flipped on a light switch and crossed to open the fridge. "It all seems to be working. What do you think?"

"It's perfect," she said, with more feeling than was really needed for the old farmhouse's kitchen.

"Great. I'm going to head upstairs and check on some things."

She got busy unpacking her groceries and pots and pans. She was making truffles for the investor reception tomorrow night along with her grandmother's candy strawberries, on request from Matt, and her own chocolate coffee toffee. She needed to get going.

For the next two hours, she enjoyed listening to Mason banging around upstairs and stomping over the back and front porches as he searched through bedrooms, the attic, closets, basement and out buildings. She'd catch sight of him through the window or passing by the doorway from time to time, but he didn't stop to chat or even steal a kiss.

Still, it was nice working knowing that he was around.

It was something she could get used to.

Which was crazy. She'd known him only a couple of days. Sure, she liked him. Yes, he made her hot and tingly with just a smile. But there was no way she could already know that she wanted him around for good.

In this house.

The thought hit her hard.

As if someone had said it out loud to her.

She was completely comfortable and could imagine herself in this house, with Mason, forever. Adrianne swallowed hard and tried to focus on the pot in front of her. She was making...it took her ten seconds to remember. She was making toffee. She added butter and sugar to the pot, stirred them together and then turned for the salt.

Through the large window by the table, she caught sight of Mason coming up from the barn. He stopped and bent to toss something into a bucket by the tree, straightened and wiped his hands on his jeans. Large streaks of dirt coated the denim and stupidly, Adrianne's heart kicked.

He looked so sexy all dirty and sweaty and...then he grinned, tipped his cap back and wiped his arm over his forehead.

She stared.

He wasn't smiling at her. She knew he couldn't even see her from there. He was simply smiling. The contentment and happiness were so obvious that she had a hard time swallowing.

A quiet hissing sound behind her reminded her she was in the middle of...something. Whirling toward the stove, she grabbed for the spoon. Oh, yeah, toffee. Dammit.

She stirred the melted butter and determined she'd caught it in time. Cussing the fact Mason could distract her so easily, she checked the temperature, stubbornly focusing.

When she had her own shop this wouldn't be a problem. There would be no sexy farmer in faded blue jeans sweating and dirty right outside the window.

The butter and sugar came to the right temperature and she moved to prepare the baking sheet for pouring it out.

Maybe she wouldn't put windows in the shop kitchen anyway. If Mason even came in for coffee or something—she frowned. Would Mason be coming in? Really? He said he wanted to stay, but there was no way he'd give Chicago up entirely. Or even at all. She went to the table and rummaged in the grocery bags for the chocolate and coffee beans she'd ground earlier for the top of the toffee.

He'd seemed really determined about it last night though. Mason Riley didn't strike her as the type to say something like he was staying without having put some thought into it. Okay, it was crazy. Definitely. But not impossible.

If he stayed, moved here, whatever, they could see each other all the time. They could date. Get to know each other. Then the ridiculous I-want-to-be-with-you-forever feelings would be okay and make sense. To everyone. Including her.

And she could make candy in this kitchen until the shop was done. Even after that. She could make candy at Christmas for their families and...

She froze.

This kitchen...at Christmas...her shop...

This kitchen was sitting on top of where they wanted to build Sapphire Hills.

If Mason stayed in Sapphire Falls, he'd be living here. In the house they were going to tear down. On the land they were going to pave over. On top of the hill—the only real hill in Sapphire Falls.

She ran a hand through her hair while rubbing the spot over her heart with the other.

Frick. Damn. Crap. What were they going to do?

This was all her fault.

The plan had been to keep Mason away from Hailey so she wouldn't screw up their chances of building Sapphire Hills.

Yeah, this was going great.

"How's it going?"

Adrianne swung to find Mason coming in through the back door.

He had dirt streaking his T-shirt and right cheek now too and he was grinning like a little boy.

Her heart thumped. God, she wanted him.

Not just physically. She wanted all of it. She wanted him to move here, to live in this house, to farm this ground.

Oh, crap.

"Is that right?" he asked, pointing at the stove.

The smoking pot barely registered. She removed it from the burner and turned to him.

"You should take your clothes off," she told him.

He quirked an eyebrow. "Yeah?" He started to unbutton. "I'm all dirty."

"You haven't even begun to get dirty."

He grinned and moved toward the sink. "Well, there's dirty and then there's dirty."

She stopped him with a hand on his arm as he reached for the faucet.

"No. Dirty."

He held up his hands. "Ad, I intend to put these all over you. Let me wash."

"You love this dirt," she said, taking his hands and putting them to her face. "Get me dirty like this, Mason."

———

He kept his hands in place when she dropped hers to his hips and brought him closer. He moved his right hand, sliding it from her cheek to jaw and down the side of her neck. Fascinated by the streaks left behind, he repeated the motion. It was strange, but seeing her covered in dirt and mud was hot. He had to be with someone who wasn't afraid to get dirty—in the original sense of the word.

"You wouldn't rather use your work as foreplay?" he asked, eyeing the butter behind her on the counter.

She grinned up at him. "That's for everyone else. This is for you."

He loved that grin. She'd been looking far too serious when he'd come in, and when she'd turned to look at him she'd seemed...stunned. At least that's how it had looked. But that didn't make sense.

She pulled her T-shirt over her head, dropped it at their feet, unhooked her bra and tossed it away.

This, on the other hand, made perfect sense.

"Put your big muddy hands on me, Mason," she said, flipping her hair back and offering her breasts.

Want pulsed through him, and it was want for everything she was—not only her gorgeous body, but her heart, her dreams, her future.

"If we're going to do this right you need to lose even more clothes," he said, resisting touching her. For now. "I want you dirty all over."

She didn't take her eyes from him as she skimmed off her jeans and panties.

"Much better," he said with approval.

She moved in and wrapped her arms around his neck, rubbing her body against his dirty clothes. She slipped her hands into his hair, against his hot scalp, and pulled him down for a kiss. "I love how you look, smell, feel, taste—" She licked her tongue along his lower lip and then pulled back. "This is the real you, isn't it?"

"Hard as a rock and ready to take you on the kitchen counter? Yeah."

Goosebumps erupted on her skin and Mason bent and licked the curve of her shoulder.

"I meant dirty and sweaty and totally happy working out there."

He ran his hands down her back, pressing close. "Yeah, that's me."

"I like it." She rubbed against him again.

He pushed her back slightly to look. Dirt streaked her chest, arms, belly and thighs.

"I do too. More than I ever realized."

He grinned and lifted her up on the counter top behind her. She immediately spread her legs and he dragged in a deep breath of air.

He ran his thumb over the streak of dirt on her face, down the side of her neck to her collar bone, down over her breast to the nipple. He drew a circle around the nipple, loving how she arched and moaned.

The dirt was faint now and there was a lot of skin to play with. Marking her like this gave him a very primal surge of possessiveness. He swiped a hand over his back hip pocket where he knew there was mud and lifted it to her breast.

The handprint he left looked incredibly erotic and he again thought some of her chocolate or the plain butter would be great.

He could at least lick that off. Not so much with the mud.

Adrianne looked down at her body and gave a little groan. "I like your handprints on me," she said. "They're the only hands I ever want on me again."

"Damned right," he said firmly. He ran his hand over her stomach.

There was all that sweet bare skin on her inner thigh and he had to mark that too.

She parted her legs for him and he could see she was already wet for him—had any woman ever wanted him like this one did?—but he couldn't put his dirty hands there.

"You'll have to use a part of your body that's been covered," she said, reading his mind and reaching for his fly at the same time.

"This doesn't have any mud on it," he said, dipping his knees before she could reach him and putting a hand on each

185

leg to keep her open. Then he leaned in and took a long lick of her.

Her fingers gripped his hair and she moaned his name. He took his time licking and sucking, making her squirm before finally straightening and letting her free his erection.

"Better than chocolate," he told her.

Without a word, she pulled him forward as she scooted closer to the edge of the counter.

He didn't argue, didn't tease, paused only long enough to roll on a condom before he cupped her ass and brought her forward onto him.

As he sank deep, they groaned together. For a moment, he paused, his forehead on hers, her arms around his neck, memorizing everything about the feel of her.

The only woman he'd ever feel like this again. Seemingly every inch of her was against every inch of him. And he still wanted her closer.

Eventually though, his body drove him to move. He withdrew with excruciating slowness. She shuddered and lifted her mouth to his. She kissed him slow and deep too, her body clinging to his as he thrust forward.

He tilted his hips so he could drag against her clit. She pulled away from his mouth to gasp and her arms and legs tightened, holding her closer to him. There wasn't even a centimeter of space between them, as if she was afraid to let go. Buried deep and pressed completely together, he could barely move except to press, rub and give short thrusts. But it was enough. His erection pulsed in her. He wanted to fill her, stretch her, never leave her.

That last thought seemed out of place, yet when she shifted against him and made that sound in the back of her throat, it really, really fit.

"This is right where I want to be forever, Ad," he managed

with the little bit of air he could pull in with her holding so tightly. "Tell me I can have this forever."

"Yes," she hissed, moving her hips to get even closer—an impossibility.

He thrust again and felt her muscles beginning to contract.

"Come for me, Ad," he whispered.

"You too," she gasped.

"I'm right with you, babe."

As her muscles gripped him, he felt release come racing from his gut through him and into her.

A moment later, he felt her finally pull in a deep breath. But her hold on him didn't relax. He kept her close, stroking his hands up and down her spine.

"Ad?"

"Yeah?" Her voice was muffled against his shoulder.

"You okay?"

"I think you should move in with me."

He pulled back and her grip loosened as she took a deep breath.

"What?" he asked

"You said you want to stay," she said. "I want to sleep with you. A lot. Actually sleep, along with this. You should move in with me."

He looked down at her, the dirt streaks on her cheeks making him want to kiss her.

Of course, her breathing made him want to kiss her.

"I'd love to live with you, Ad. You can move in here."

"So you are moving here?"

"Of course. I'll have to make trips to Chicago periodically, but yes. And this house is great. You can do your candy here. Maybe go online with it. I'll farm and—"

She sat up straight. "You're going to farm?"

"Yes." He felt it in his bones. That was what he wanted—to grow things that had nothing to do with the lab or IAS. He wanted to grow things that didn't require him to tinker and test and trial. He wanted to plant good old seeds and watch them come up. He wanted to have crops he didn't have to meet with anyone about, plans he didn't have to have conference calls for. "Farming here, being with you, this house, this land, is what will make me happy. This is what I want." He squeezed her and smiled. "I can hang out downtown at the diner with the other guys at lunch and we can play ball and go to barbecues."

"You don't play ball," she pointed out.

"Maybe I can learn."

She shook her head. "I don't think so."

He pinched her butt. "Thanks for the vote of confidence."

She looked up at him with a mixture of surprise, happiness and worry. "This is what you want, huh?"

"This. You. Adrianne—"

"Does the shower in this joint work?" She let go of him and slid to the floor.

"It should. But are you—"

"Let's go." She grabbed his hand and headed toward the front of the house. "Why don't you grab that jar of caramel sauce too while you're at it."

————

Over an hour later, they were back in the kitchen. Mason was stirring the butter and sugar on the stove for the second try at the toffee while she finished the truffles.

"Why'd you leave Chicago?"

She paused in the midst of swirling white chocolate on the top of the dark chocolate Kahlua truffles.

"I got tired of it," she said, semi-honestly.

"Not tired of the candy."

She smiled. No, never the candy. "Selling the candy, the pace, the pressure, competing with my brothers."

She took a deep breath and looked up. How much sh̶ should she tell him? How much mattered? Not many people in Sapphire Falls—really just Phoebe and Matt—knew all the details. Hailey knew she'd gotten sick and chosen Sapphire Falls to be healthier and slow down, but Hailey didn't know about the heart attack.

But if this was the man she wanted to be with forever—and she was more sure of that all the time—then she needed to let him close.

She finished the swirls and laid the decorating pen to the side.

"I pushed hard," she said, wiping her hands on a towel and facing him. "I was top seller but it wasn't easy staying there. I preferred making the candy, inventing new recipes, playing in the kitchen. I loved being in the stores too—seeing customers trying our stuff. We have a huge factory, of course, but attached to it we still run the original Scott Candy Shop that my great grandmother started. It's this great, old-fashioned candy shop with wood floors, high ceilings, huge windows and glass display cases."

"Scott Candies?" Mason asked. "As in Adrianne Scott?"

Everyone knew Scott Candies. They hadn't over taken Hershey or Mars, but they did enough business that the top companies watched out for them.

She nodded. "My family's business. My great-great grandfather started it. It's a huge thing, to be a part of it."

"But you left it?"

"Yes. I have three brothers who all intended to take it over, make it bigger, push it forward."

"And you couldn't keep up?"

She hated that was his assumption, though she could admit that it was probably an obvious conclusion to jump to. "I was the best of the bunch. Biggest sales, the most contacts, the board loved me."

"But?"

"But it can be harder to stay on top than it is to get there. They were all watching me, waiting for me to screw up, trying to get to things before I could, constantly pushing and criticizing." She rubbed her hand over her heart. "It sucked."

"They're your brothers," Mason said with a scowl.

"Yes. But they believed they were doing what was good for the company, and therefore for all of us. Pushing each other resulted in new products, new accounts, new ideas. And they figured that if I could do a great job—wonderful, but if one of them could do better—wonderful. They still compete with each other."

Thinking back made her chest, her stomach and her temples tighten. She missed some of it. She missed the product development. She loved having ideas about new things they could try, brainstorming with the candy makers, doing the taste testing and focus groups and the thrill of finding something new that people liked.

But her father had insisted she and her brothers be more involved in sales. No one knew or cared about the business like they did, he contended. Who better to be out there selling Scott candies than the Scott family themselves? Anyone could mix ingredients, not everyone could sell. Or so he maintained.

She didn't miss the frustrations in dealing with him. She didn't miss the headaches and stomachaches her brothers gave her. She didn't miss the jet lag, the need for sleeping pills at night and massive doses of caffeine in the morning, the kissing the asses of people she didn't even like. She definitely didn't miss the nicotine withdrawal from her attempts to quit four times a year or the sense of guilt and failure when it didn't work.

"This is pretty different from what you did with Scott Candies," Mason said.

"It is. It's good. I was in the fast track in Chicago, but I wasn't happy or healthy. This is better all the way around."

"Can you open up your own shop? Don't they have rights to the candy recipes?"

"Of course they do." What did he think? Her family was a bunch of idiots? "My grandmother helped with product development and had some ideas that were never approved. She passed those recipes to me when she died. I'm going to use those to start and then develop my own."

She leaned back on the counter behind her. "I learned the ins and outs of the business and the kitchen before I was even twelve. Selling the candy was always the fun part—helping people find what they want, seeing them try it—I mean it's candy. What's better than that?"

Mason was still stirring but his attention was fully on her. "You're better at the candy making than the selling?"

Adrianne picked up a pink decorating pen and started on the cherry chocolate truffles. They had a hint of cherry in the chocolate and a rich cherry center. "Nah, I'm a natural seller. I worked hard, long hours and stuff, but it wasn't difficult. I was great at it. I took off right away and everyone, myself included, assumed that's where I should be. I missed the creating— which I'm also good at—but I could sell ice to an Eskimo as they say."

She looked up to find Mason smiling at her. "What? Keep stirring."

He did but said, "I'm trying to imagine you in a conference room in a suit. The jeans and ponytail are so you."

She shrugged. She'd successfully shed all of that and felt very comfortable in her new persona. "I look damned good in a skirt and heels."

"Hey, at the end of the day I'll gladly strip you out of whatever you choose to wear," he said with a sexy grin.

She grinned back. "Well, no more suits. I love blue jeans. I don't want high-pressure meetings, high stakes, long hours, traveling—I'm over all of it. I love small town, quiet and simple."

"What about short trips and a skirt once in a while?"

She looked up from the pink squiggles. He'd stopped stirring again.

"Mason." She pointed to the pot. When he started moving the spoon again, she said, "You mean like vacations?" Sure, if they could drive to their destination. She didn't fly anymore. Not since her heart had stopped beating on a plane two years ago. "Because I'll do sundresses, no problem."

"That or trips to Chicago or DC with me."

Chicago was drivable. DC—not as much. She raised her eyebrows. "You want me to go?"

"I don't want to go without you."

She felt her heart flip. "That's...nice." To be with Mason she'd figure something out. She could drive to DC if she had a few days head start. "Yeah, I'd go for a few days. I'd even wear a dress."

"When I go its more than a few days."

"How long?" She wasn't sure she wanted to hear.

"Two weeks minimum."

"You'll have to be gone for two weeks or more at a time?"

He frowned slightly. "Yes. Projects will need overseeing. I'll need to meet with the key players. If there are problems I'll have to stay until those are resolved."

Just then the smell of burnt butter hit her. Again.

Dammit.

She crossed to the stove and moved the pot to the back burner. So it was only going to be truffles for the reception. They were out of butter so no toffee and the jar of caramel sauce was now only half full.

"Mason, I—" She swallowed hard and turned to face him. "I

can't. I told you that I left Chicago because I wasn't healthy. I wasn't kidding—or being dramatic. I had a heart attack."

She leaned against the counter, gripping the edge and awaiting his response.

He stared at her.

"Mason. Did you hear me?"

He took a deep breath, the lines between his eyebrows creasing deeply. "I heard you."

Okay. She waited.

Finally, the look on his face eased from confused to concerned. "Are you okay?"

She was. She knew that. Everyone kept telling her she was. And Mason needed her to be. "Yes. I'm fine. Fully recovered. Have been for a while. But it's part of the reason I love and need Sapphire Falls. It's quiet here. Peaceful. Slow paced. All the things I want now. I can't leave for long periods of time." She swallowed hard. "I don't want to."

He reached out and she took his hand. He hauled her in and enfolded her in his arms. "God, Adrianne," he muttered in her hair, stroking his hand from her crown to the back of her neck. "God."

She wrapped her arms around him and squeezed him tight. "I'm okay, Mason."

He leaned back too, her face in his hands, and kissed her.

It was the sweetest, most heartfelt, most amazing kiss of her life.

When he lifted his head, he stared into her eyes. "Thank you for telling me."

She nodded. "I—"

Her phone rang "It's Raining Men." That was okay. She'd had no idea what she was about to say to Mason. He let her go as she reached for it. "Hi, Phoebe."

"Hey, Hailey's bringing the other investors to the farm. Should be there in about fifteen."

"Thanks." She sighed and disconnected. "We'll have to move this party to my house," she told Mason.

She started to tell him why but paused. He'd said no to Hailey that morning. But she was still bringing investors out? Did she not realize he was saying no to the donation and to selling the farm? Did Mason not realize she didn't know that?

Adrianne really didn't want to get into this now.

She didn't need her—was he her boyfriend?—well, whatever Mason was, she didn't want him upset. She didn't need her boss—who was sort of a friend—upset.

She needed her candy made.

And more butter.

Simple things. Things she could do something about.

"We need to go to the grocery store," she finally said.

He looked around. "Okay. You can leave this stuff here if you want."

Leaving the finished candy would be easier—and faster since Hailey was on her way.

"Great. Let's go." The investors wouldn't come in the house. As far as they were all concerned the house would be demolished.

Adrianne felt a twinge in her heart at that thought. She liked this house. Mason loved it.

Dammit.

She was sure to take different roads than Hailey likely would on the way back to town.

But as she did it, she realized this had gotten complicated. She didn't like complicated.

Worse, it had the potential to be her absolute least favorite thing—dramatic.

Back roads and lies weren't going to save her forever.

———

"He's staying?" Phoebe asked. "Wow."

"Yeah. And on the farm. In the house Hailey wants to knock down."

They were back at Adrianne's contemplating finishing the rest of the candy she needed to make. She'd encouraged Mason to call Drew and see what the guys were up to, knowing that she had to get the candy done and certain that with him around it wasn't going to happen. She'd burned far too much butter as it was.

But mostly she needed to talk to her best girlfriend.

Adrianne was eternally grateful that her best friend was a teacher and didn't pick up part-time work in the summer. She needed Phoebe to be able to drop everything and come listen to Adrianne's problems at a drop of a hat. Apparently.

"Wow."

"Because of me. At least partially. Mostly, I guess."

"Wow."

"Stop saying that!" Adrianne snapped. "That's not helpful."

"I don't know what else to say," Phoebe said.

Adrianne blew out a breath. "Yeah. Me too."

"You want him to stay?"

"Yes." She knew that for certain. "But..."

"But what? You're in love, he's in love, he wants to live here, you want to live here. Sounds perfect."

Adrianne nodded. It did. She should be ecstatic.

When he was with her, all she could think about was how much she wanted him, how head-over-heels she was. But when she had some space, she realized how crazy it all was.

"What about the shop, the project, the town, Hailey?"

"Oh, screw Hailey," Phoebe retorted.

"Easy for you to say." Hailey was her boss. And her sort of friend. At a minimum, she'd trusted Adrianne to have the town's best interests at heart.

"Practice it a few times, it gets easier," Phoebe replied. "You cannot live your life around what Hailey Conner wants and thinks."

"No, but I had—have—a responsibility. I'm on the committee—"

"Screw the committee too," Phoebe said, waving her hand. "Who cares about the committee?"

"The rest of the committee," Adrianne said dryly.

"I'm serious," Phoebe said, pinning her with a stare. "I promise you that there will be another committee. This is Sapphire Falls. We can't even put up a flag on the Fourth of July without a committee meeting about it."

Adrianne gave her a little smile. "What about the shop?"

"Ad, it's just a shop. It's just candy."

"Hey."

"You know what I mean," Phoebe said, unconcerned by her offense.

"Not really. It's my shop. How I'm going to make a living. What I want to do with my life."

Phoebe raised an eyebrow. "Really?"

"Hey." Her candy was great. It made her happy. It was a fine dream.

Phoebe sat forward on Adrianne's sofa. "Okay, owning your own business and making candy is fine. Nothing wrong with that. But it's so..." She obviously hesitated.

"What? It's so what?"

"It's so safe," Phoebe finally said. "It's fine. It really is. But it's more like...a hobby for you. I get the impression you do it because it's what you know. It's..."

She trailed off and Adrianne sat forward with a suspicious frown. "Yes?"

"It's easy," Phoebe said with a shrug.

It was easy. That was the point. Life was too short to go to a job every day that made her crazy. "My family got quite wealthy from candy and—"

"Yeah, but you don't intend to make it a multi-million-dollar business. You're using it to fill in the gaps."

Adrianne had trouble swallowing as she stared at her best friend. "The gaps?" she asked softly.

"The gaps where you feel like you should be doing something but you're too scared of most things that occur to you."

"Phoebe, I—"

"Adrianne, businesses, money, bosses, that all comes and goes. Love doesn't. You can live without Hailey, candy and money. Can you live without Mason?"

There was that swallowing problem again. After she'd cleared her throat, she asked, "You've turned into quite a Mason Riley fan."

"Oh, I've always been one. Now that's he's making my BFF so happy, I'm the president of his fan club though. He deserves you, Ad. I love it. The justice is perfect really." She sat back against the cushions and chuckled. "You know that saying about the best way to get back at your enemies is to live a good, happy life? Mason's doing that and then some."

Adrianne frowned. "He had enemies?"

"Well, no," Phoebe consented. "But he should be flaunting his success to some people for sure. And now he's not just able to live a good, happy life, but he's doing it right in front of Hailey. Without Hailey. He's in love, but not with her. He's going to live and be totally happy right smack dab on top of where Hailey wants to put something that would make her totally happy."

"Okay." Adrianne took a deep breath. "I need to finally hear this story."

Phoebe seemed glad to comply. "He was in love with her for years. Everyone knew it."

"Uh huh." She wanted to hear this story. Honest, she did.

"And then there was that night when he gave her a ride home."

Adrianne swallowed her mouthful of tea, feeling like it was battery acid going down. She couldn't bring herself to even grunt in response.

Phoebe went on, happily.

"According to some, she invited him over, did a strip tease and they had hot sex. Others say once they got to that point, he couldn't perform. Others say he turned her down. No matter what happened in that house, we all know what happened at school the next day."

Adrianne was glad she had her cup. She needed something to throw up in.

"We were standing around in the commons before school and he approached her. He had this huge grin on his face. He... Lord, I almost can't think about it without shuddering," Phoebe said.

"He what?" Adrianne prodded. For some reason, she wasn't sure she wanted to hear the rest, but she was very sure she needed to.

"He kissed her cheek."

The tea/battery acid churned in her stomach. "What did she do?"

"She turned to him, asked him what the hell he thought he was doing."

"Oh, God." Adrianne put her head down on her hand.

"He didn't back down at first. He narrowed his eyes and said, 'I'm kissing you. A PG version of what I did to you last night.' He looked her straight in the eye, in front of everyone and said that. I couldn't believe it. No one could."

Adrianne lifted her head.

"But then it got worse."

Adrianne's heart squeezed.

"Mason said, 'You were sure glad I pulled over and picked

you up last night.' And Hailey's boyfriend, Mark, said, 'How glad?' and before Mason could say anything, Hailey laughed and said, 'Don't worry. A normal guy would have made a move but this is Mason. No worries, right?' and Mark laughed and said, 'Good point. You'd need test tubes instead of tits to get him excited'."

Adrianne had the urge to kick Hailey's ass on a weekly basis as it was, but this was enough for her to want to hunt her boss down and do much more damage than that. Permanent damage. That would show in photos.

Maybe she wasn't as accepting as Mason thought.

Well, she was. Except for Hailey. No. She was accepting of Hailey too. Maybe especially of Hailey. Dammit.

Adrianne closed her eyes. "That bitch."

And one thing was now for sure—she and Hailey were definitely not friends.

———

Mason could walk the sidewalks of Sapphire Falls blindfolded. Or evidently with his thoughts fully occupied by the memory of Adrianne in the shower. He hadn't noticed one detail around him since leaving Adrianne's house...

Caramel sauce dripped from her index finger onto the tip of his *erection and then slid slowly down the length. Adrianne was on her knees in front of him and her gaze followed the caramel's path. Mason fought to stay still. He wanted to grab her, lift her against the shower wall and thrust.*

"This is gonna get messy," she promised him as she unscrewed the lid of the jar. They hadn't turned the shower spray on yet. It was going to be a little while.

When the sticky trail reached the base of his shaft, she leaned in with her tongue. He groaned and tangled his fingers in her hair. But he kept still otherwise.

"Sweet stuff is my specialty. Just stand there. No moving," she instructed, dipping her finger into the caramel.

"Sweet stuff is your specialty all right," he quipped as the warm sauce touched his skin. From there he was pretty much speechless.

When she reached his tip, she swirled her tongue around, gathering all the sugar. Then she scooped more from the jar and painted a stripe down the center of his shaft. She followed it down slowly with her tongue, then back up, sucking when she reached the top.

Soon sticky caramel was spread all over both of them—and that was when he stopped following the rule of not moving...

H is thoughts and forward motion both came to an abrupt stop as he ran smack into someone rounding the corner.

His phone went flying, her phone went flying—as did a couple of expletives.

"Dammit, watch what you're...Mason!"

His eyes widened as he realized he'd almost knocked Hailey Conner on her ass. "Hailey. Sorry." He retrieved both phones and handed hers over.

"Hi." She seemed to immediately forget that he'd nearly knocked out her front teeth with his chest. "I'm glad I ran into you." She gave him an adorable smile that he knew she'd perfected years ago.

"Are you?" he asked, eyeing the front of the café over her shoulder. He was meeting the guys to go golfing. He was only a few feet away.

"Yes. I have to ask you something and I wanted to do it in person but privately."

Oh, boy. "I'm meeting the guys right now—"

"I know." She waved her hand as if the guys were unimportant. "I saw Drew. He said you were on your way."

"So I really should go—"

"This will only take a minute." She reached out and touched his arm. "But you have to promise to be honest."

Mason shrugged. "Sure." He had no reason not to be totally up front with Hailey.

"Are you saying no to the donation to Sapphire Hills because you're still mad at me from high school?"

Okay, he hadn't been expecting that. He thought about her question though, and he realized it was fair. "You know," he said. "It would make sense if I was, wouldn't it?"

Her eyes widened a bit. "I suppose."

"I mean, you really did a number on me back then. Public humiliation. Calling me out on my biggest vulnerability. Rubbing in the fact that I didn't fit in."

Hailey had the grace to look a little sheepish.

"And that wasn't even the worst part. I stopped and gave you a ride. I gave you someone to lean on. I was there when no one else was."

Hailey's eyes had narrowed slightly by now and she crossed her arms.

This was fun.

"And then there was what happened at your house. You started that whole thing. Then you lied about it. You made me look like a fool. Looking back, that was really—"

"Okay," she cut in. "I screwed up. I was a jerk. I'm sorry."

Mason gave a short nod. "Okay."

"Okay? As in, I'm forgiven?"

He looked at her closely. "Do you want to be forgiven?" It had never really occurred to him that she might feel bad about what had happened. But it could be true. Everyone grew up and matured. That certainly could have happened to Hailey.

"Yes, I want to be forgiven," she said.

"Because I might give you money then?"

She sighed. "No. I'm sorry for what I did with or without your money. But I wouldn't be upset—or too proud to take it—if it did make you more inclined to write the check."

He chuckled, appreciating her candor. "I'm not donating to the project because I don't think it's a good investment, Hailey. Not because of high school," he said honestly, as promised.

"Okay. But I'm not giving up."

"Okay." He could keep saying no.

She stood looking at him for another long moment. "Do you know why I told everyone that nothing happened at my house?" she asked.

"Because you were kind of a bitch and didn't want anyone to know the truth?" he asked.

She grimaced slightly at the kind of a bitch but didn't deny it or defend herself. "It was because I was trying to protect you."

"Protect me?" Yeah, having everyone know that he'd kissed Hailey Conner would have been so bad for him.

"Mark would have beaten the crap out of you. You have to realize that."

Mark, her boyfriend, had been starting defensive lineman for the Sapphire Falls football team. "You think so?"

"I know so."

It was likely completely true. "And that's why you denied the whole thing?"

"Yes. I know that's probably hard to believe."

It was.

"But I didn't want him to freak out on you. You didn't do anything wrong. You were helping me out and I...went a little too far in thanking you."

He gave her a half grin. "Yeah, well, I was never upset about that part."

She returned his smile. "So we can be friends?"

"Why not?" A lot stranger things had happened since he'd returned to Sapphire Falls.

"Great."

This time the adorable smile seemed a lot less practiced. And as she walked away, Mason reflected on the fact that not getting what you wanted could lead to getting exactly what you needed.

9

"I'll get it," Phoebe offered, surrendering her wooden spoon to Adrianne. "Keep going there."

Adrianne attempted to stir both pots at once. She had five dozen of the eight dozen truffles done and the toffee well on its way, but she definitely needed Phoebe's hands. In fact, she could have used four more. But when Mason had called to say the guys had invited him to golf again, he'd been so happy that Adrianne had refrained from asking for his help. Or inventing any emergencies for anyone. Barely. She had, however, answered all his questions about the Sapphire Falls football team.

She heard Phoebe open the door and ask, "Can I help you?"

"You're not Adrianne Scott."

Adrianne didn't recognize the voice and she leaned around the corner to look down the hallway to the foyer.

"How do you know?" Phoebe asked, propping a hand on her hip. She sounded amused.

"Because Mason isn't into redheads."

Mason? A woman who knew what he was into? Adrianne

forgot the candy—but did turn the burners off—and headed for the door.

"Yeah, well Mason doesn't know what he's missing," Phoebe informed the woman.

"Is this Adrianne Scott's house?" the woman asked, seemingly annoyed.

"Yes," Adrianne answered as she came up next to Phoebe. The woman standing on her front porch asking about Mason was gorgeous. "Can I help you?"

"You're Adrianne." It wasn't a question. "Definitely Mason's type," she added, glancing at Phoebe.

"Yes, I'm Adrianne. And you must be Lauren." Adrianne leaned against the doorframe, not inviting Mason's best friend in but not shutting her out.

Lauren's eyes narrowed. "He's talked about me?"

"Of course. You're his best friend."

That seemed to take her aback a little. "Yes, I am. That's why I need to talk to you." She held up the cardboard carrier with four cups. "I brought coffee."

"I like her already," Phoebe said. She pushed Adrianne out of the way, took the coffee and ushered Lauren into the house.

"Mason isn't here." Adrianne shut the door, admired Lauren's Gucci platform sandals and followed them to the kitchen. "He won't be back for a while."

"I know. That's why I'm here to talk to you now."

Ah, she had something to say that she didn't want Mason to hear. This could be interesting.

Phoebe passed out coffee cups, keeping two for herself, and went to the fridge for creamer.

"You're concerned," Adrianne said. That much was obvious.

"Very," Lauren replied

"That he's having the best time, and the best sex, of his life?"

Lauren leaned her hip against the counter. "Yes."

"Because he wants to stay here and keep doing it?"

"Yes." Lauren said it with feeling.

Yeah, she'd figured. It was crazy to Adrianne that Mason had decided to uproot his life and move to Sapphire Falls after only three days. She could only imagine what it would sound like to someone who hadn't been there to see how things had evolved.

"Listen, Adrianne, here's the thing. I've known Mason very well, for a very long time. I think it's natural I have some concerns when he leaves for a weekend high school reunion and then suddenly calls to tell me that he's turning his whole life, our work, everything upside down to move to the town he hasn't had a single desire to see in over a decade."

Exactly.

"I do understand," Adrianne said. "But if you—"

"I think it's great that he's having a good time," Lauren broke in. "I'm thrilled, in fact. You're a nice perk of this little weekend getaway. He hasn't been this happy in a long time."

Warmth spread through Adrianne's stomach with those words. But then she frowned. She was a perk of a little weekend getaway?

"But," Lauren continued, "he's...overreacting. You have to agree."

Adrianne started to respond—with what she wasn't sure—then she realized Lauren was talking to Phoebe.

Phoebe paused in the midst of stirring hazelnut creamer into her coffee cup. "Why are you looking at me?"

"You're her friend, aren't you?" Lauren asked, gesturing toward Adrianne.

"Yes. Which means I'm happy that she's happy," Phoebe said. "I think it's wonderful that she found a great guy."

"It's been three days," Lauren said. "Come on. He's letting his apartment in Chicago go to move to a town of less than a thousand people, giving up his career, pissing the Vice President of the United States off—again—all because he's finally feeling popular."

"The vice president?" Phoebe asked, her eyes wide.

Adrianne sighed. That was what Phoebe was focusing on?

"I—" she started.

"I understand how he's feeling," Lauren went on. "I was like him in school. An outcast, a misfit, a nerd. Then I moved to a new school my junior year of high school and I took the chance to start over. I realized that if I could look and act like everyone else, it wouldn't matter if I thought like everyone else. And it worked. For two years, I was kind of normal and I loved it. I went a little crazy. I smoked. I drank. I dated. A lot. I did all the things I thought normal kids did."

"That's all very nice for you," Phoebe said, one eyebrow up. She leaned her elbows on the center island. "But Mason isn't a teenager, or a kid for that matter. He's a grown man with more than enough brains. He can make his own decisions. I don't think he needs a babysitter."

"Mason wants normal. Or he thinks he does," Lauren insisted. "And he's never really had that. Especially here. But until he came back, he had accepted that being...abnormal was a good thing." She shrugged. "He's found a place where he fits in perfectly. The scientific and agricultural communities look up to him, people seek him out, he's been praised and rewarded over and over. For not being normal."

Adrianne scowled at her. "He's normal. There's nothing wrong with him."

Lauren studied her. "Of course there's nothing wrong with him. But he's not like other men. He's better. And until you came along, he believed that."

Adrianne mouth dropped open. "Hey."

"She hasn't done anything but think he's awesome," Phoebe protested. "She's spent a ton of time with him, she admires him, she hasn't done anything but—"

"Chill, Red," Lauren said. "I'm not saying she's a bad person. She's just bad for Mason."

"Hey," Adrianne said again. "Mason is very happy here with me. So happy he wants to stay if you remember."

Dammit, who did this woman think she was? But right on the heels of that thought came the answer—she was Mason's best friend and partner. She knew him. Had known him a hell of a lot longer than Adrianne had.

"That doesn't mean it's a good idea," Lauren returned. "To Mason, normal people farm and have barbecues and have girlfriends. So that's what he wants." She focused on something over Adrianne's shoulder for a moment and sighed. "Normal people do not work for days straight in a lab, forgetting to eat, not even knowing what day it is sometimes, blowing off dates to work on a bunch of seeds."

"Seeds?" Phoebe asked.

That seemed to shake Lauren out of whatever thoughts she had going. She sat up straighter and frowned at Adrianne. "Do you have any chocolate?"

Adrianne looked closer. Lauren seemed truly upset. She took three of the finished truffles from the counter top by the stove and laid them on a napkin in front of Lauren. She immediately picked one up, bit into it and moaned. Then she took a deep breath and focused on Adrianne again.

"Normal people don't put their own lives on hold for months at a time to go to a painfully poor country that's been devastated by a natural disaster, political unrest and disease. But Mason's doing that. So I, for one, am glad he's not normal. As is the US Government, Outreach America and most of the population of Haiti."

"Haiti?" Phoebe asked.

"Adrianne, I'm thrilled—and jealous—that he came here and got to be normal for a while. But it can't last. It shouldn't last. If he stays, he'll change your life. But if he goes, he'll change the lives of thousands."

Adrianne had a hard time swallowing. He'd already changed her life. And it made her heart pound to think of all the people he was going to help in Haiti, and God knew where else.

"He deserves to be special," Lauren said. "Mason Riley doesn't deserve to just be normal."

Holy crap, Scott Candies should look at hiring Lauren in the sales department, Adrianne thought as she tried to process everything. "So you're saying that he can't work in Haiti and also have barbecues," she said dryly.

Lauren smiled. "Buying a grill and eating bratwurst once in a while won't change who he really is. Like I figured out in high school—you can look and act normal even if you don't think normally. But then in college I figured something else out."

"That bratwurst is a terrible food?" Adrianne asked.

"That no matter how much I dressed him up, no matter what I taught him, there was something about Mason I couldn't cover up. And then he started showing me the stuff he was figuring out with conservation and recycling and alternate energy sources and then these damned seeds." She said it with an affectionate smile. "And I realized that being special trumped being normal. So he helped me too. He made me want to do big, fantastic things and I helped him feel more comfortable and...we balance each other."

Adrianne blinked hard and pressed her lips together. She didn't really want to like Lauren. She was convinced that Adrianne and Mason were moving too fast and that she wasn't good for him. At the same time though, it was quite obvious that Lauren loved and believed in Mason. How could Adrianne not like her for that?

"Wow," Phoebe said to Lauren. "You sure you're not sleeping with him?"

Adrianne's eyes flew to Lauren. When Mason had talked about Lauren it hadn't seemed like a sexual relationship, but she wouldn't mind a bit if Lauren would deny it out loud.

Lauren leaned forward and ran her fingertip over the back of Phoebe's hand. "Mason's not my type. But I am into redheads."

She was into...oh. Adrianne turned to her friend with wide eyes. She hadn't seen that coming.

Unfazed, Phoebe grinned. "Everyone's into redheads," she said. "They just don't all know it. And I realize it will be a crushing disappointment to you, but I like the outies."

Lauren nodded. "Me too sometimes."

Adrianne was trying to keep up. Maybe outies didn't mean what she thought. "The outies?"

Phoebe answered. "The parts that stick out rather than the parts that go in."

Adrianne rubbed her forehead. How had they gotten on the topic of sexual orientation—and possible changes to that orientation? "So you're not a lesbian?" she asked Lauren, just to clarify.

Lauren smiled. "I'm open minded."

"You go both ways?" Phoebe asked, eyebrows high.

Lauren gave her a wink. "I like to have lots of options."

Adrianne wasn't sure what to say to that.

Thankfully, Lauren's attention shifted back to the main topic at hand. Mason. "We have to be in DC next week," she told Adrianne. "And in Haiti in two weeks."

"Two weeks." She swallowed. That wasn't very much time. She felt like Lauren had blown into her kitchen like a tornado and spun everything around. She'd had a hard time believing that Mason really wanted to stay. Now she was being told all the reasons he couldn't. And they made sense. At that point, all she could really do was nod. "Okay."

"What's going on in Haiti exactly?" Phoebe asked.

"Our company is working with the White House and Outreach America to bring an innovative planting program to Haiti," Lauren said, glancing at Phoebe. "We'll be going to some very rural areas of Haiti and implementing the program by teaching farmers to plant and tend the crop as well has how to reproduce the seeds on an ongoing basis."

"Wow." Phoebe was staring at her. "I have to say, I'm kind of fascinated by you."

Lauren gave her a wink. "Lots of people feel that way. Wait until I get some liquor into you." Then she turned back to Adrianne. "I hope I've helped you see that there's no way that Mason can give all of that up for you. No matter how much fun it is here, how good he feels, how great the sex is, there is a lot bigger picture."

Adrianne felt like she was in a haze. Of course there was a bigger picture than Sapphire Falls for Mason. That had been true for the past eleven years. She'd known that when he'd said he wanted to stay. "I don't expect him to give anything up for me."

Lauren laughed lightly. "Right. Nothing except his apartment, his job, his life in Chicago."

"No." Adrianne shook her head. "None of that was my idea. I was as surprised as you are."

"Good. Okay," Lauren took another sip of coffee. "So then you need to break up with him now before he blows the whole thing in DC."

Adrianne started. "Break up with him?"

"Yes. Today. He needs to be on a plane with me this evening."

"Today?" Adrianne felt like Lauren had slapped her. "But—"

"Whoa, hang on," Phoebe said. "No one said anything about breaking up. Adrianne's totally supportive of Mason and his work. She'll still be here when he gets back."

Adrianne smiled at her friend. Right. She'd be here when he got back. That wasn't so bad. It wasn't as good as seeing him every day, but she'd survive for a few days.

"Mason will be in Haiti for a month the first time," Lauren said calmly.

Phoebe turned to Adrianne. "Oh. Okay, well that's not so bad. There's the phone, texts, email, Skype."

Adrianne took a deep breath. This was big. This...made sense. A strange, rational part of her brain told her that it was completely logical that Mason had a huge project to work on and that it would take more than a long weekend. But her heart still hurt.

"Right. A month is no big deal. I'll see him when he gets back," she said.

"He'll be gone for at least six months after that," Lauren said, watching Adrianne closely.

Six months.

Okay.

Half a year.

Great.

Adrianne sat down hard on the chair at her kitchen table.

"Ad, breathe," Phoebe ordered, coming to stand beside her. "Listen, there are military families that are apart for longer than that. I'm sure there are aid workers with the Red Cross that are gone for long periods. You can do this."

But she wasn't so sure. "You're right. It's what he needs to do."

"No." Lauren crossed her arms. "He'll never go for that. He'll never leave her for six months. People are stupid when they're in love."

No one in the room could argue with that.

"And this is his first time," Lauren went on. "He has years of pent-up stupidity that's all going to come spilling out now.

"Okay then." Phoebe sat in the chair across from Adrianne. "Then she'll go with him."

Adrianne felt like she was moving in slow motion as she turned her head toward her friend. "Are you insane?"

"You would go with him?" Lauren asked over the top of Adrianne's question.

"Of course she would." Phoebe grabbed Adrianne's hand. "You're in love with him."

"Alex would have never even thought of that," Lauren muttered. "Okay," she said to Adrianne. "Then we've got a lot to do really fast. Do you have a passport?"

"No." Adrianne felt like she had to push her voice out of her throat.

"I can probably speed that process up. We also have to get you a physical and a background check. I'll need to call Ben and see what else—"

"No," Adrianne said with more force. "I'm not going to Haiti."

Phoebe squeezed her hand. Hard. "You can do this, Ad," she said. "This is awesome. What a cool opportunity to see what Mason does up close and personal, to help out in a big way in Haiti. Talk about a departure from your life in Chicago."

Adrianne didn't even try to return Phoebe's smile. "I'm scared to eat French fries," she told her friend. "I gave up a four-day trip to a posh resort in Hawaii last year. And you think I'm going to go to Haiti for six months?"

"With Mason," Phoebe said, her tone stern. "It's a big adventure, yes, but you'll be with Mason. You'll be fine."

"It's Haiti," Adrianne said, feeling just short of panic. She could feel her chest tightening and her voice getting higher and louder. "They barely have clean water. Most of the people are homeless. There's a cholera epidemic, for God's sake."

"They have ways of cleaning the water that prevents

cholera," Lauren said. Then she turned to Phoebe. "What the hell is going on?"

"I have a bad heart." Adrianne pulled her hand from Phoebe's before her friend crushed her fingers. "I can't be gone that long, away from my doctor and my pharmacy and...home."

"Oh, for the love of..." Phoebe muttered, slumping back in her chair.

"A bad heart?" Lauren looked confused. "Seriously? You might not even pass the physical."

"See?" Adrianne asked Phoebe. "I might not even pass the physical."

"You would too," Phoebe snapped. She looked up at Lauren. "She's fine now. She had a mild heart attack two years ago, they think brought on by stress. It's why she moved here."

"Haiti's a tough place," Lauren said with a little frown. "You have to be in good shape—mentally and physically."

"Mentally is definitely questionable," Phoebe muttered.

"Are you healthy enough to go or not?" Lauren asked Adrianne.

Adrianne started to shake her head, but Phoebe jumped in, "Yes. Her doctor has told her over and over that she's fine."

"It doesn't matter," Adrianne finally said. "I'm not going no matter what the physical says." She hadn't told anyone all the details of her heart attack, but she hated that her friend thought she was weak.

"But you—" Lauren started.

"I can't fly," Adrianne said.

Phoebe's hand slapped the table top. "Come on, Adrianne."

"The last time I was on a plane was two years ago. I was sitting in first class like usual," she said, studying Phoebe's manicure instead of meeting her eyes. "Everything was going as usual. I had a drink. I'd just gotten off the phone with one of my brothers. I was exhausted and upset. And then I started feeling funny." She took a deep breath, remembering the feeling of her chest pressing in on her lungs and heart, feeling like she couldn't move.

"We weren't even to cruising altitude," she went on. "My chest got tight, my arm started aching—all the classic signs." She looked up. Phoebe was staring at her. "I passed out. They did CPR on me until they could turn around and make an emergency landing." She swallowed hard. She could still remember the panic. She couldn't breathe, everything hurt and she knew exactly what was happening—and that being on that plane was the least safe place she could be when it did. "They said later that if we'd been any higher or farther into the flight it might not have turned out as well."

"Shit," Phoebe said, sitting back. "I didn't know all of that."

"I know," Adrianne said. "I...it never mattered." She shrugged. "The life I have now means I don't do anything that means I have to fly."

Lauren sighed. "Chicago's a long drive. Driving to DC is almost ridiculous. To Haiti, impossible."

Adrianne nodded. "Exactly."

"Dammit," Phoebe added.

"Does Mason know any of this?" Lauren asked with a frown.

"He knows about my heart, but that it was a long time ago and that I'm fine now," Adrianne said quickly. "But he doesn't know about the plane. If I tell him that's why I can't go with him, he'll decide not to go too."

"Right." Lauren crossed her arms and looked down at Adrianne. "So you care enough about him to agree that he can't stay here?"

Adrianne nodded. Mason couldn't shine in Sapphire Falls. He deserved every chance to show how extraordinary he was. And people needed him. More than she did.

She rubbed at the spot on her chest but knew that this pain went even deeper than skin and bone and organ.

"And you, evidently, aren't willing or able to go with him?" Lauren asked.

"Adrianne, we can get you over the fear of flying," Phoebe said. "The chances of a heart attack on a plane must be a million to one. The chances of it happening again, especially with you in such good health now, must be a gazillion to one. You have to take a chance sometime."

"We have to figure out a way to convince Mason to leave. Without me," Adrianne said to Lauren without looking at her friend.

"Fine." Phoebe shoved back from the table and stomped to where her purse sat on the counter. "You don't deserve him then." She spun back to face Adrianne as she pointed at her. "Remember those gaps in your life we talked about?" she asked. "The ones that are there because you want to do things but you're scared? Well, this is the perfect way to fill those in. This is about loving Mason. And about doing some-thing that matters. Both of those things will do more for your heart than any exercise or medicine could ever do." Then she stomped to the front door and made sure to slam it on her way out.

Lauren stared after her for a few seconds before turning back to face Adrianne. "I know this is hard. I'm sorry. And I know it's fast. But I need him in DC on Wednesday."

"Tell me more about the meetings and the project," Adri-anne said. She wanted to know every detail of what Mason would be doing. She had to know that it was big, huge, much more important than she was.

Lauren took the seat Phoebe had vacated. "Okay. We're going to DC on Wednesday to convince Vice President Forrester that we do want to partner with Outreach America and the White House even though Mason told him and O.A.'s director that they are self-centered pricks before storming out of his office about a month ago."

"Mason said that?" Adrianne was impressed in spite of herself. That didn't sound very nerdy. "Why?"

"They were debating how to spin the story about our new seeds being used by O.A. The White House felt that they should get some PR out of it too."

"Why?"

"The White House is helping get us in and providing military escorts while we're there."

"Why do you need military escorts?" Sure, she needed the idea that Mason might be in danger on her mind too.

"Haiti has a long history of political and social unrest. Since the earthquakes it's gotten worse. The majority of the island lives in poverty. If there is something of value coming in, there are people who will want to get a hold of it."

She was sorry she'd asked.

"But the White House wants PR out of it?"

"Of course. Have you ever met a politician that didn't want good PR?"

Good point. "Seems like a lot of egos getting in the way of the important work. Including Mason's," Adrianne commented.

Lauren rolled her eyes. "You have no idea."

"Can't you take your seeds and everything into these countries on your own? Why do you need Outreach America?"

"Technically, yes, but there is a lot of politics, not to mention money involved in something like this. And O.A. has already established relationships with the people themselves. It was going smoothly until the White House wanted a piece of the PR. But working with them is the fastest way to do this, even with all the BS... It would take us too long to figure out our contacts and shipping and get enough staff in place to get the seeds where they need to be, in the ground and growing along with the teaching and training that has to go on."

"Why O.A. then?" Adrianne asked, wanting every detail. "Why not another group?"

"O.A.'s the biggest, they already have agriculture programs in place, which means they have staff who know what they're doing, and...well, they want us."

"Others don't?" Adrianne frowned. "That's crazy. With what you can do and offer them—"

Lauren smiled. "A lot of them are struggling just to do what they do. They don't want to take on new projects like this. And besides, we have an in. A friend of mine worked for them for four months right after the quake hit and recommended us. It's ready made for success."

"But you need Mason."

"Definitely. Mason has to smooth this over and he has to head the project. I know a lot about a lot of what we do, but this one is his baby. He's the problem solver. And there will be problems in Haiti. It's inevitable with something like this. But with Mason there, they'll be solvable."

"I wonder if this is what it feels like to be in love with a super hero," Adrianne said with a sigh. "He'll never fully be mine because the whole world needs him."

"I'm sorry this happened," Lauren said. "I'm the one that suggested he come—insisted in fact."

When Adrianne looked at her, the other woman did look a little sad. But Adrianne couldn't quite bring herself to be sad that she'd met Mason. She was in love with him and breaking things off was going to hurt like hell, but she wouldn't trade the time she'd had with him.

Besides, they'd known each other three days. That had to be better than having several months, or years, of loving him before losing him.

She shivered. She would love to have months or years of memories with him. Even if it ended in heartbreak.

"I have to convince him to leave," Adrianne finally said, breaking the silence.

"I know." Lauren sighed. "You have to make it good. It can't be that you think he should go to Haiti, or that it's more important than you are. He's in love for the first time. He's going to hold on tight."

Adrianne swallowed against the tears she could feel building. "The only way he'll leave is if he believes I don't really want him to stay."

"Right."

"I have to break his heart."

Lauren looked pained at the idea too. "Yeah, I guess so."

They were quiet for a moment. Then Lauren asked, "Any ideas on how to do that convincingly?"

Through the kitchen window, Adrianne saw Hailey's car pull into her driveway.

Adrianne felt like she was going to be sick as she said, "Yeah, I think I do."

———

"What the hell happened?" were Hailey's first words to Adrianne. Her second sentence was, "Who the hell are you?" when her gaze landed on Lauren.

"Dr. Lauren Davis. Mason's partner."

Hailey looked Lauren up and down. Lauren let her. They reminded Adrianne of two lionesses circling, trying to determine if the other was a threat or an ally. The stand-off took only a few seconds before they seemed to come to some sort of silent acceptance of one another. Thank God. The last thing Adrianne needed was Hailey getting her panties in a twist.

Adrianne took a deep, calming breath. Supposedly calming anyway. "What's going on, Hailey?"

"Drew called me from the golf course. Mason told the guys that he's moving here. To be with you. That you're going to live on the farm so there's no way he can give up the land. He wants to plant corn, Adrianne. What the hell is going on?"

Okay, so Hailey's panties were in a twist anyway.

Adrianne's heart wanted to flip. Mason was telling everyone. He wanted to stay with her. He was in love with her. At the same time, she felt like someone had put a brick in her chest. All she had to do was say yes and she could have all of it—all of him.

At the expense of a few thousand lives, including the ones in Sapphire Falls.

No, the hopeful business owners here wouldn't die without their shops, but their dreams would. And her friendships would. And that was all small potatoes compared to the lives in Haiti that would be affected.

And then there was Mason. What was really best for him?

Heartache seemed inevitable. But better her than all of them.

Adrianne straightened her shoulders. "There's been a...misunderstanding."

"Who's misunderstanding?" Hailey asked.

Adrianne almost couldn't say it. "Mason's."

Hailey's shoulders relaxed a little and she took a deep breath. "I told Drew that was probably what happened."

"Mason's just jumping ahead. I'll talk to him."

"Okay." Hailey sighed. "That's what I wanted to hear. Right after Drew called, Ken Stevens called and said that the price on his land by the highway has gone up ten-thousand dollars. He knows we don't have any other options. And he's still insisting on Eddie having his taxidermy shop."

"Isn't taxidermy stuffing dead animals?" Lauren asked.

Hailey frowned at her but didn't answer her question. "On top of this mess with Tyler, I'm feeling like things are falling apart," Hailey went on.

"I don't think you should put a taxidermy business in this new shopping area," Lauren said.

Hailey glared at her.

"What about Tyler?" Adrianne asked, trying to keep Hailey focused—and not going for Lauren's throat.

"He won't return my frickin' phone calls," Hailey said with a scowl. "And then after I left my sixth message, he posted something on Twitter about six unreturned phone calls being pathetic and that a woman should never call more than twice without hearing back. He's such a jerk."

Hailey's scowl grew and Adrianne had to fight a smile for a moment. That jerk was the guy Hailey had been gushing about to all the investors earlier that week.

"You follow him on Twitter?" Adrianne asked.

Hailey didn't answer that. "I'm not calling him because I'm in love with him or something," Hailey said. "This is business. He's being an ass." She picked up a truffle and shoved the whole thing into her mouth before picking up another.

Adrianne watched with some fascination. She'd never seen Hailey riled up over a guy. She'd seen Hailey eat chocolate only a handful of times. This was...weird.

Adrianne handed a cup of coffee to Hailey.

"Maybe I'll start a blog. Tyler Bennett Is Full of Shit," Hailey said, accepting the cup and drinking. "That guy is so full of himself. So he won a dumb medal. Big deal. And it was only a silver."

"You know Tyler Bennett?" Lauren asked. "The hot Olympian? I didn't know he was from here." She frowned. "Mason never tells me anything."

Hailey opened her mouth to reply and Adrianne rushed to interrupt.

"Well, he is the first American man to ever medal in the triathlon," Adrianne said. She caught Hailey's glare and added, "If that matters."

"It doesn't," Hailey said firmly. "He thinks he's God's gift and I'm starting to think he's just messing with me. He's taunting me, seeing how hard I'll work for this, what I'm willing to put up with."

"Did you sleep with him in high school too or something?" Adrianne couldn't help but ask.

Hailey finally focused on her directly again. "You have to make sure we have that land. We have to get this thing going. I'm going to hold Tyler Bennett to his verbal commitment. I'll take him to court if I have to."

That wasn't a confirmation or a denial of her past with Ty, but Adrianne really couldn't worry about Hailey's sex life and how it might be interacting with their plans. Her own was messing things up enough.

Adrianne rubbed her forehead. "I'll take care of it, Hailey." Like she did everything else. It only made sense that this would fall to her too.

But even if Hailey was willing to be the one to get Mason to leave town, it wouldn't work. There was only one person who mattered to Mason here.

Three hours ago, the knowledge that she was that important to Mason had filled her with joy and hope and tingles in all the right places.

Now it made her nearly sick to her stomach.

If he wasn't in love with her, she'd have no power to get him to DC to do the right thing. Now she was going to have to use his feelings for her against him.

Right then another car pulled into her driveway. At the same moment her phone started to ring. Hailey's cell phone began beeping as well and Lauren had just answered hers.

Adrianne closed her eyes, again breathing deep. All hell was breaking loose. Deep cleansing breaths were the only things she was still sure of.

She reached for the phone and grabbed it on the fourth ring. "Hello?"

"Is this Ms. Adrianne Scott?" a man's voice asked.

"It is."

"This is Brandon Johnson. I am with the office of Secretary George Williams."

Adrianne's heart thumped and she rubbed her chest. She would have never recognized the name of the US Secretary of Agriculture if it weren't for the articles she'd read on Mason.

"I'm looking for Dr. Mason Riley. We have this number as a backup number."

"Why would you have this number?"

"Dr. Riley notified us that he would be in the process of moving his residence over the next several days and gave us this number in case of emergencies."

"I see." She didn't. At all.

"Ms. Scott," Brandon said. "This is an emergency. We need to speak with Dr. Riley immediately."

"I, um..." She rubbed her chest harder as the ache increased. "He isn't here at the moment. Can I take a message?"

"Please tell him that Secretary Williams is insisting that Dr. Riley keep the meeting next week as planned."

"He cancelled the meeting?" What the hell was he thinking?

"He first requested a conference call. The secretary will not grant that request," Brandon said. "Secretary Williams has also denied Dr. Riley's request to reschedule the meeting. Tell Dr. Riley we are expecting to see him."

Adrianne rubbed her forehead. Mason had tried to have his meeting via conference call? What was he thinking? And then he'd tried to reschedule? Until when? Once Haiti was back on its feet? He needed to be there for that to happen. He wasn't going to singlehandedly restore all of Haiti, but he was part of the solution. He was not going to be part of the problem if she had anything to say about it. And she did.

"Of course. I'll be sure he gets the message," she told Brandon.

As she disconnected, Greg Porter and Jennifer Jensen, two potential business owners at Sapphire Hills, came through her front door.

Greg spoke first. "What the hell is going on, Adrianne? I heard at the lumber yard that Mason said no to the building site because you're going to live there?"

Oh, this was bad. "Well, I—"

"Hailey said the time you were spending with him was for the project," Jennifer added.

"Yes, he knows all the details, he's seen our plans," she assured them as the ache spread from her heart to her stomach.

"And he's saying no," Greg said. "He knows the details and is saying no."

"Because he feels the project isn't right for us," Adrianne said. "It doesn't have to do with me or us living there."

"Why didn't you head the meetings with him?" Jennifer rounded on Hailey. "This wouldn't have happened if you'd been in charge."

Hailey lifted her hands and shook her head. "Adrianne's my friend. When I realized he was in love with her, I backed off."

Adrianne rolled her eyes. She wasn't sure she'd classify Hailey's actions as backing off.

"He knows all the details and you're sleeping with him and he still said no?" Greg asked Adrianne.

It was all unrelated, dammit. How could they not understand that? They'd fallen in love. It wasn't about the project. It was about wanting to be together.

"That's enough, Greg," Adrianne said sharply. "My relationship with Mason has nothing to do with the building project."

"Which is very disappointing," Greg muttered.

Adrianne's head ached now too. She rubbed her chest with one hand and her temple with the other.

"Everybody needs to shut the hell up." Adrianne and everyone else turned as a group to face Lauren as she stepped forward. "I don't really care if you try to sell specialty coffees to people in the middle of nowhere or not, but you all need to back off of Adrianne a little. She said she's going to handle it and she will. Having you all yapping at her can't possibly be helping."

Adrianne was shocked by Lauren's defense. She started to answer with something, but Hailey turned to her with her mouth open. "Who is that?"

"Mason's business partner."

"So Mason really does want to stay and grow corn?" Jennifer asked, apparently not interested in advice from the stranger.

Adrianne sighed. "Yeah."

"And you're really going to marry him, move onto the farm and grow corn with him and forget about what the rest of us want?" Greg asked, also completely ignoring Lauren.

Adrianne wanted all of that so badly she could taste it. Well, except for the part about forgetting what the rest of them wanted. The guilt would be oppressive. The peace she'd feel sitting on the front porch at the farm would be tainted by the thought that she was sitting precisely on the spot that would have made a lot of people very happy. "There's nothing to worry about," she said miserably. "I'm taking care of it."

She was taking care of all of it. All of them.

Hailey didn't have to worry about her political career. Greg could make his rocking chairs. Jen could sell tons of cards. The people in Haiti would have a crop and even the White House would get their way.

Everyone was going to be fine. Except her. But she was one person, one heart. And she would have what she technically had wanted all along—a quiet, simple life. No one showing up and yelling at her in her foyer for one. No one blaming her for the economic demise of their town. No visions of starving children in Haiti keeping her from sleeping well at night. And no one making her heart nearly burst with love and happiness.

A safe life and a safe heart.

"What do you mean you're taking care of it?" Hailey asked. "If making him fall in love didn't work, how do you know—?"

"Just shut up, Hailey," Adrianne snapped.

Hailey, Greg and Jennifer stared at her.

But wow, telling Hailey to shut up felt good.

"The truth is," Adrianne said as she started the biggest lie of her life. "I never said yes to the farm or to being with him."

That wasn't the lie. She hadn't—very much on purpose. But she was implying she didn't want to say yes. That was the lie.

"If last night is how you treat people you're going to turn down, I'd love to see what you do for someone you want to keep around."

Everyone, again, turned as a unit toward the new voice—except Adrianne. She reacted slower than the rest. It was Mason. And he'd overheard that.

While his tone was conversational, his words were harsh, and she didn't want to face him.

She suddenly wasn't sure she could do this. She looked for Lauren and found the other woman looking as concerned and nervous as Adrianne felt. Mason had to believe that Adrianne truly wanted him to go.

She had to do the sales job of her life.

10

Finally, Adrianne turned. Mason stood in the doorway. His expression and stance—hands in his pockets, weight shifted to one hip—appeared casual, but as soon as she looked into his eyes, Adrianne knew he was anything but.

His gaze was focused on her but she quickly broke eye contact. She was so glad the others were here. Yes, it would be more painful with witnesses, but she had to hurt him and she'd never be able to do it if they were alone.

Heck, she had her doubts about pulling it off anyway.

She crossed her arms, not wanting to let him get too close or he'd see in her eyes how she really felt.

"I never said I was for you keeping the house and farm, Mason. I never said I'd move out there with you."

He looked at her for a long moment and she had to bite the inside of her lip to keep from blurting out the truth that she'd imagined them together at the farm too. Mason didn't argue, he didn't call her bluff, he simply nodded.

"You're right. You never said you'd do that."

She swallowed hard. "If you move to the farm and keep the

house, I don't get my shop. I can't forget all those plans and dreams and you shouldn't expect me to."

"I thought I was offering you a different dream. Maybe even a better dream," he said evenly.

"I've known you for three days, Mason. And what about everyone else? I can't want you to move here knowing that it's taking away their dreams. You're asking me to choose a three-day fling over friends and neighbors I've had for years."

His expression was shuttered and she knew it was painful for him to do this in front of an audience like this. She hadn't been there eleven years ago, but she could imagine how everything with Hailey had gone. It was painful enough hearing someone tell you they didn't want you. It was far worse in front of a crowd. Which was no doubt why Hailey had done it. And why Adrianne was doing it now. This had to sting. This had to be bad enough that he'd leave and not want to come back.

Of course the others were keeping her from caving too.

She thought about that as she watched him watching her.

Had Hailey done it with witnesses because it was meaner or had she done it to keep from throwing herself at him and forsaking her popularity, her plans to stay in Sapphire Falls, her plans to live the life she now had?

"I wouldn't be moving here for a fling, Adrianne," Mason said easily even as his eyes flashed with anger.

Her heart felt like someone was pulling a jagged piece of glass through it. He loved her and that was what allowed her to hurt him like this.

"I like you, Mason," she said. "We've had a great time. But I want Sapphire Hills. I want my candy shop."

"I'll buy you a fucking candy shop," he said, his temper finally breaking through. "I won't let that keep us apart."

She swallowed. He was angry. He'd told her himself that he only got emotional when he was really passionate. She was the only woman who could do that to him.

"I want it more than anything." She was shocked she could say that without choking. She really was good at sales.

"That doesn't make sense," he said with a scowl. "You love me. I know you do."

And things always had to make sense to Mason Riley. She almost smiled in spite of the pain.

"We just met. We're attracted but it's not..." she almost choked again but pushed to finish, "...it's not normal to fall in love that easily."

Complete silence met her words. No one but Phoebe knew Adrianne knew the story of what had happened between Hailey and Mason. Adrianne would have never said something like that to anyone else with that past. Normal Mason was not. He was so much better. But he wanted to be normal. She knew that.

"You're probably right," Mason finally said. "I don't know much about being normal."

She was barely holding it together as it was and hearing him say that was her second-to-last straw.

He reached into his pocket and withdrew a checkbook. Adrianne's gut cramped and she hugged her arms over her stomach to keep from throwing up. But she stayed quiet. This was making everything okay for everyone else. She could do this. It was almost over.

Mason's pen moved over a blank check. The sound of him tearing it from the rest of the book was thunderous in the silent foyer. When he took a step toward her, she flinched. He held it out. It was for the requested hundred thousand dollars.

"Trust me," he said coolly. "You were worth every penny."

She couldn't look past the top button on his shirt. She also wouldn't reach for it. If she let go of herself she was going to fall apart.

After five seconds ticked by, he handed it to Hailey instead. Adrianne gratefully turned her attention to her boss.

"I'll have my lawyer look into the land situation," Mason said. "Who should he contact when we get a deal ready?"

"Me," Hailey said softly.

"No." Mason's answer was quick. "I don't want this to be personal at all. Lawyer to lawyer."

Hailey nodded. "Okay, we'll have Mike Little handle it," she said, naming a Sapphire Falls attorney who had served on the city council in the past.

Adrianne wasn't sure if Mason nodded or sighed or frowned, but she felt his eyes on her before he stepped around her.

Lauren didn't even flinch as he reached out and grasped her upper arm. She seemed resigned as he started for the door with her in tow.

"Excuse us. I need to confer with my partner."

Lauren gave Adrianne an apologetic shrug and went with Mason.

The screen door slamming was like a gunshot and Adrianne tried to pull a deep breath in and couldn't. She felt like her ribs were shrinking, crushing her heart and lungs.

———

"What the hell just happened in there?" Mason demanded of his best friend—who he was less shocked to see than he probably should have been.

"Adrianne broke up with you," Lauren said, meeting his gaze steadily.

He let go of her before he squeezed her arm too hard. "Is it a coincidence that you're here and all of a sudden she breaks up with me?"

"Not really." Lauren crossed her arms and risked looking belligerent. "I told her about Haiti."

Of course she had.

"And I believe I warned you about not making me come here," she added.

"What did you tell her?"

He could only imagine. Lauren got passionate about their work, but never as much as she did about the project in Haiti. They'd been there twice already, for two weeks each time. And while it wasn't an easy place to visit, it was also a hard place to leave. There was so much need there, and the idea that they could do something about some of it had hit them both hard, but Lauren had, for some reason, really gotten fired up.

"I told her the truth," Lauren said firmly. "I told her about the project and everything you've worked on and what it's like there and what they need. She wants you to go. Very much."

He believed that. Adrianne believed in him, in what he did. But there was something not right. Something didn't fit. "I want her, Lauren. I don't want to be without her."

"I offered to let her come with us," Lauren said. She met his eyes and he knew she wasn't lying. "I offered to call Ben about her background check and passport. But she said no."

He tried to process that. "No to what exactly?"

"Going with you. Being with you." Lauren paused and then said quietly, "She said no to you, Mason."

"But I..." He really didn't know what he'd meant to say. Adrianne had said no to him.

"She wants you to go," Lauren said gently. "She wants you to make things right in DC and then go to work in Haiti."

"Does she know how long I'll be gone?"

Lauren nodded. "I told her everything."

Something still didn't feel right. She loved him, he knew it. She'd said it wasn't normal to fall that fast but...

That was what didn't fit, he realized a moment later. Adrianne would never say something like that to him. She didn't believe he was abnormal or strange. So she'd said that specifically for a reason.

And then it occurred to him that she knew the story. The story of his public humiliation at Hailey's hands.

Maybe Hailey had told her the story. Or maybe not. There were at least thirty people in town who had personally witnessed the whole thing. Including Phoebe and Matt, come to think of it. Hailey had used the words not normal too. Or had implied them. Hell, he couldn't even really remember any more and he didn't care.

But it seemed that Adrianne thought he cared enough about the past that a repeat performance would be enough to push him away for good.

She really wanted him to leave badly. He'd seen how she was shaking, how hard that was on her. She loved him—he knew it, even if it had only been three days—and there had to be a damned good reason for her to be willing to hurt him like that.

"Fine," he finally said. "She wants me to go? Fine. I'll go. I'll do this thing. But this isn't over."

"Yeah," Lauren said. "I was afraid you were going to say that."

———

"You don't look so good," Hailey said with concern.

"I need you to take me to the hospital," Adrianne managed.

"I'm coming too."

Adrianne looked up to find Lauren had come back in.

"Is he gone?" Adrianne asked.

Lauren nodded. "He went to get his things and is flying out tonight."

Adrianne felt like bawling but her chest wouldn't expand even enough for that. "Is he...okay?"

"He's hurt. He's confused. But he's going." Lauren looked tired as she said it.

Adrianne respected that. Mason was her friend. Seeing him hurt, going through this, had to be hard on her too. Even though they both knew it was for the best.

"He said this isn't over between you," Lauren told her.

Adrianne shook her head. "He can say whatever he wants. Once he's back in Chicago and back to work he'll snap out of it. He knows what he's doing there is more important than golfing and corn in Sapphire Falls."

Lauren didn't answer.

On the drive to the hospital, Adrianne prayed for quiet. Her head was pounding and she almost wished she could just pass out to get away from the pain.

But the silence lasted only until they were on the highway. Which in Sapphire Falls only took four minutes.

"What the hell was that?" Hailey demanded.

"I got the money and the land. Now shut up," Adrianne said from the back seat. She rested her head against the window and shut her eyes.

Not that Hailey listened. "But you said you wanted Sapphire Hills more than Mason. That's crap. Obviously. Everyone knows it."

"Yeah, well, Mason's the only one who has to buy it," Adrianne said. "Now shut up."

"Mason's a genius, Ad. No way did he buy it."

"He paid us and left, so who cares?" she snapped. "Now shut up."

Hailey stopped talking to her. She turned her conversation to Lauren.

"Everything was fine until you showed up. What's going on?"

"Hey, I happen to have a pretty high IQ too," Lauren informed her. "No way am I getting into the middle of this."

Adrianne's cell rang. Was it Mason? Her heart rate picked up again, but then she used her IQ and realized that there was no way it was Mason. He was never going to speak to her again.

As it should be. As she wanted it to be.

Besides, it was Phoebe's ringtone. She seriously considered not answering, knowing she could not explain this event to even her best friend without crying. Finally though, she picked up. "I'm on my way to the hospital, I'll call you later," she said before Phoebe could speak.

"I know. Hailey texted me. Want me to come?"

"God, yes." And Adrianne promptly burst into tears.

An hour later, she was fine. Or as fine as she was ever going to be again.

Mason was still gone, her heart still hurt, but her blood pressure was down to the normal range and her headache was mild. Dr. Carthan told her she was fine. Four times. He also told her that he was startled to see her this worked up. He'd often praised her for how well she managed her stress and the diligence with which she followed her health plan.

She burst into tears again at that.

Her heart was in trouble, hurt, was broken in spite of the fact that for two years she'd followed every bit of advice she'd been given, read or researched.

All thanks to Mason Riley.

"Do they make medication that will help me forget the past twelve hours?" she said.

"Yes, it's called alcohol," Dr. Carthan said.

"But I can't drink."

He sighed and put her chart down. "Yes, you can. In moderation. You can also eat potato chips and sky dive and enjoy your life, Adrianne."

"I'm trying to be careful," she said grumpily. Didn't he realize that it had been a sacrifice to pass up wine and chips for the past two years?

"There's a fine line between being careful and being miserable with these things," he said. "And I think maybe you've stepped over it."

She frowned at him. "And to think that staying near you has been a consideration of mine."

"Staying near me for what?"

"For you to take care of me and my heart."

"Oh, sure." He nodded. "It's important to stay near a doctor who can so effectively take care of a perfectly healthy heart. It's not like every physician in the universe can do that."

He gave her a wink, gave Phoebe a grin, nodded to Hailey and Lauren—both of whom leaned a bit to watch him leave the room.

Adrianne looked from one woman to the next. Her best friend, her boss and Mason's best friend. All women she happened to like at least a little. All women who had headed straight for the hospital with her without question.

"Nothing to say?" she asked them.

"I'd like to go on record as agreeing with him," Phoebe said. "And simply add that you could get hit by a bus tomorrow and all the sacrifice and deprivation wouldn't matter then anyway."

Adrianne's eyes widened. "I hope that's not supposed to be a pep talk."

Phoebe shrugged. "It was short notice."

"I would have to agree with her," Hailey said. "Life's short. There are just some things you can't go without."

Adrianne tried not to show how interested she was in that answer. Did they think she should go after Mason? Was Hailey saying that her being with Mason was more important than Sapphire Hills? What about DC and Haiti?

"I think it's obvious what needs to happen now," Hailey said.

"Absolutely," Lauren agreed.

"Oh? What's that?" Adrianne asked, trying to seem nonchalant. Surely she could still catch him at the airport. There was no way he'd had time to cancel his move yet.

"We need to get you drunk," Phoebe said.

"Definitely," Hailey agreed. "To hell with moderation for tonight."

———

"You know," Lauren said as they settled into the limo that would take them from the White House to the hotel. "I'm thinking a policy that states we don't call anyone we work with a prick might be in order."

Mason scowled at the back of the driver's head. "I agreed to do the interview with Newsweek. I agreed to talk at the press conference. But I'm not babysitting a bunch of reporters in Haiti. And he was being a prick about it."

So he was the vice president. That didn't mean he got to tell Mason what he did with his project and team.

Except that it did of course when he was making the project happen.

"Yeah, well, he wasn't the only prick in there," Lauren muttered.

Mason scrubbed a hand over his face. He was exhausted. He was beyond frustrated. He couldn't do anything right.

"You look like crap," Lauren finally said.

He knew that. "Then I look better than I feel."

"What did you have for breakfast?"

"Coffee."

"What did you have for dinner last night?"

"Coffee."

He had no appetite and all he felt like doing was sleeping so coffee seemed a logical choice.

Lauren made a frustrated sound. "I came to get you in Sapphire Falls because I needed you. And you're fucking this all up. Maybe I should have left you there."

"Yeah, maybe you should have left me there," Mason snapped. But his gut cramped as he said it. He hadn't left Sapphire Falls because of anything Lauren had said or done.

"Mason, I..." Lauren trailed off. Then she turned to face him fully and tucked a foot underneath her. "You need to snap out of this."

"Just like that? Forget all about the only woman I've ever loved?"

"Well...I told you so."

"What are you talking about?" He wasn't sure he had the energy for this. He barely had the energy to stay sitting upright.

Lauren sighed. "Adrianne. I really didn't think she was until I met her. Then I thought she definitely could be. Now I'm pretty sure she's not."

Mason frowned at her. "What the hell are you talking about?"

"Adrianne isn't good enough for you."

He closed his eyes. "I can't do this, Lauren."

"No, Mason, I have to tell you this because you've got to get your ass in gear." Lauren touched his arm.

He rolled his head to look at her, forcing his eyes open.

"Adrianne did want you to leave Sapphire Falls."

"Yeah, she made that pretty clear," he said dryly. He'd been trying everything he could to not think of her and focus. He had work to do. When it was over, he was going to allow himself to really wallow. And throw things. And get completely inebriated. But right now he was trying to concentrate. Which Lauren should be helping him with instead of...this.

"She wanted you to leave for your sake," Lauren said. "She

believes in you and knows you need to be in Haiti. But she was adamant about not coming with you."

"I remember," he said darkly.

"But you don't understand why."

"And you do?"

"Yes." Lauren met his gaze. "She's afraid to fly. Terrified, in fact."

Mason felt her words jolt through him. There was a real reason Adrianne wouldn't go with him? Other than not wanting to—not wanting him enough? But why wouldn't she tell him that?

In the next moment, he shook his head. "She traveled—flew—all the time for her job in Chicago before she went to Sapphire Falls."

"Yes, before Sapphire Falls," Lauren said, watching him. "Her last flight was the reason she left her job and moved to a smaller town with a slower pace."

"What happened?" Mason asked, feeling his heart rate kick up. There was something here. Something big, he could feel it.

"The last time she flew she..." Lauren seemed to hesitate on the next words. Finally, she said, "She had a heart attack, Mason."

He stared at her. He knew about the heart attack. He was still having trouble truly accepting it and now...it had happened on a plane?

Lauren continued. "I looked it up after I found out. It's rare in a woman her age, but she was doing everything wrong—sleeping pills, too much stress, smoking, all of that. She's changed her life now, but it scared the shit out of her. Which is legitimate, I guess."

Mason let the words roll around in his head. On a plane? Good God, she could have died.

He closed his eyes and let the new knowledge sink in.

Of course she could have died. Her heart had stopped. But

she'd been on a plane. He didn't care that the flight attendants were trained in CPR and that the planes all had defibrillators. Being on a plane complicated an already dangerous situation, period.

She could have died. He would have never met her.

He thought about her smile, how it felt to hold her, how she kept everything going, how she came to his rescue. She was so soft and warm—in every way.

And she could have died.

A shudder went through him.

But she hadn't died. She was alive. And well. And wonderful.

"Is she okay?" he asked Lauren. "She told me she is, but... maybe she was making me feel better."

Lauren frowned. "She's fine. Evidently. Phoebe said her doctor has told her repeatedly that she's fine, that she doesn't have to live the way she does."

"The way she does?"

"Scared. Worried all the time. Not getting on airplanes with the guy she's crazy about."

Immediately, he shook his head. He was in a daze for sure. But something didn't feel right about that. "Maybe it's better. She's safe this way. She has what she wants." His heart hurt a little with that realization. She had the life she wanted in Sapphire Falls. The life where she was safe and free from worry. Then he came along and within three days was changing everything. "Why didn't she tell me about the plane?"

Lauren looked at him with her you're-kidding-right? look. "You know the answer to that."

"I would have..." Been tempted to wrap her in bubble wrap and never let her go anywhere. Damn. He certainly wouldn't have expected her to fly to Haiti. Or live in Haiti. He shook his head. "I would have wanted her to stay in Sapphire Falls."

"And you would have been determined to stay with her,"

Lauren said. "Which she knew. Which was why she didn't tell you."

"There was something in her eyes," he said. "When she was saying she didn't want me to stay. I knew there was something else there, something more."

Lauren nodded. "I know. I thought so too. But now I'm wondering."

"About?"

"Her. Her feelings. You." Lauren shrugged. "I know she's scared, but the truth is she's healthy, there's no reason for her not to fly. I really thought—hoped—that for you she'd get over it. I expected her to be here by now."

"That's asking a lot." But a weight seemed to have settled on his chest.

"Being in love requires a lot," she returned. "You have to fight for it sometimes. Even if you're fighting yourself."

The weight on his chest turned cold. Adrianne didn't want to fight. She wanted peace and quiet and calm.

"You don't think she's coming?" he asked Lauren who'd had a much more detailed conversation about all of this than he had.

Lauren looked like she regretted having to say it. "I don't."

"Because she loves me and wants me to go to Haiti?"

"That's what I want to think."

"But you're not sure now?" He wasn't sure why he was torturing himself like this. Wasn't it bad enough that she wasn't here and wasn't coming? Did he really have to delve into why?

Apparently, the answer was yes.

Lauren's expression hardened. "I'm becoming more and more sure that she's not coming. And that she doesn't deserve you."

"A heart attack is a big deal," he said.

"You're a big deal," Lauren shot back. "And I really thought she got that. But I guess not. Which means you're better off without her."

Right.

That made sense.

She wasn't willing to step up and be brave for him, so maybe she wasn't the one.

Alex hadn't been willing to give anything up for Lauren. She'd wanted her life to stay the same—normal—and if Lauren wanted to be a part of it, she had to give up Haiti and their work. Lauren probably was better off without Alex.

Adrianne hadn't asked him for that. She hadn't expected him to change. And maybe she had a better reason for wanting her life to stay the way it was. But the bottom line was still that she didn't want her life to change. Not even for him.

So he was probably better off without her.

Yep, that was likely the reaction a normal person would have.

Which would explain why he didn't feel that way at all.

———

Adrianne paced across her kitchen and glared at the new box of butter she'd pulled from the fridge. She should work on her candy. That was simple, made sense and would definitely be sweet in the end.

Instead, she held her phone to her ear and chewed on her left thumbnail as she waited for Lauren to answer. Calling Lauren to check on Mason was complicated, confusing and could pretty much go either way as far as being sweet or bitter in the end.

It was Thursday. Mason had left Sapphire Falls on Monday. It felt like an eternity.

"Dr. Davis," Lauren finally answered.

"How did it go?"

Lauren apparently knew who it was. "Let me put it this way —the vice president has banned Mason from his office indefinitely, and Mason hasn't done one bit of productive work since leaving Sapphire Falls."

"You left not even quite seventy-two hours ago," Adrianne pointed out, slipping right into protect-Mason mode.

"You have no idea what Mason Riley can do in seventy-two hours when he's on," Lauren informed her.

Hearing his name made Adrianne feel antsy. She wanted to be with him, dammit, and she was going to do this.

If she died on that plane—and she did acknowledge the fact that the chances of that were small—at least she'd died taking a risk for something big.

That was better than sitting safely in Sapphire Falls with only her regrets.

"So he's not willing to work?" Adrianne asked, wondering if it was okay to feel flattered by that. She knew she should feel guilty—and she did—or worried—which she also did. But it was nice to know that Mason seemed as messed up without her as she was without him. She knew he needed to leave. But she didn't want him to like it.

"He's trying, I think," Lauren said. "He was in the lab all day Tuesday. But it's not working. Something's not clicking. He knows this is important to you and he knows we need this fertilizer figured out before we get to Haiti but..." Lauren trailed off. "You know what I think?"

Adrianne didn't respond to the question right away. "He knows this is important to me?" she asked, standing in the center of her kitchen and staring at the jar of caramel sauce she'd had to replace.

Lauren paused. "Yeah, he...he knew something was up, Adrianne. He knew that you were making him leave because it really mattered to you rather than because you didn't want him."

She wasn't sure what to say to that. That was...incredible. Mason knew her, after three days, enough to trust that she loved him in spite of all she said and did to the contrary?

Wow.

"Okay, so you think he's just distracted or what?"

"Maybe," Lauren said. "But I'm wondering if it's more than that. It's like...he put so much heart into his work before that now that his heart is with you, there's not enough left for the lab."

Um, wow again. "That...doesn't sound like you at all," Adrianne said. She didn't know Lauren well, but the other woman gave the definite impression of being tough and practical and not all that sentimental.

Lauren laughed. "I know. But it's the only explanation. He's worked through illness, distraction, fatigue and almost everything else."

"I might have a solution," Adrianne said, her heart rate picking up.

"Good. 'Cause I don't know what the hell to do."

"I'm coming to Chicago. But I need to know where—well, where should I go? Should I go to his place? Yours? The lab? And I need addresses for all of those and times to be there. Things like that."

"You're coming?" Lauren said.

Adrianne took a deep breath and felt the rightness of her answer clear to her toes. "Yes."

"Oh, thank God. Don't move."

The next thing Adrianne heard was nothing. Lauren had hung up. She didn't answer when Adrianne called back.

Ten minutes later, there was a pounding on Adrianne's front door.

"Oh, for God's sake," Adrianne said when she opened the door to find Lauren on her front porch. "You were already in town?"

"Yeah. I was with Phoebe trying to figure out how to convince you to come to Chicago."

Adrianne looked over Lauren's shoulder to find Phoebe and Hailey coming up her front steps.

"How did that plan look?" Adrianne asked dryly.

"I'll admit that it involved a lot of alcohol."

"For me or you?"

"Both," Lauren confessed.

"I've been reading up on the fear of flying," Adrianne said.

"I have too," Lauren said with a laugh. "And minor heart attacks in young women."

"You have?" Adrianne was stunned by that. And a little touched.

"He's my best friend, Adrianne, and he needs you," Lauren said with a lift of a shoulder.

"Are you going to let him come back to Sapphire Falls?" Adrianne asked.

"Are you?" Lauren challenged.

Adrianne didn't hesitate. "In between trips to Haiti. And wherever else he needs to go."

"Good answer," Lauren said with a nod. "Let's get you on a plane."

"I only need to pack my bag."

"Then we're right on time," Lauren said to Hailey. "This is Chicago and DC, not Sapphire Falls we're talking about here." She glanced at Adrianne's blue jeans. "You want to handle makeup? And hair?" she asked, taking in Adrianne's pony tail.

"What are you doing here anyway?" Adrianne asked her boss.

"It occurred to me that I like you better happy. You do more for me when you're in a good mood," Hailey said.

"Of course this is about you," Adrianne muttered.

"I'm kidding," Hailey said, holding up a hand. "Mostly anyway."

Adrianne started to reply but Hailey jumped in. "I'm really here because Lauren came to the office wanting Phoebe's address. She told me she was here to talk you into going to Chicago. It occurred to me that you've spent a lot of time making me look good and maybe it was time I returned the favor."

"How are you going to make me look good?" Adrianne asked with some sarcasm.

"I'm not completely talentless," Hailey protested.

Adrianne drew herself up tall. "Are you seriously thinking that I need a makeover?"

"Honey, like I said, you're not going to be hanging out in Sapphire Falls," Lauren said. "You need to look more like Hailey than Phoebe. No offense," she added to Phoebe.

"Oh, none taken," Phoebe said sarcastically. "Why would I take offense at your criticizing my clothes, shoes, makeup and hair?"

"No, I mean..." Lauren trailed off. "Sorry."

"For your information," Adrianne said, stepping forward. "I can out-Hailey even Hailey Conner when it comes to clothes, shoes, hair and makeup. If I want to."

"Well," Hailey said, stepping forward to meet her with a smile. "It might have been a tie. In the old days."

"Oh, really," Adrianne said, her eyes narrowed. "You ever dressed for a business meeting and dinner in London or New York?"

Hailey didn't answer, but Adrianne added, "I don't need help looking good. If I want to."

Lauren was looking back and forth between them. When they both looked at her she said, "Seriously?"

"Yep, and I can prove it." Adrianne turned and headed for the stairs.

Phoebe grabbed her suitcase from the hall closet while Lauren and Hailey followed her to her bedroom closet.

Five minutes later, her suitcase lay open on her bed and was quickly filling with outfits, underwear and bras and shoes.

Too many shoes.

"It's only a few days," Lauren said taking two of the six pairs out.

"She needs to stay longer than that," Hailey said, adding a pair of boots.

Lauren rolled her eyes. "Fine, but it's DC She still won't need the boots." She took them out.

Hailey took them away from her. "You never know," she insisted, putting them back in.

Phoebe added lingerie.

"That's not even mine," Adrianne protested, grabbing for the black teddy Phoebe had apparently brought along.

"It is now." Phoebe grabbed it back and stuffed it under the boots.

"I thought I was going to Chicago, not DC," Adrianne said. When no one responded—Hailey and Lauren were disagreeing over a pair of red three-inch heels Adrianne hadn't even seen in two years and Phoebe had moved to her jewelry box—Adrianne said louder, "Why am I going to DC?"

"We'll go to Chicago first and get Mason, but he has to go back to DC and apologize. Again. If you're there with him, he's more likely to do it."

Adrianne frowned. "What is he apologizing for this time?"

"He got pissed when the vice president said Mason needed to allow press with him on the initial trip to Haiti," Lauren said.

"What did he say?" she asked hesitantly.

"Mason said he's not babysitting reporters, the VP said you

will if I tell you to, Mason said, 'there you go being a prick again' and walked out."

Adrianne groaned and closed her eyes. This was not good.

"I need you to come and calm him down, talk him into an apology."

Adrianne frowned at her. "He shouldn't have to apologize." She grabbed the tank top Phoebe held out. "His job is to get those seeds in the ground and growing, not stand around posing for photo ops and giving quotes so Newsweek can sell more copies. In fact," she said as she tossed her T-shirt aside and pulled the tank top on. "The best thing would be for them to interview people about Mason. They'd get the right flavor but it wouldn't bother him and getting the job done and he wouldn't say something—unfortunate. Then they can..." She trailed off when she noticed the other women staring at her and one another with amused wonder.

"What?"

"I know exactly who you need to talk to," Lauren said. "And it's not Mason after all."

———

L auren used her outrageous stock of frequent flier miles to get Adrianne a first-class seat on the same flight she was taking that evening. Adrianne was grateful not to have more time to think and worry about the flight. Trying to sleep that night would have been impossible. Better to take a deep breath and get it over with.

At the gate, they talked about Haiti—anything to keep Adrianne's mind off of eventually boarding a plane. For the first time in two years. For the first time since she'd almost died.

It wasn't the magic solution, but it was interesting information.

Lauren told her about how most people on the island were

still in tents and shacks. Relief workers sometimes had rudimentary buildings—generally put up by whatever organization they worked for—but running water was hit and miss and electricity was sporadic, depending on how hard the wind blew.

Even with four walls and a roof, workers still slept in tents to protect themselves from bugs, primarily mosquitoes. Only the more affluent side of Port-au-Prince had air conditioning and the team's time there was short. Lauren and Mason and their team were needed in the rural areas. The poor rural areas.

Still, Adrianne only had to think of Mason's smile and she figured she could deal with the heat and sleeping on the hard ground. Like Phoebe kept telling her, she was fine.

Fine was the last thing she felt forty minutes later when she took her seat in 3A however. Lauren was supposed to sit across the aisle, but she leaned on the back of the seat in front of the man next to Adrianne in 3B.

"You wouldn't mind if my friend and I sat together would you?" she asked, giving him a sexy smile.

The man smiled. "I could probably be talked into it."

"I'd appreciate it. She's a little freaked out about flying and I want to hold her hand."

The man glanced at Adrianne, who barely managed a tight smile.

"I wouldn't mind holding her hand," he said with a grin.

"Yeah, well, she's all mine." Lauren gave him a little wink.

With one eyebrow raised, the man looked from Adrianne, back to Lauren. "Ah. In that case, I'm happy to move. And sit right across the aisle from you two lovely ladies."

He stood and stepped into the aisle, letting Lauren slide into the seat next to Adrianne.

Adrianne tried to take a deep breath. She forced her chest to expand, to pull air in, then relax and let it out. In and out. They just had to get off the ground. In and out. Once they were on their way, she really thought she'd be okay. In and out. She needed to get past the point she'd been last time.

Lauren forced her fingers to uncurl from the armrest and held her hand. "You'll leave a dent," she said lightly.

She ran her thumb back and forth over Adrianne's knuckles. "You know," she said, turning in her seat to face Adrianne. "Mason and I have always had similar tastes in women. We both love blonds."

The stewardess stepped into the aisle to demonstrate the safety features of the plane. Adrianne tuned it out and focused on Lauren. She didn't want to think about needing safety features of any kind. If they started going down, she was going to freak out, pass out and not know the difference anyway.

Lauren reached up and fingered the curl of hair near Adrianne's jaw. "Alex, my last girlfriend, was blond. Her hair was straight but about the same shade as yours."

Lauren's eyes roamed over Adrianne's face and Adrianne found herself riveted by how thick her eyelashes were.

"Alex really liked my eyes," Lauren said. "And she had great skin." She ran her finger over Adrianne's cheek. "So do you, but I think your best feature is your mouth. You've got great lips."

Adrianne held her breath as Lauren slid the pad of her index finger over her bottom lip. She had no idea how to react or what to say. Lauren was beautiful and confident and put off a very sensual vibe. She also smelled great. But Adrianne wasn't into women. It had never even occurred to her. She'd never been hit on by one that she could recall, and the simple fact was she wasn't interested.

Lauren gave her a soft smile. "You're very beautiful, Adrianne."

Though, wow, if anyone could make her consider trying something new, it might be Lauren. She practically oozed the promise of a good time.

"I'm guessing Mason would say it's your hips and butt—

which are fantastic by the way—but for me it's definitely your lips."

Then she leaned in and kissed Adrianne.

Adrianne gasped at the soft, completely foreign texture of a woman's lips, glazed with strawberry lip gloss, touching her own.

It didn't feel...bad. But it was certainly different.

Lauren tipped her head, cupped the back of Adrianne's, and increased the pressure, opening her lips slightly.

Adrianne didn't push her away, but she had no idea what to do. Kissing Lauren felt weird, and Adrianne had a suspicion that it was more about the fact that she didn't want to kiss anyone but Mason than it was about Lauren being a woman. Though that was a little weird too.

A moment later, Lauren pulled back and settled into her own seat again.

Adrianne pressed her lips together, still tasting strawberry. Once Lauren shifted, Adrianne could see the guy in 3C was watching with wide eyes.

Lauren glanced over at him.

"Best seating arrangement ever," he said with a grin.

Lauren grinned back and then turned to Adrianne. "You okay?"

"I'm...stunned. I'm flattered too, but...stunned."

Lauren reached for the People magazine she'd brought on board with her. "Relax. It was a diversionary tactic."

"The kiss? What?"

"I was trying to distract you from the fact that you're lifting off in an airplane," she said as she flipped the cover open and perused the contents page. "I didn't have time to get you drunk, so I had to improvise with what I do have."

"That would have definitely worked," Adrianne admitted, slumping back in her chair and crossing her arms.

"It did work," Lauren said, pointing at Adrianne's window.

Adrianne looked out.

Sure enough, they were airborne. Nearly at cruising altitude. She'd made it.

She swung back to face Lauren. "Thank you."

"Hey, it's not like it was a sacrifice," Lauren said still looking at the magazine. She licked her lips as she turned a page. "Not at all."

11

Mason had been to the lab on Tuesday when he'd returned to Chicago. He'd waited to go in until long after he knew everyone else would be gone, knowing that he would be horrible company and not convinced he could contribute anything meaningful to anything.

He'd stayed for twenty minutes.

He was so restless he felt like he was going to crawl out of his skin. The lab seemed to be mocking him—it was everything he'd done, worked for, accomplished. Everything he was known for. And he hated it all in those twenty minutes.

This was keeping him from normal. This was what was in his way of having a normal life.

If it wasn't for this fucking lab, for the tests and trials and projects, he could have Adrianne. And Sapphire Falls and everything he wanted. He could golf and have coffee at the diner and go to the town festival without worrying about Haiti and Outreach America.

If it wasn't for this fucking lab, he wouldn't have developed his seed project. Without that, Outreach America would have never been interested in talking with him. If they hadn't talked to him, he'd know no more about Haiti than Drew or Tim or Steve. Without that knowledge, he could have been content to donate money to the Red Cross and know he'd done some good that way.

But now he knew. He knew what was happening, he knew what was being done about it and he knew that he fit into that.

Frustration welled up and he'd tried to throw a glass container of the almost-there-but-something-was-missing fertilizer against the wall. But he couldn't even bring himself to do that. He'd never been the violent type and he'd worked hard on that mixture. It wasn't perfect, but throwing it away didn't make sense.

It wasn't like it would change anything.

Nothing had changed.

He'd gone to Washington with Lauren. He'd had the meeting with the vice president.

That hadn't changed anything either.

The truth was, from here on out everything he'd worked for —even if it all went perfectly—wouldn't be quite enough.

He'd finally found a woman who understood and admired what he was doing in Haiti—so much that she shut him out of her life so he'd go do it.

She wasn't returning his calls, she wasn't responding to texts or emails. Phoebe and Hailey weren't even calling him back. And Drew and Tim—no surprise—weren't a hell of a lot of help.

It was now Friday and he was back at the lab.

Adrianne wanted him here. She believed in his work. Maybe those thoughts would make being here tolerable. Or at least he could get this fucking project going, get to Haiti, launch the project and then head back to Sapphire Falls. He'd be needed in Haiti again, of course, but he was going to see Adrianne before that happened.

He needed to see her, hear her, touch her—reassure himself

that she was healthy and well and...happy. Even if it was without him.

"Dr. Riley!"

He was immediately greeted by the three lab assistants. Spencer was a grad student working on his PhD in agricultural engineering like Mason. Nadia had finished her master's degree and was starting her PhD program that fall. Todd was in his last year of his undergraduate degree in microbiology and was fascinated by the work Mason and Lauren were doing. He'd begged for a position in the lab and had been a huge asset. All three were accompanying them to Haiti.

"I'm so glad you're back," Nadia told him, giving him a big smile. "I've been dying to bounce some ideas off of you but didn't want to bother you while you were on vacation."

"I've got some seedlings going from that tomato crop we were playing around with," Todd said from across the room. "You have to see this."

Mason took a deep breath. Damn. This was like being greeted by the guys at the coffee shop times ten.

He felt like a rock star.

"I've started packing some of the seeds," Spencer said. "But I wanted you to check the boxes."

These kids were excited. They were ready to take the challenges and make the world a better place. And they looked up to him—nerd tendencies and all.

The least he could do was try to pull it together enough for them.

———

"I don't think I can do this," Adrianne whispered to Lauren as she smoothed the front of her skirt and licked her lips.

She'd had to buy the suit she now wore—the weight she'd

gained in Sapphire Falls meant that none of her previous work suits fit anymore.

She liked the black skirt and the red and black jacket. She hadn't missed heels though.

"You can do this," Lauren said confidently. "You're a natural."

Adrianne looked at the woman sitting in the leather wing-back chair adjacent to hers, flipping the pages of a People magazine. "Thank you. I think."

Lauren smiled. "You know how to sell and you believe in our product. Secretary Williams is going to be eating out of your hand."

Adrianne felt her pulse slow and she took a calming breath. She was fine. She'd even enjoyed the flight—Lauren had booked them in first class, which certainly helped—and the five-star hotel last night. She hadn't been in bed with five-hundred-thread-count sheets in a long time. She'd swum, had an egg-white omelet and fruit for breakfast and had on a new pair of Gucci heels. All in all, she had nothing to complain about. Money made it easier to travel healthy—if she wanted to put in the effort.

Today she did.

"This product isn't exactly like a box of candy," she told Lauren.

"No," Lauren agreed. "It's something you feel even more passionately about than candy." She flipped the page on her magazine.

Watching her, it was hard to believe this woman was one of the foremost authorities on water and soil conservation in the United States.

She looked like a fashion model. It would be easy to under-estimate her. Adrianne needed to keep that in mind.

Adrianne pulled her notes out of her bag. She was here to do a job. This was essentially a sales meeting. She was convincing someone to take a chance on her product. She'd been in this position hundreds of times.

In this case, it was a little different product. Today she was selling Mason Riley. To the Vice President of the United States. Well, to one of his advisors anyway. Still, this was the chance to help them understand the best way to get what everyone wanted and needed.

"Dr. Davis, Ms. Scott? Mr. Gavin will see you now."

"It should be the White House's priority, from a PR perspective at least, to keep the best interests of the people of Haiti in mind," Adrianne said twenty minutes later. "And I can assure you, Dr. Mason Riley is the Haitian people's best interest."

Daniel Gavin made a final note and then met her eyes. "I'm meeting with the vice president later this afternoon. But I do want to say that I believe it's in everyone's best interest to have you remain in charge of Dr. Riley's PR, Ms. Scott."

He rose, shook their hands and escorted her and Lauren to the front office. "I'll be in touch, Dr. Davis. It was nice to meet you, Ms. Scott."

They were in a cab before either woman spoke.

Lauren let out a long breath. "You were amazing."

Adrianne finally let her smile go. "That went very well." She slipped her shoes off and leaned her head against the back of the seat. "I think they'll give Mason everything he wants. And they won't expect PR from him." She sighed happily. She was great at reading body language and other non-verbal cues. She'd impressed Daniel Gavin today.

Lauren laughed. "He won't need to do anything more than show up and point to what he wants after that meeting, Adrianne."

She rolled her head to look at Lauren. "Yeah?"

"Yeah." Lauren shifted in her seat to face Adrianne fully. "So let's talk business here with you. What can I do to keep you around? Our company could use you doing PR. Not marketing

—we don't have to sell ourselves to customers. But public relations could help us. Not just with government and agencies, but there are people in the public who don't understand what we do. They worry about us mutating seeds, messing with the natural order of things, messing with the environment. We could use a front person, a face, who's not a scientist but who gets it, believes in it and can explain it in lay terms."

Adrianne stared at Lauren, aware of her heart thumping crazily—but not in a bad way.

She'd be perfect for that job.

Lauren's cell rang before Adrianne said anything.

"This is Dr. Davis." She paused and then glanced at Adrianne. "Okay, that's not a problem." She disconnected and leaned toward the driver. "We need to go back."

"Back?" Adrianne said. "To see Mr. Gavin?"

"No," Lauren answered. "To the West Wing."

———

Vice President Forrester was shorter than Adrianne expected. That was all she had time to register before they were ushered into seats around a conference table and the vice president pinned her with a direct stare.

"Dr. Riley makes me nervous," he said.

Adrianne nodded. "From a PR perspective, I can understand that. But from the perspective of what you need him to do, there's absolutely nothing to be worried about. There's no one better to lead this project, I can assure you."

He looked at Lauren, who simply smiled, and then back to Adrianne. "I understand his expertise is the science, the hands-on work, but it's important that this project be presented to the media and the public a certain way. My advisors insist that the American public would find this story encouraging and interesting."

"And I understand the White House wanting to be connected to something encouraging and interesting," Adrianne said. "As a member of the American public, I can guarantee you that's true. Not only is it something hopeful happening in a part of the world we're used to seeing beaten down and devastated, but it's something everyone can understand. Planting crops, the heartland of our country going to the heart of theirs. Beautiful." She took a breath and leaned her arms onto the table, meeting the vice president's eyes. "The White House needs to think big here, sir. You could develop a program that could go into grade schools and talk about the science behind this project. The water and soil conservation focus will inspire conservation here. The human interest stories alone will be—"

"I told you she was good." Daniel Gavin pushed away from the wall where he'd been leaning. The vice president was looking at her with grudging admiration.

"Dr. Davis," he said, rising from his chair. "We'll want a preliminary team to go in two days. This has already been pushed back enough that we need to do some fast PR."

"I don't think there's any way—" Lauren began.

Adrianne cut her off. "That's a good idea. It will take a few weeks to get everything in place, but sending you and Mason over with a few reporters will kick things off, satisfy the media and the White House and then leave things quieter for the full team's arrival in a few weeks."

Vice President Forrester nodded. "Fine. We'll do our part." He started for the door but turned back after a few steps. "As long as she keeps Dr. Riley on a short leash in front of the reporters." He headed for the door that Daniel Gavin held open for him but he paused at the threshold. "Dr. Riley's lucky," he said to Adrianne.

She took a deep breath and a chance. "Mr. Vice President?"

He turned back. "Yes?"

"Dr. Riley is a brilliant scientist and a wonderful person with a huge heart and a hell of a lot of passion for what he does. He's not lucky. You are."

Michael Forrester looked at her for several seconds. Then he gave her a nod. "Agreed. But I was referring to him being lucky to have you."

The door swung shut behind him as Adrianne stared at the dark wood. Slowly, she smiled.

"See, even the VP knows you love him," Lauren said.

Adrianne's smile grew. "Evidently."

"How's your heart doing?"

"Never better."

———

M ason frowned at the back of Ryan McDonald's head as the White House Press Secretary was running down what was going to happen at the press conference in ten minutes. The man took fourteen paragraphs to explain the simplest thing.

They were standing on the tarmac outside the hanger where the private plane was housed that would take them to Haiti the next morning.

The Secretary of State and Secretary of Agriculture would each make a statement—something along the lines of how great this project was to bring two countries together and challenge the United States to use their vast resources to blah, blah, blah. Mason and Lauren were available for questions for fifteen minutes. Then they would be getting their team ready for the trip. Which is what they should be doing. That was the important part.

He was only here because of the fucking PR consultant.

He didn't need a fucking PR consultant. He didn't need anyone telling him that insulting the Vice President of the

United States was a bad idea. But Lauren had hired someone to do it anyway. And thanks to that person, he was now getting ready to speak at a press conference.

Wonderful.

And he was paying this person. Quite well according to Lauren.

Even better.

Mason rolled his head and shoulders, listening to the pops and cracks. He was tense. He knew it. He didn't need a health consultant to tell him that—or that it was lack of sleep, lack of exercise, lack of giving a fuck about anything that was doing it to him.

Instead of tense, he should be excited. He should want this trip to Haiti. He'd wanted it for months, years really. He'd been working for it for a long damned time.

And now he didn't care.

It wasn't about this circus around the White House. Though he hated it, he understood this was smoothing the way. The team would be more effective and efficient with the White House behind them. That was a no brainer.

His irritation was not about where he was—but where he'd rather be.

Though he planned to return to Sapphire Falls the minute he touched US soil again, every hour he was away was a heavier and heavier weight on his heart.

She still wasn't answering her phone, even at her office. According to everyone, she was out of town.

They were all lying for her.

He needed to be in Sapphire Falls. He needed to be with her. He'd be there this minute if he didn't have to go to Haiti.

But he had to go to Haiti. It wasn't guilt, it wasn't interest. He had to go. It was a pre-visit visit for the public relations and media angle of the story. According to the new PR consultant, it would keep the reporters away when the rest of the team showed up, which meant they could get right to work.

That was the only reason he was here. The sooner they got to work down there, the sooner he could come back.

That and the fact that Lauren had threatened to put him in charge of their Facebook page and Twitter account if he no-showed.

He knew the Facebook and Twitter thing were because of this PR woman too. What the hell did they need Facebook and Twitter for?

Rebelliously, he'd left his suit jacket and tie in the car. No denim, she'd said. How had she known he'd considered blue jeans? He'd only started wearing jeans again regularly since Sapphire Falls.

Also, to show this PR nut who was really in charge, he intended to use the term zoonotic diseases during the Q and A. It wouldn't be relevant to anything but he was going to throw it in so that everyone would scramble to look it up.

That would show her.

"Dr. Riley?"

Mason tuned back in as the questions started.

"Larry Chilver, The Examiner. Wondering how you answer the questions about the importance of this project?"

"No one's asking me about the importance of the project," Mason said. "I guess the people I hang out with get it."

Larry didn't seem to find that funny. "Some say that the Haitian people have bigger, more immediate concerns in light of the housing situation and cholera epidemic sweeping the country."

This was exactly what annoyed Mason most about these press conferences. He didn't want to answer questions about if they should go, not go, what it meant socially or psychologically. What was he, an idiot? Of course there were questions and issues, but that wasn't his deal. He had the science and the

Haitian government and Outreach America wanted it. It was up to everyone else to work out the political, economic and cultural issues.

"That's not my problem," Mason said into the mic. "Talk to Ryan here about how this impacts them socially and what their agenda and priorities are. Ask me about what we're going to do when we get there."

"So IAS doesn't care about the living conditions or health conditions in Haiti?" Larry returned.

"Yes, that's exactly what I said," Mason answered sarcastically. "All we care about are plants that will allow this country not just to eat but to stabilize economically and socially—"

"Of course IAS cares about every aspect of life in Haiti," a woman said, stepping forward and pushing Mason away from the microphone. "Really, Larry, what kind of question is that?"

She laughed lightly and Larry even smiled.

"You know that Dr. Riley knows and understands every aspect of what life's like in Haiti. But feeding this country, giving them back the opportunity for economic stability, are huge priorities of the Haitian government—who have asked Dr. Riley to come and share his work."

The woman was dressed in a red suit and heels and she obviously knew not only what she was talking about, but how to work a crowd. The reporters were smiling and nodding, listening raptly and taking notes as she went on about how the local Haitian farm economy depended on viable crops. That grassroots stability, of course, spread to form a foundation for the entire country to build on, including their exports. In time, with the right help from Outreach America, the US government and IAS, Haiti would be able to truly recover.

Mason realized that having a PR person on his side might not be such a bad thing.

Especially if she looked like that and so obviously believed in what they were doing.

Especially if it was Adrianne.

Adrianne was here. Surprisingly, it took that fact a while to sink in. She loved him. He'd known it all along.

As she stepped away from the podium, turning a question over to Ryan McDonald, Mason pulled her up against his side and said in her ear, "No denim, huh?"

"You have to admit," she said with a smile, still facing the reporters, "I look damned good in this suit."

"I have to admit I want to see you out of that suit ASAP." He knew they had to keep facing forward with friendly, composed expressions and mannerisms as if they were discussing nothing more than work. Mason didn't want the media in his work and he definitely didn't want them in his love life. But it was damned hard not to grab her and kiss her right there in front of them all.

An incredible sense of relief and rightness swept over him as her scent drifted up to him and he breathed deep. She was here. She'd gotten on a plane—

"You got on a plane?" he demanded, turning toward her with a frown.

She elbowed him in the ribs. "Smile, Mason."

Gritting his teeth, he faced the reporters and relaxed his face. He wasn't quite able to pull off a smile. "You flew to get here?"

"Of course," she said. "I'm fine."

"I know about your heart. I know that—"

"I'm not afraid anymore."

He turned toward her. "What happened?" He was thrilled, of course. But this was big. Something had changed her mind.

"You happened, Mason." She glanced up at him with a smile. "You're worth every risk. Without you, my heart wouldn't be whole anyway."

No one had ever said something like that to him before. He

started to reach for her, but she nudged him. "Answer the question."

The question...

Mason turned to the reporters and answered a question about the shortened growing season for his seeds. Then Adrianne kept him from losing his cool when asked about the skeptics who wondered if IAS was playing God.

His response was that those skeptics would be praying to him for help if an earthquake took their homes, friends and livelihoods.

Adrianne's response was much better. "Innovative Agricultural Solutions is still, of course, working within the confines of the natural world. While what they do certainly seems miraculous, Dr. Riley and his team still answer to Mother Nature. Soil, water, light, pests all still play a role."

That might have been the sexiest thing he'd ever heard.

That the love of his life not only understood and supported him, but was willing and able to go on record with it...that was the miracle.

"As a layperson myself, I understand that it's hard to grasp what they're doing, but I am smart enough to know that I should be thankful—to IAS and to God for giving them the brains to do this wonderful thing."

Adrianne stepped back next to him as Ryan moved to the podium again.

"You know it's killing me to stand here next to you and not touch you," Mason said.

She reached out and hooked her pinky finger with his.

"You always broadcast everything you feel for me. Wish you were broadcasting right now," he added.

She kept her face toward the crowd. "My feelings right now are that this is a hell of a project and neither of us is going to mess it up. If I have to keep the fact that I'm madly in love with you under wraps for a few minutes, I can do it."

"I don't care what these reporters think," Mason said.

"I do. I want them to make you look really, really good. Because you are really, really good. But," she added after a pause, "the minute we're alone, I'm going to be very outgoing about how I feel."

He tightened his finger on hers and fought to keep from putting his hand on her butt. At least.

"You could have told me about your fear of flying," he whispered.

"No, I couldn't."

He opened his mouth to reply and then shut it. She could have but it would have changed everything—exactly what she didn't want.

"And now?" he asked. She was here. Something had happened.

"I told Lauren I wanted to do this and she helped me find a way to get over my fear."

"How?"

She gave him a mischievous smile. "I'll show you later."

He frowned. Adrianne and Lauren as allies should make him happy. Instead, it made him nervous. The only two women in the world who really knew him were teaming up...that could only be trouble.

"Smile, Mason."

He tried.

"I love you, you know," she said conversationally, smiling at the small crowd before them.

Pleasure and want seemed to explode in his gut. It was the first time she'd said it directly and he was standing in front of a crowd of reporters trying to act professional and intelligent. He groaned. "Not fair, Ad. Do you have any idea what I want to do right now?"

"Yeah, I'm pretty sure I do." She smiled but kept her eyes

forward. "We have all night and then it's a long flight to Haiti. You can show me later. Repeatedly."

"Long flight?" he repeated. "But—"

"I'm going with you to Haiti tomorrow," she confirmed.

"No."

She glanced at him and he realized he'd said it loudly.

"No scowling, Mason."

He consciously relaxed his face. "You're not going."

"Yes, I am." She faced their audience again.

"Your heart—"

"Is fine."

"But your doctor—"

"Practically wrote me a prescription for the trip and for the sex," she said. "And I met the physicians for the team. Neither are concerned. And Mason," she said, turning to him as the last question was answered and the reporters began gathering their stuff. "It'll be harder on my heart to be away from you anyway."

"Cheesy," he said. "But I appreciate the sentiment. And feel the same, by the way. But I'm only going to Haiti for the first week and then I'll be back in Sapphire Falls. At least for a while until I need to go check on things." But he couldn't deny that the idea of having her with him was tempting.

"Then I'll go with you for a week and we'll go back to Sapphire Falls together after that."

"I don't want this to be too much," he said, pulling her closer.

"I know. Me either. But I've already dealt with the press, the Vice President of the United States and Lauren, Phoebe and Hailey ganging up on me. I can handle anything after all of that."

Mason pulled her in and hugged her, awed, grateful and completely in love.

And like that the answer to the fertilizer mix came to him.

"Do you have a pen?" he asked.

She pulled back, not looking a bit surprised. She reached into her jacket pocket and handed him a felt tip. Then she pushed her sleeve up.

He grinned at her and quickly jotted down the notation.

"Hey, Lauren," Mason said as his friend joined them. "You're going to have to grab a cab."

"You're going to have sex in the limo?" she asked with a groan. "Come on. It's only like twenty minutes to the hotel."

"That's twenty minutes I don't want to waste talking with you about the press conference and Haiti," Mason told her.

"I am a very good friend," she informed them both. Then she gave them a wink and headed after Ryan McDonald. No doubt to talk the young press secretary into giving her a ride home.

"Please tell me you're not wearing panties," Mason told Adrianne as they slid into the backseat of the limo.

"A thong," she told him with a giggle.

"I can work with that."

"I brought you a present though," she said, reaching into her bag. She pulled out a jar of caramel sauce.

He went from aroused to ready in three seconds. "I didn't think I could love you any more than I already did." He took the jar from her. "But in this moment, I do." He unscrewed the top and dipped a finger in. "Let's see some skin, babe."

She shrugged out of her jacket and started to unbutton her shirt. A minute later, he was pulling the cup away from her breast—where he fully intended to start with the caramel—when an entirely new equation popped into his head.

"No," he groaned, letting his head fall back against the seat.

Adrianne laughed lightly. "It's been a few days. There's a lot to shake loose."

"Where's the pen?" he asked, licking the caramel sauce off his finger so he could write.

She held it up. He took it with a sigh and uncapped it. "You better keep undressing. This is a big one."

She shifted and moved to straddle his lap. "I know."

He couldn't believe it was all coming together like this. Except that he could.

He started writing as she undressed, scribbling notations he hoped he could read later over her stomach. She unhooked her bra and let it slide down her arms, obstructing his view. He switched locations to her right breast.

"Good enough," he said when he had the basic idea down. He'd remember the rest. Or not. He really didn't care once Adrianne dipped her finger into the caramel and swirled it around her nipple. He took the hard, sweet tip in his mouth and in that moment wasn't sure he could even remember how to spell Haiti.

Adrianne got rid of the caramel jar and tangled her fingers in his hair as he sucked harder, arching into him and moaning.

"I love you so damned much," he told her gruffly.

"Show me."

She lifted up off of his lap and quickly undid his belt buckle, pants button and zipper. She pulled his throbbing erection from his underwear, rolled on a condom and then reached under her skirt to move the thong to the side. As she sank down on him, their groans were almost loud enough to rattle the partition between them and the driver. She was hot and wet for him, as ready as he was.

"I love you, Mason," Adrianne gasped as he shifted, causing sweet friction and intense heat.

"I'm going to need reminding of that for the next sixty years or so." He held her hips as he thrust upward.

"My pleasure," she gasped, lifting and lowering herself in rhythm with his thrusts.

He was in the midst of making love to her and he was hungry for her. Unbelievable. Giving her pleasure, making her make those sounds he'd never get enough of, causing that look of love and lust on her face, would now forever be a part of what he needed too.

Mason pulled her down for a deep, slow kiss and then held her gaze as he surged up into her. "You're mine. Tell me you know that."

She barely had breath but managed, "You know, being demanding and possessive isn't very nerdy."

He thrust up hard and she groaned.

"Maybe you've saved me from my nerdiness again," he told her. "Because I intend to be very demanding and possessive." He thrust again to show her. "Come for me, Ad."

She groaned. "Yes, Mason."

"Yes, you're mine or yes, you're about to come for me?"

"Both," she gasped.

And she did. Right along with him. Just as they pulled up in front of the hotel.

Mason tipped the maid extra the next day when they checked out. He was sure the caramel sauce made the sheets pretty sticky.

The week in Haiti wasn't easy—physically or emotionally. The devastation was still clear and the living conditions were far from ideal.

But Adrianne loved it.

Watching Mason in action was inspiring and made her positive that with him, wherever that was, was exactly where she wanted and needed to be.

She ate strange food, had a very weird routine and certainly hadn't seen a treadmill, but she was sleeping wonderfully next to Mason every night and feeling better than ever.

Her chest hadn't hurt since seeing him in DC.

They met with local farmers, talked with relief workers and discussed their plans with scientists from other countries.

They also posed for pictures, gave interviews and basically let the reporters follow them around for three days.

Finally though, Adrianne could tell Mason had had enough.

"Julia, I have someone you have to meet," Adrianne said to the reporter who had cornered Mason by one of the trucks. She took the other woman's arm and started walking her away from Mason. "There's this woman who's been making hats for all the children since the earthquake. Each hat is unique and enables each child to have something that is their very own that's different from everyone else's. She believes this gives them hope that they haven't been forgotten and that they matter."

It was a true story and Adrianne felt it was one that should be told. Julia was one of many reporters who should be picking up on these human-interest stories—and leaving Mason alone to get some work done.

"There you go saving me again," he said, slipping his arms around her from behind as Julia knelt next to the Haitian woman and Adrianne waved over an interpreter.

She rubbed her hands over the backs of his. "I always will too."

He set his chin on top of her head. "Someone has to."

She laughed and turned in his arms. "You've saved me just as much."

"Yeah? From what?"

"Never having a golden wedding anniversary party thrown by my five children and eleven grandchildren."

His eyes crinkled at the corners. "Ah, Ad, of course I'll marry you."

"There's one condition."

"Uh huh."

"We have to get married in Sapphire Falls."

He pulled her in close and hugged her. "Of course we do."

"At the new site of Sapphire Hills."

"You have a new site?" he asked. "Ken Stevens sold you the land?"

"Yes, clear on the other side of town." She didn't mind a bit. That farm was now in her heart as much as it was in Mason's.

"Oh, that's too bad," he said sarcastically. "It's closer to the highway. People might actually stop and buy something now,"

She grinned. "Well, they won't be stopping in for taxidermy services at least."

Mason chuckled. "How'd you get the rest of the money?"

Her grin grew. "Dr. Lauren Davis."

Mason's eyes widened. "You know, I really think I need to hear what happened between you and Lauren on your way to DC."

"It's a little crazy," Adrianne warned him. But she was smiling as she said it. They could handle crazy. They could handle anything as long as they were together.

"Bring on the crazy," he said, his own smile huge. "I don't know much about being normal anyway."

———

Thank you for reading Mason and Adrianne's story! I hope you loved Getting Out of Hand!

And there's lots more sexy, crazy fun from Sapphire Falls in Phoebe and Joe's story, **Getting Worked Up!**

See what happens when millionaire city boy Joe shows up in Sapphire Falls to to win back his would-be fiance from the country boy who's stolen her heart.

But he's going to need some help from a local girl to fit into small town life. Fortunately, Phoebe is the perfect coach.

These unlikely partners in crime will absolutely pull this off— as long as they can keep their hands off of each other and remember which hearts they're trying to win over.

Grab Getting Worked Up now!

———

<u>The Sapphire Falls series</u>

Getting Out of Hand
Getting Worked Up
Getting Dirty
Getting Wrapped Up
Getting It All
Getting Lucky
Getting Over It
Getting His Way
Getting Into Trouble
Getting It Right
Getting All Riled Up
Getting to the Church On Time

Find all of my books and a printable BOOK LIST at
and more on the books page at
ErinNicholas.com

———

Join in on the fan fun too! I love interacting with my readers and would love to have you in the two places where I chat with

fans the most--my email list and my Super Fan page on
Facebook!

Sign up for my email list! You'll hear from me just a couple
times a month and I'll keep you updated on all my news, sales,
exclusive fun, and new releases!
http://bit.ly/ErinNicholasEmails

Join my fan page on Facebook at Erin Nicholas Super Fans! I
check in there every day and it's the best place for first looks,
exclusive giveaways, book talk and fun!

ABOUT ERIN

Erin Nicholas is the New York Times and USA Today bestselling author of over thirty sexy contemporary romances. Her stories have been described as toe-curling, enchanting, steamy and fun. She loves to write about reluctant heroes, imperfect heroines and happily ever afters. She lives in the Midwest with her husband who only wants to read the sex scenes in her books, her kids who will never read the sex scenes in her books, and family and friends who say they're shocked by the sex scenes in her books (yeah, right!).

Find her and all her books at
www.ErinNicholas.com

And find her on Facebook, BookBub, and Instagram!

CPSIA information can be obtained
at www.ICGtesting.com
Printed in the USA
LVHW041952091022
730311LV00003B/393